STUD MUFFIN

A SEXY ROMANTIC COMEDY

LAUREN LANDISH

Edited by

VALORIE CLIFTON

Photography by

ALEX WIGHTMAN

I want to give a huge special THANK YOU to some very special ladies. Valorie, Staci, and Donna, I appreciate all the work you do to help me along the way! <3

INTRODUCTION

**From Wall Street Journal & USA Today Bestselling Author
Lauren Landish.**

I'm so done with men. I don't care if he looks like Ryan
Gosling with a ten-inch cucumber in his pants and says he
wants me to have his babies.

Just, no. I'm done. I can't pick them.

To make matters worse, the real estate investment company I
work for is on the verge of collapse. There's one deal that can
save it, and it's all up to me. I make this deal or look for a
new job.

Problem is, I'm competing with the arrogant jerk who
started my whole bad luck streak with men.

His smoldering green eyes have haunted me for more than a
year, and if it weren't for his cockiness, I would've been
screaming his name during our first encounter.

He's the competition now, and I can't let him get to me. I have too much to lose.

But what if I want to have my studmuffin and eat it too?

Want the FREE Extended Epilogue? Sign up to my mailing list to receive it. If you're already on my list, you'll get this automatically!

Other books in this series:

Irresistible Bachelor **Series (Interconnecting standalones):**
Anaconda || Mr. Fiance || Heartstopper
Stud Muffin || Mr. Fixit || Matchmaker
Motorhead || Baby Daddy

*T*he chimes of wedding bells are like a golden symphony to my ears. *If I ever have a wedding, I want it to be as beautiful as this one*, I think to myself. The stunning hall on the edge of the sea, the whole place bedecked in white and gold—it's like a true fairytale wedding. I smile as I watch my best friend, Roxy Price—excuse me, Roxy Stone—having a blast with her new husband, Jake. They are just too cute together. I might have been wrong about them at first. I was too caught up in stupid office politics shit, but looking at them now, I know the truth. They're perfect, made for each other. It makes me want to reach for my camera.

"Now Mary Jo, I don't give a single fuck about what the doctors say. If I want to get out there and show these kids a thing or two about how to rodeo on the dance floor, then I'm going to do it!" Roxy's grandmother, Ivy Jo, says. "You know, it was these hips that got you into the world!"

I laugh as I wistfully take in the dynamics of Roxy's family. They're foul-mouthed, even more than Roxy, and Ivy Jo, in

1

particular, has zero filter on expressing her opinions. I love them all, and I wish I had more people like them in my life.

My skin pricks when I feel eyes on me and turn my head. The man looking at me leaves my heart skipping in my chest as I take in his magnificence. The feeling of his sea-green eyes feasting on me has my blood rushing through my veins, and I feel myself flush, smiling without even thinking.

God, he's fucking handsome. I almost feel like he's familiar. Something about him . . . he looks like someone I know. I can't really focus, though, as he smiles at me, the kind of smile that says he takes what he wants. There isn't a question of yes or no because nobody says no to him. The way he's looking at me, my body is already tingling, and I feel like I might just give in to him now if he asks.

He keeps throwing looks at me, and I try to look away, not letting on to what he's doing to me. The music changes, and I'm pretending to be preoccupied with Roxy's joyous twerking in her wedding dress when I hear a deep voice behind me.

"Hello, lovely lady." I nearly swoon at the sound of his voice. It seems to reach right through my ear and to my stomach, where I feel a tight ball of desire form. I swear his voice is smooth like honey. I want to drown in it.

I turn around and my heart flares. He's even more gorgeous close up, and I recognize him. He's related to Roxy's brother-in-law, Oliver. They've got the same eyes.

"H–hello," I reply, aghast as I stammer. *What the fuck, Hannah?* Since when do I get tongue-tied over a man? They've always been easy as 1-2-3. Pop the hip, bite the lip, and I control the dick. But this one takes my breath away.

He gives me a cocky smirk as if he knows every little uncertainty running through my head. His eyes seem to pierce me straight to the heart, and I feel my fingers start to tremble. "I don't think I need to tell you this because it's obvious, but you're fucking gorgeous."

Damn, it's corny, but someone bring the fire hose already. This man is burning me up and he hasn't even taken off his shirt yet. I duck my head. "Thank you," I say in a sweet voice. If Roxy saw me acting like this, she'd swear up and down I'd gone senile at an early age.

"What's your name, gorgeous?" he asks, sipping at a flute of champagne.

"Hannah. Yours?"

"Anthony. But people call me Tony."

As soon as he says it, I remember Mindy mentioning that they'd invited Oliver's brother. I remember she told me a little about him, but right now I'm too lost in his dark hair, startling green eyes, and lean, chiseled jawline.

"I like that name," I say softly, sarcastic comments flying out of my head as fast as they appear. I just can't seem to make a joke about 'Tony Steele' in the power of those eyes.

"Do you?" he murmurs, drawing in close. I can feel the heat emanating from his body, and the magnetic pull of his personality draws me a step closer, to the point I have to fight the urge to run my hand over his chest. I want him. God, after watching Roxy get her man, I fucking need him.

With an ironic twist that I can't deny seems to show that the Almighty is sensing my needs, a fast dance song comes on. Cascada . . . okay, not bad.

"Would you like to dance?" he asks me. After the year I've had, he's lucky I don't grab him by the hand and take him someplace private.

Not trusting myself to speak, I nod, and Tony grins. He finishes off his champagne and takes my hand, leading me out on the dance floor. It feels like everyone is looking, but it's probably just my sudden anxiousness. Either way, I'm ready to get down and I'm going to give him everything I've got. I move to the rhythm, alternating between facing him with a hand behind his neck and turning my back to his chest, my ass grinding against his crotch. Maybe it's a little much for a wedding, but this is Roxy's soiree and since she's the one who taught me the moves, I think she'd approve of a little down and dirty on the dance floor.

We dance until the song is over, and as the notes fade away, I find myself covered in sweat. Tony's glistening too, his skin alight with a sexy glow that has my heart not slowing down but speeding up. His intense gaze speaks telepathically to me. He wants me. He needs me. On his lips, I feel the words barely held back. He wants to take me right here and right now. If things keep going like this, he might just get what he wants.

"I need a drink!" I beg into his ear when the song is over. *And something else.*

He grins, grabbing my hand. "Well then, let's go."

We walk over to the punch bowl, where he gets me a drink. I don't take it slow, gulping it down. Maybe if I slam down this stuff fast enough, I can distract myself from the burning desire inside me. I hold out my glass, desperate to get some sort of balance back. "More, please?"

Tony gives me a look but refills my glass. "You really know

how to dance. The most beautiful woman in the room and one of the best dancers? I think they've got the wrong star here today."

My cheeks turn a rosy red. *A charmer, huh?* "Thank you. You're sweet." Hmm, maybe he's a Don Juan type, but if he is, he knows just what to say to make my panties wetter than they already are. "You asking for another dance with that compliment?"

Tony chuckles, smirking with a confidence that I'm not quite sure yet whether it turns me on or pisses me off. "Close. I was thinking more along the lines of, should I pound you from behind or make you ride me all night?"

Shock flares through me, then anger. Yeah, I'm sure now—it pisses me off. I glare at him in disbelief. Never in all my life has a guy been such a gentleman then an absolute douche a minute later. "You just ruined your chance, bastard!"

My hands fly out before I can stop them, and I splash punch in his face. Unfortunately, my glass slips from my fingers at the same time and falls to the floor. The crystal shatters like a bomb and the music stops. All eyes are on me, and I stare in shock, seeing Mindy staring at me, her mouth wide. My cheeks burn with embarrassment. I see Oliver turning red next to her, and I realize what I just did. Oh, my God, I just splashed punch on my best friend's sister's husband's brother at her wedding!

Damn, that sounds like a line from *Spaceballs*.

In the silence, I quickly look around the room, grateful at least that Roxy and Jake have already left to consummate their marriage and didn't see this. Still, I'm sure they're gonna hear about it.

"Wait!" Tony tries to stop me, but I'm not listening. I'm not even mad at him. I'm more embarrassed than anything. I turn and run from the room, hiking up my dress as I go to give myself some extra speed. I head for the door and don't stop to look back until I'm already in my car, the engine roaring, and I'm driving away. In my rearview mirror, I see Tony in the driveway of the reception hall, and my lip curls.

Fuck that arrogant asshole.

CHAPTER 1

HANNAH - PRESENT DAY . . .

"*I*'m so done with men!" I declare over the phone to my six months pregnant bestie, Roxy. "Finished! I swear to God, I'm going lesbian!"

I'm at work, sitting at my desk, doing everything but my job. I know I should be working, but I'm in too shitty of a mood. It certainly doesn't help that the rat bastard's portrait is sitting right in front me. That smooth golden skin, those suave brown eyes, the looks that made me ignore all of his bullshit. The picture of the asshole who used to make me smile now only seems to piss me off. "I don't care if he looks like Ryan Gosling with a ten-inch cucumber in his pants and says that he wants me to have his babies all while promising me the pleasure of a thousand orgasms," I growl. "I don't care. I'm turning him down."

Roxy laughs. "It must be bad! What the hell happened this time?" She pauses, chuckling. "Or do I even want to know?"

"Screw this shit!" I snatch the portrait off my desk, taking it out of the frame. Snarling, I rip up the picture of the two of us and crumple it into a ball. "Roxy, it's the craziest shit you'll ever hear." I toss it into the wastebasket with one hand. "Score! LeBron ain't got shit on me!"

"Enough fucking around. Tell me!" Roxy commands immediately. "Now you have me curious."

I take a deep breath, anger twisting my stomach as I think about last night. "You won't believe it. He has mommy issues!"

"For real?" Roxy gasps. "What does that even mean?"

My eyes go big even though Roxy can't see them. "I mean, he's got legit Mommy issues, girl! We were going at it, and suddenly, he starts asking if he's been a bad boy and if I would punish him!"

Roxy laughs in disbelief. "Seriously? That's nuts!"

"I shit you not. I thought the whole time he was calling me *Mami*, like Latino style? I mean, he's from Miami, right? No, the guy literally meant Mommy, as in . . . he even asked if he could put on a diaper!"

"No way!" Roxy chokes with laughter.

"Way! After I heard that, I was like, fuck this, I'm outta here!" I shake my head in disgust. "Seriously, Rox, this is five in a row who've turned out to be either a jerk, a freak, or a damn pervert. I'm starting to think there's not a man out there for me."

Roxy laughs. "Come on, Hannah, don't become jaded. The right guy will come along and knock you off your feet eventually. You'll see."

"Ha! That's easy for you to say, Miss I-Just-Got-Nominated-For-A-Kids'-Choice-Award. Let's see here," I say, starting to count on my fingers. "Lance was a drunk jerk, Hank was a cheater, and Troy never could keep it up without drugs or closing his eyes . . . talk about a boost to your self-esteem. And then there was that prick To—" I stop short of saying his name. We were never dating. But he still adds to the line of terrible luck that I have. I shake off the thought of him. "Meanwhile, the right guy came along for you and you just fucked him to death to make him love you."

"I did not!" Roxy protests. "We didn't even get our clothes off on the first try!"

"I'm just kidding," I say with a mirthless snort. It's not what I remember her telling me, but that's beside the point. Still, Jake's a good catch. While my life has been on replay, Roxy's gotten out. Not a superstar yet, but at least she's got a man she loves and has every weekend to do what she always dreamed of—singing.

I feel like I'm going through the motions. Since quitting my job at Franklin Consolidated, I tried out photography for a little while, and while I enjoyed it at first, I quickly realized it wasn't for me when I was taking a lot more pictures than I was selling. Besides, with Roxy moving on to be with Jake, I was starting to drain my savings, even if I did downgrade my living situation. So I picked up this job at Aurora Holdings and have been here since.

Aurora's a good job, and it does allow me to travel, which is something I've always wanted. Real estate research and scouting for rich investors is actually fun. And I do still have my camera, even if the only people who see my work are my Facebook friends. Still, it's not where I want to be.

"Yeah, well, you don't have to be angry about me and Jake,"

Roxy says, and I can hear that she's not really hurt, but still a little peeved.

"I'm sorry," I say. I'm coming across as bitter and I don't mean to. "I don't want to seem like I'm being Princess Pissy Panties over here. I'm happy for you, Rox. It's just that . . . I thought I might have had something special with Josh." I bite my lower lip. "While I felt creeped the fuck out about the whole thing, at least I hadn't invested a lot of my time into the relationship. What's that saying, better now than later? I'm more upset about another failed venture. Another waste of my time."

"Oh, honey, I understand," Roxy says emphatically. "But you'll get through it. As you like to remind me, you're that bitch who turns bad boys into choir boys."

"Girl, I feel more like 'that dumb trick who gets nothing but shit' right about now."

"Oh, stop it," Roxy says before burping loudly. "Sorry, I'm blaming that on the baby."

I laugh, having heard Roxy let loose some wall rattlers before. "Seriously. I've decided I'm cursed when it comes to men. So maybe I'm going to hang up my coat for a while. Hell, I'll even break out the granny panties and let the garden grow since no one will be breaking and entering any time soon."

"I don't believe you. You'll be back to riding dick in a week." Roxy snorts a laugh. "You need it like the rest of us need water."

"Just watch me. I'm serious."

Roxy giggles, unconvinced. "Well, other than dicks with dicks, how are you doing? Liking the job?"

I shrug, though she can't see me. "It's good. I like my boss, I directed some good sales last quarter, and most importantly, I still get to travel and take pics. Especially awesome that I get to do that on someone else's dime."

Sharp voices interrupt my words, and I hear footsteps approaching from outside.

"Shit. Okay, boss coming. I got to get off quick."

Roxy tries to get out a quick, "Bye, Mommy—" in a baby voice.

I hang up before she can finish, vowing I'll get her back the next time I see her, and pretend to start working. Bringing up my desktop screen, I pull up a recent property on my computer along with a few websites about the area. As I do, the two voices become clearer.

"Just give me the chance, Mrs. Sinclair," I hear Cassie White, my twenty-one-year-old, relatively new coworker say as the two women walk into view. My boss, Myra Sinclair, is dressed sharp as a tack, as usual, in a slim-fitting white pantsuit, her grey-white hair cut into a trendy side bob. She has money, and I gotta give it to her—she built it the old-fashioned way. She's used her own sweat and genius to become the head of the property division of Aurora Holdings. Now, she's always wanting the world to know it. Cassie, in perfect minion fashion, has on a grey pantsuit, her dark blonde hair pulled back into a sophisticated ponytail. It's not that Cassie doesn't have skills. She's smart when she wants to be. She just seems to still be in the 'make a good impression' stage and hasn't quite figured out that she needs to move on.

Sinclair spins sharply on Cassie, causing her to nearly stumble back and fall to the floor. "Absolutely not! I told you already that you're too inexperienced. There's too much riding on this, and I wouldn't be comfortable with only you there."

"But I can do it," says Cassie enthusiastically, flashing her dimple-filled smile that I'm sure melts the hearts of men but does nothing for Myra.

"Funny you say that when you nearly botched your last assignment. I seem to recall your spilling coffee into Mr. Balding's lap. He had second-degree burns on his balls and we narrowly avoided getting sued."

Cassie bites her lip, looking guilty. I remember that day. It had been my quick thinking—and a nearby pitcher of iced tea—that had stopped the burns from being worse. "That was an accident."

"That's one of the main reasons I don't want to send you alone. You lack grace and experience." Cassie scowls at Myra's insult, but she pretends not to notice. Myra shakes her head sadly. "Besides, my bosses have someone else in mind . . ." Myra goes silent and looks my way, and I pretend to be preoccupied with the paper I'm scribbling on.

"Hannah," says Myra in an almost singsong voice.

I look up from my computer. "Yes, Mrs. Sinclair?"

"Our quarterly report just came in," she says, brandishing the stack of folders in her hands. "And do you know what it says?"

I beam with pride. Damn right, I do. That, at least, I can take pride in. "That we're doing great, better than we expected."

Myra lets out a laugh. "Oh, dear, that's a good one!" Her smile fades fast, leaving me confused. "Apparently, Aurora Holdings has lost its holdings, pun intended. The shedding of our properties in Puerto Rico and Europe has hurt our shares, and several divisions are under threat of becoming extinct."

She doesn't have to say which divisions she means. I was responsible for the selling of the European properties, but the market was crashing, the properties were old, and there was no way we were going to get a better price. It was the right thing to do. Still, my mouth goes dry. I thought we were doing great. "We had that company conference call," I protest, thinking of last week's call. "The CFO was talking a good game."

Myra snorts, flipping a dismissive hand. "Jason Randal is a braggart used car salesman and nothing more. The damn fool wouldn't know his asshole from a hole in the ground. It was all talk, Hannah. That's what it was, designed to keep our shareholders appeased and the company from panicking. We've already taken a pounding in the market. We start a shareholder revolt, and we're in deep shit."

I gulp. I've never heard Myra be this brutal before. "Mrs. Sinclair . . ."

"The truth is, our company is close to bankruptcy," Myra says, a note of doom entering her voice.

Her words hit me like a semi-truck in the chest and the office goes totally silent. I clutch the edge of my desk as Cassie turns white in the face, dread gripping my insides. I thought for sure we were doing amazing things. I just secured a contract on a property in a new market that's going to be super hot within ten years. Even Myra said I'd done a great job in closing the deal.

Ugh. This couldn't have come at a worse time.

I was so confident after the last deal that I signed a new lease for an upgraded apartment. There's no way I can afford to lose this job. I don't care if I have rich friends. I'm not asking for a handout.

"So what's going to happen?" I ask, feeling slightly nauseous.

Myra shrugs. "If we don't get a few things falling our way . . . it's not looking good."

I bite my lower lip as I watch Cassie grab herself by the arms. She looks like she's about to cry.

"But," Myra says, giving me the eye of the tiger, "there's an opportunity."

"What's that?" I feel both motivated and frustrated at the same time.

Myra tosses the folder on my desk. "Hawaii. We've tried to secure this in the past, but the man never seemed ready to sell."

I flip through the papers, skimming the details. "Wow," I say as I look at the photos that are included. They're not professional, but still, the property is so impressive it doesn't need pro photography. "This could be big."

Myra nods. "And it could be the thing that saves us. I just need someone competent to go seal the deal. I've worked hard and told the suits that this division can handle it. They were impressed by how you secured the Hastings deal. They want you on the task."

"Me?" I say incredulously. "I'm not sure I'm the one for the job with so much at stake."

Myra clucks her tongue reprovingly. "They won't be happy to hear that. But if you insist, I'll tell them."

"I'll do it," I say immediately. It's my ass on the line too, and if it goes south, at least I can't blame anyone but myself. I try to regain my confidence, squaring my shoulders. "I'll take care of it. I know the island market . . ."

I go silent as Myra gives me a bemused and worried look. "It's not what you think. You see, the owner is an eccentric man by the name of Wesley Mobber." Myra picks up the folder off my desk and flips through it, turning pages until she pulls out a glossy photo with a page paperclipped to it. She hands me the photo of a middle-aged white man smiling through a week-old beard with a twisted knot of dreadlocks on top of his head. "He's not going to let just anyone have the property."

I stare. The guy looks like something out of a parodied Internet meme or something. "What's that supposed to mean?"

Myra sighs. "Wesley is not a motivated seller. From what I gather, he'll sell, but first, he has to like you. Like I said, people have been trying to secure this property for a while. He's not doing anything with the land, so he's basically losing money. But he doesn't give a shit. He's got enough to sit on the damn thing until your grandchildren are geezers. And so far, his eccentric ways have proven quite . . . difficult. He's granted us a meeting though, so you have to work your magic and seal the deal."

"I can handle eccentric," Cassie boasts immediately, as if she knows exactly what that means. I damn sure don't. "I'll do my Cassie Charmer and have his head spinning so fast that his dreads are going to—"

"I don't think so. You can stay here," I try to say. If it's this important, I can't risk Cassie screwing this up. Besides, the first surfer hottie she sees, she's going to be distracted for the rest of the stay.

"But this will be good for me!" Cassie pleads, turning to Myra. "You say Hannah is great at her job, you've mentored her yourself. Let me learn from her, maybe she can mentor me?"

Myra bites her lips, thinking thoughtfully. "Maybe…"

I shake my head gently, "Myra, if this contract is do-or-die for the company, I need to focus 100%, not spend time teaching Cassie."

Cassie ping-pongs her head between the Myra and me, finally settling on Myra. "That's the best time to learn."

Myra scowls, and coalesces, "I'll give it some thought, Cassie." Myra turns her gaze back to me. "I need you to go through the report, do your research, and then get back to me asap on your plan of attack so we can book your trip."

"Right away—" I begin to say.

Cassie cuts in quickly. "How am I supposed to get the experience if you don't give me the chance? Please, Myra, I won't let you down. I'll just watch, learn, and follow Hannah's instructions."

Myra pauses, staring at Cassie thoughtfully.

Seeing a hole in Myra's armor, Cassie presses her advantage. "I can play fetch, help her with research . . ."

Myra holds up her hand. "Okay, you know what, Cassie? You're going, but you're going to be Hannah's assistant. Whatever she needs, you do, and nothing more."

"Thank you!" Cassie lets out a squeal of delight, coming

forward to give Myra a hug, but stops dead in her tracks when Myra fixes her with a frosty scowl.

"Don't thank me. Just do your job well," Myra growls. She turns and nods at me. "Report to me when you're done. I'm counting on you." She walks out of the room and enters her office, closing the door behind her.

I let out a groan and mutter under my breath, "Just great . . . she's saddling me with the motor mouth from hell."

"Oh, come on, Hannah," Cassie says, flashing her dimples at me. "You've got the wrong impression about me. You'll see."

I point a stern finger at her. "I'm serious, Cass. I don't want you to even breathe without my approval. We can't screw this up."

Cassie's smile only widens. "You got it, boss."

"And no fetching coffee!" I have to add, remembering the narrowly avoided lawsuit. "I don't want any more fried balls on my watch."

Cassie salutes me. "Got it. No more fried ballsacks!"

Staring into her smiling face, I can see disaster just over the horizon, but I'm hoping I'm wrong. If Myra says for her to go and watch, I'll go with it.

CHAPTER 2

ANTHONY

"ucking asshole!"

Smack!

My head turns slightly to the side, a burning sting on my cheek. Clenching my jaw, I slowly turn my head around to gaze at the furious little minx dressed in a skintight blue dress who's practically foaming at the mouth.

Why does it always seem like chicks can't wait to slap me? Do I have a sign on my face that says *Slap Me*?

"This is the second time you've humiliated me!" Samantha fumes, clenching her hands and standing up on her tiptoes to try to get in my face. She still barely reaches my chin, and that's in three-inch heels. I've heard that short chicks can be feisty, and redheads even feistier. I guess I should have known that going out with a five-foot-tall redhead was dangerous for my health. "I was waiting here for an hour and everyone was looking at me like I was crazy!"

Well, you are crazy.

"Calm down," I say placatingly, glancing around at the crowd of people flowing around us. We're in a shopping mall square. I'd just gotten here and barely had the chance to approach Sam before she goes all MMA on my ass. "Something unexpected came up. I'm sorry I didn't call."

I don't bother telling her I was handling business for Oliver, my big brother. Yeah, I should've called, but I lost track of time. It didn't seem like it took that long. I know I'm at fault here, but Samantha hasn't seemed interested in my job before. She's only wanted to know that I'd be there to show her a good time and then fuck her until she passes out. Usually, I've delivered on both.

I would've tonight, too, but Oliver cockblocked me. I went into town to check out an eightplex, nothing major, and got held up by an overzealous lady who wouldn't stop talking. She wasn't even interested in selling the property. She just wanted to have someone to pour out her life story to. I bet her tenants know better than to hand-deliver the rent checks.

"An hour!" Sam screeches, causing heads to turn as she jerks me out of my thoughts. "We had a date, Tony! A date!"

I scratch at the stubble on my jaw. This is turning left quickly. The biggest problem is, I find myself not really caring that she's mad. Especially since she just bitch slapped my ass.

"Well, I'm sorry," I half mutter.

Samantha scowls at me, crossing her arms across her chest. "Sorry isn't good enough. You know what my girlfriends say? That I made you up. That you are a fictional character whom I only dream about being amazing in bed, and I named you after the vibrator that I carry around in my purse."

I know I shouldn't, but I laugh. "You carry a vibrator around in your purse?"

My laughter only enrages her. "That's funny to you?" she snarls. "It was one damn time, and now you gotta jump on my back too?"

I try my best to hold in my grin, and I hold my hands up in surrender instead. It does me no good. "No, I didn't mean to—"

"You know what?" Sam yells, cutting me off, "Fuck you! I'm done!"

Her dismissal is broadcast to everyone and their grand-mother, and she spins on her heel and disappears in the crowd. A few of the guys walking by give me commiserating looks, but a few are also smirking—single guys who are probably thinking, fuck it, it's my chance now, homey.

For a moment, I stand there, debating on whether to go after her. After a moment, I shrug. It just isn't worth my damn time. We've only been going out for a month, and she already thinks I owe her the world. The only thing I've owed her is what I've given back, toe-curling orgasms that leave her knocked out in bed. But she seems to think my getting her off is some sort of privilege. I don't need that drama. Honestly, it feels like I've just been going through the motions.

But the truth is, I've been in one failed relationship after another. I always do something fucking stupid. I guess this is another one of those situations. A few times, it was because I was scared to commit. I saw the relationship my father had with my mom. I saw how he left her and how Mom struggled for years, refusing the crumbs from his table. I don't want to be that dude.

21

I run my hand through my hair, looking around. I still feel bad for Sam. I honestly didn't mean to be late. But it's actually best that we part ways now rather than later. I could already tell she wasn't the one, so why prolong it?

I rub my cheek. It still burns from the slap, but another girl comes to mind. I fucked that up within a few minutes of talking to her. Shit, I thought I was feeling a naughty vibe from her and figured she'd dig it. I remember the night of the wedding and how she felt for that one dance. The way she looked, and then I went and . . .

I push the thought out of my head. Hannah's far gone, in another city and probably with a guy who treats her right. Hell, she could be knocked up by now. I only knew her for a second. It was just heated lust.

Fuck it, the night is ruined. I could go catch the movie we were supposed to see. I'd talked her into something decent . . .

My phone buzzes and I pull it out. It's a text from Oliver.

Hey, I need 2 C U asap.

Sighing, I tap out a response.

Can it wait? Rly not in mood to talk biz right now.

No. It's important.

Fine. Have it ur way. Be there in 20.

I groan, putting my phone away. There are good and bad things about working for my brother. He's taught me a lot, and that is something I'm grateful for. But still, part of me hates working for Oliver. He's so ambitious, and sometimes it's hard to keep up, present day included. I don't know how he finds time for his family. He's a machine.

I leave the mall and get in my car. On the way downtown, I have my windows and rag top down on my convertible Jag and let the wind ruffle my hair. The moon is out, huge and orange in the sky. It's the kind of night that would be magical except I've fucked things up again.

It takes me just over twenty minutes to get to Oliver's building. I gotta say it looks good. Mindy's Place is on the first floor, and the small sign for his investment business is on the second floor of what's still sometimes called the Flaming Dragon building. Despite the funky ass location name, business has been booming off the charts for Mindy. But right now, everything is dark and closed down. Parking out front, I go around the side and down the stairs to the basement, where I find the steel security door open and a dim light filtering underneath the swinging regular door.

I push my way through the door and see that the only light on is the long LED that illuminates what Oliver likes to call the 'laboratory', the metal table where he, Mindy, or others try to find new recipes. Oliver's standing, his chest and head slightly shadowed as he turns toward me. I expected that, but I'm not expecting the guy sitting at the table waiting with him.

"Caleb?" I ask as he nods in greeting at me. "What are you doing here?"

Caleb Strong, my childhood best friend and one of the few I knew who stuck around in this small town. I haven't talked to him in a couple of days, and he gives me a grin that I've known for years, the one that usually means *just wait and you'll see*. "I'll let Oliver explain."

I nod and look over at Oliver, who gestures with his head. "Sit," he commands.

I bristle, as I always do when he uses this tone with me. "Dude, what the fuck? I'm not your servant."

I hate when he pulls the big bro shit on me. It might have worked when I was in my teens. But I'm a man now, and I don't like being pushed around. Sure, he might have millions of dollars, and yeah, I work for him, but it's nearly ten o'clock on a Friday night, and this isn't the White House.

Oliver, as usual, gives zero fucks. "Sit," he repeats.

I sit down just so we can get on with it. "I let him play big brother sometimes," I tell Caleb, who only grins. He's seen Oli and me bump heads before. He knows the game. I turn my attention to Oliver. "It's Friday night. This couldn't wait?"

Oliver shakes his head. "I've been busting my butt, but this concerns us all. I've been waiting months for an answer on this. You needed to know now so you can rearrange your schedule."

What the fuck is this? I mean, Oli's always got a lot of projects going. He's the sort of guy who loves having about a dozen irons in the fire, but he's making it sound like a goddamn state secret. "My what?"

"How did the look at the property go?" he asks, cutting in before I can complete my question.

"No-go," I reply. "The lady wasn't looking to sell. She was looking for someone to talk to."

Oliver frowns. "Oh, really? And what about the Gallino deal? That one fell through as well."

"That was bad luck," I say. "I couldn't help the owner wanted to pull out at the last second."

"Maybe . . . what about the Doughtry project?" Oliver asks.

"We actually signed the contract on that one, only to find out afterward that the property wasn't zoned for what we wanted to develop it for. Now we're sitting on the damn thing for another year or more while we wait for someone to look over our application."

I shift in my seat, squaring my shoulders to display confidence. "We'll still be able to get back our—"

"I'm getting worried, Tony," Oliver says, cutting me off. You started off hot, man, but lately . . ." His voice trails off, but I get the message.

I can tell where he's coming from. I used to be a major fuckup that loved to party. But those days are behind me. I'm not that guy anymore, with the credentials to prove it. Just lately, I've had a string of bad luck. "So I've hit a rough patch, Oli. Even you've told me that not every property, every business you've touched turns to gold."

"I know," Oliver says, then he chuckles. "Remember when I told you about my sure-fire plan on investing in that deal in Montana? I fucked that one up royally, so I know you can't be perfect."

"Exactly. Hell, I even got you that Lakeside deal for a helluva bargain. So what are you so worried about?"

"Relax, Tony," Oliver says, "I know what you're getting at. And I don't think that. I respect you too much to beat around the bush. I don't think you're just slacking off. That's why I want to send you to Hawaii."

I frown in confusion. "Hawaii?"

"There's a property there," Oliver says, and for the next twenty minutes, he fills Caleb and me in about the place. Caleb knew the gist but not details. "Here's the bottom line.

Gavin and I both want to invest, to turn the property into something that can set both of our families up for life. Tony, if this deal goes right, the Steele family is going to have 'fuck you' money for generations."

"I'm glad you have faith in me," I say confidently. Oliver's worry about my slipping back into my old habits has me irritated and wanting to prove him wrong, regardless of whether he says he doesn't believe that. I'm not a fuckup, nor will I ever be again.

I'll go there, break this bad luck streak, and put all of that to rest.

Oliver looks relieved that I agreed so readily. "Good . . . because Mindy's pregnant again. It'll be a huge weight off my shoulders."

The news hits me like a punch in the chest. I've loved being Uncle to Oliver's two children. "Congrats, man! When did you find out?"

"About two hours before I found out about the Hawaii deal," Oliver says. "It was like a double-whammy."

"Damn, that must be something," Caleb says. "I can't imagine having kids right now."

Oliver grins. "They're a handful, that's for sure." He clears his throat, his gaze returning to me. "So yeah, I'd be going with you if not for that. But I'm counting on you to make this happen, brother."

"Don't sweat it. The deal is as good as done." I nod at Caleb. "And what role does he play in all of this?"

"I've hired him for Steele Solutions. He's smart, and he's helped me on some other properties that needed rehabbing.

He's got an eye for creative ways to solve problems as I'm sure you know from your complete disregard for rules for most of your lives. He's going to be your wingman, not for chicks like you used to do, but for this… With the two of you working together, you should have no problem closing this deal."

CHAPTER 3

HANNAH

"*D*oes this make me look fat?" I ask Roxy, stepping out of the dressing room. It's a black dress that hugs my curves, but it's still professional and businesslike.

"You look like every horny office worker's wet dream."

I roll my eyes even as I agree with Roxy. I do look smoking in this. We're inside Neiman Marcus, checking out new outfits for me. I checked the weather, Hawaii's total tank top and short shorts weather, which I already own, but I need a couple of tropical weight business outfits that won't break the bank. I don't know what this Wesley Mobber guy is like, but I want to make sure I look my best. "Come on, seriously, Rox. Do you think this is too sexy?"

Roxy stares at me for a moment before leaning so far forward in her seat to get a good look at my butt that I think she's gonna fall and faceplant. She taps a finger to her lips. "Hmm, I seem to recall a certain person always talking about my big ass, but it looks like you've been on a Krispy Kreme vacation lately. Got a little more sand in your hourglass."

I scowl. I know she's joking, but she's right. I've been eating unhealthy lately, and while it hasn't been Krispy Kreme, I have done my fair share of late-night Taco Bell runs. But I haven't put on more than five pounds. At least I think . . . I've been avoiding my scale. "Hey! I've been busy and I've gotten in too much of a habit of picking up something quick to eat! It's not fun cooking for a party of one."

Roxy laughs. "You know I'm just playing. You look beautiful, and you've filled out in all the right places, actually. Besides, I'm not one to talk. I've found a couple of new lovers by the name of Ben and Jerry. Jake doesn't mind. He's freaky like that."

I laugh. Roxy knows how to make me feel good. "Yeah, but you have a reason. You're pregnant."

"Speaking of which," Roxy says, rubbing her belly. "I'm having urges now. Baby's saying we want some Chinese, and I saw a Panda Express in the food court."

Before I can reply, Cassie comes out of the dressing room beside me in a two-tone, two-piece bikini. I brought her along for the shopping trip as a chance to get to know her as more than Myra's Minion, and I'm sort of regretting it. She nearly talked our head off on the way here, starting with telling Roxy how much she loves Heartstopper, Roxy's hit song, as soon as she realized that my friend really is *that* Roxy.

"Wa-la!" Cassie says, throwing her arms up and doing a little twirl. "How do I look?"

Roxy places a hand over her mouth, trying to contain the giggles. "My God, leave something to the imagination. I think I can see your uterus."

"Brings a whole new meaning to 'camel toe'," I agree. "I don't know if I'm looking at a muffin or an apricot. By the way, speaking of fruit, that split peach ass of yours is a total no-go."

Cassie places her hands on her hips and huffs in exasperation while stomping her feet. "Dang it! I really liked this one, too!" With another twirl of her barely covered butt cheeks, she goes back into the dressing room.

I shake my head after she closes the door. "Lord, help me. Was I ever that young?"

"She seems like a nice girl," Roxy whispers. "A little cheeky."

I make a face. Roxy's puns are horrible. "Yeah, she's nice. But she talks so much that she drives me nuts. You saw how she was in the car on the way here. It's just how she is, talk, talk, talk, then flash those dimples, and boom, she gets away with it."

"I hear you guys talking about me!" Cassie yells over the dressing room door.

"We're just talking about how sweet you are," I say. "How you bring so much to the office."

"Mhmm. Sure. By the way, I do have more than dimples! I'm just smart enough to know when and how to use them for the biggest bang for my buck."

Roxy chuckles. "She seems fun." Leaning back, she rubs her belly and sighs wistfully. "Hawaii. I sure wish I could go, but Jake would never go for it with my being pregnant. He's turned into a mother hen worrying about me. If I say I want to go to Hawaii, he'd have a fit."

"Well, I'll live it up for you," I say, turning to look at myself in the mirror and running my hands along my side. Roxy's right. I do look good in this. "You definitely don't want Jake worrying. And I promise, I'll bring back lots of good photos. Besides, this trip is supposed to be mostly business."

Roxy's eyes narrow and she gives me a look that reminds me that regardless of whether she's a budding pop star on hiatus or not, she's got as much brains in her head as junk in her trunk. "Oh, yeah, tell me about that again."

"Honestly, I still don't know much. This rich man owns a piece of land that could potentially be worth who knows how much if it's developed right. He's apparently open to selling, but only to someone he approves of. He doesn't really need the money. He just wants to see it in the right hands. What those right hands are, we have no damn clue. My boss seems to think I can charm him though," I say, still trying to wrap my head around it. Myra's file had a ton of information on the property itself and damn near a biography on Mobber, but not much on the development plans for the property, although I've got my ideas. "I guess she's sending me for my personality."

I expect a wisecrack from Roxy, but she surprises me. "I'm sure you'll come through. Who wouldn't like you? Besides, I've never known you not to be able to wrap a guy around your finger in two minutes flat."

I think about the information on Wesley Mobber and shake my head. "I don't know if he'll be susceptible to my charm. Something about him . . . he's just . . . unique."

"Whatever, it doesn't matter. You've got this," Roxy says with conviction.

The doors to the dressing room bang open again, and Cassie comes out, twirling for us on one pointed toe. Her suit's certainly different. She's gone with a white monokini that doesn't look too bad. At least half of her ass is covered.

"How about this one?" she says with that dazzling smile I both admire and get frustrated by. She sashays around, her hands on her hips like she's working the runway.

"Much better," Roxy and I almost say in unison. "I won't be embarrassed to actually be seen in public with you in that thing."

Cassie lets out a squeal of delight. "GREAT! Now I get to try on my party dress." She disappears back into the dressing room.

Roxy shakes her head. "I sure wish I were twenty-one again," she says wistfully. "I'm gonna have a hell of a time getting the baby weight off so I can go on stage again. Her, you can bounce a penny off her butt."

"Ha!" I laugh, looking over at Roxy. For a woman who says she's only having fun with singing, she sure takes it seriously, but I know it's because she loves it. "Speaking of butts, how's everything going with yours?"

"I've already scaled back on singing at Club Jasmine, and no more dancing. Taking it slow, doctor's orders. Jake is having a blast at the company, and his little sister, Sophie, has been kicking ass her senior year of high school. So all I need to be is a lady of leisure—sit on the couch and eat bon bons while watching my stories," she says with a faux snooty affect.

I shake my head, laughing. "I'm jelly. Are you hoping for a boy or girl? It's going to be a girl," I predict. "Knowing your family, you're gonna have a little princess on your hands."

Roxy grins and bites her lower lip. "I hope so too. Of course,

Jake is hoping for a boy. A boy would be great, but I do want a little girl."

I head back into the changing room, and we continue trying on outfits. At Cassie's and Roxy's insistence, I even grab up a new bathing suit, a string bikini, but it does cover a lot more than what Cassie was trying on. I don't think I'll do much swimming, but maybe I'll get in the water at least once. After getting everything we need, we head to the food court and catch lunch.

As expected, Cassie is in her element, talking the whole time, and Roxy tosses me gazes here and there over the gigantic milkshake she somehow thinks goes with sweet n' sour pork. After we clean up, we leave the mall. Roxy insists on driving, and we talk about the upcoming trip. But Roxy catches me off guard when she brings up a sore topic.

"Think you'll be needing protection?" Roxy asks as we come up on a stop light.

"I know I will!" Cassie chirps from the backseat.

I ignore her and give Roxy an appalled look. "How many times do I have to tell you? I'm through with men. This trip will be about business, and business only."

Roxy shakes her head as the light turns green and she takes us across the intersection. "Are you sure? I don't think you are. You can't be celibate for the rest of your life."

I turn my nose up, wanting this to be over. "I just might, yeah. I'd rather wear an iron-locked chastity belt than to deal with the assholes I've had the past few months."

Roxy sighs. "You're so going to end up like Good Girl."

"Huh?" I ask, knowing she's talking something pop culture.

You know, the thing I've been too damn busy to keep up with.

"It's that movie with Jennifer Aniston," Roxy explains, "where she works as a store clerk and then ends up screwing this young guy's brains out because she's sexually repressed and is as horny as a monkey on ecstasy? That one. That's gonna be you."

I laugh, I can't help it. "You're fucking crazy."

Cassie sits forward in her seat, poking her head between us. "How about just getting a Mr. Rabbit and calling it a day?" I give her a look, and she asks sweetly, "What? At least with rechargeable batteries, he'll never let you down. Always hard and ready to jam."

Damn, sweet little Cassie might be a freak. I feel a long-missed sarcastic grin creep to my lips. "Sounds like you're speaking from experience."

Cassie bites her lip naughtily and grins. "I might be."

Roxy glances at Cassie as she turns a corner. "So what . . . never mind. I'm not even going to ask."

We exchange amused glances as we pull up to Cassie's apartment building.

"Wow, thanks for letting me come along, girls," Cassie says. "So I guess I'll see you at the airport Sunday! It was so awesome meeting you, Roxy!"

"Nice meeting you too!" Roxy says, smiling at her. "Hey, when you get back, stop by Club Jasmine. I'll get you VIP tickets to a show, if I can still sing!"

"You were right," Roxy says when Cassie's gone. "She's a talker, but she's sweet as can be."

I nod, grinning for a second before I go more serious. "So . . ."

Roxy glances over as we turn out onto the main road again, her brow furrowing. "Talk to me, babe. What's going on?"

I sigh. "Just . . . there's a lot of pressure. I mean, the whole damn division is resting on my shoulders, and numbers don't mean anything to this man. I've got a lot on my plate."

"If anyone can handle it, you can," Roxy says quietly. "Hannah, you're strong as hell. Forget Good Girl. I should call you Wonder Woman."

"Thanks," I reply, touched. "You think so?"

"No doubt," Roxy says before grinning. "Still, now that I think about it, maybe Cassie was right. Maybe you need to get you a purple friend so you can relieve some stress."

"Roxy!"

She laughs, turning right. "Come on, they even have USB rechargeable shit!"

We get back to my place, and I grab my bags from Roxy's trunk while she looks around at the building. It's a step down from where we lived, and I know she wants me to move to a better place. "Hey, Hannah?"

"What?" I ask as I close the trunk. "Trust me, Rox, I'm getting out of here soon. I've already signed the papers. So let's hope I pull through."

"I wasn't thinking that," she says. "Just . . . try and enjoy yourself. Have some fun, too."

I shake my head, chuckling. "With the pressure, it'll be hard, but I'll try."

"You'll handle it," Roxy says, stepping close and giving me a hug. "Hey, remember, I found my perfect man right about the time I was feeling the same way you are right now. Have a little faith. The right guy's gonna drop right into your lap, you just watch. Enjoy yourself, pretty please? And take some good pictures for me while you're at it. I've always wanted to go there."

I toss her a smile and try to feel confident, even if it's just for her. "I will. I'll call you from Hawaii."

CHAPTER 4

ANTHONY

"*H*and me that hammer," I say to Caleb, steadying myself on my ladder. "The claw one . . . yeah, and the box of nails?"

"Sure," he says. The two of us are up on my mom's roof repairing some old shingles. We're supposed to be getting ready for our trip in two days, but Mom said she had a leak. The weather reports say that there's a good chance of heavy rain in the next two weeks, and I'll be damned if I come home to find she's been flooded out of her own kitchen. Mom's stubborn. Oli and I could easily upgrade her living situation, but she refuses. She loves this place and is intent on staying.

A droplet of sweat runs down my forehead, stinging my eyes. The sun is high in the sky and bearing down on us with unbearable heat. Caleb tosses the hammer as I'm wiping at my eye. Thankfully, I catch it, barely keeping it from cracking my front teeth. "What the fuck, dude? You trying to make me look like the Joker?"

Caleb shakes his head, sweat trickling down the side of his face as he grips his ladder. "Sorry, man. I almost lost my balance and sorta had to wing it."

"It's all good," I reply. I shake my head, aligning a shingle and picking a nail out of my pocket. "You know, I still can't believe my brother hired you. What do you know about property research or contracts or any of that shit?"

I still don't know how I feel about going to Hawaii. Oli put a lot of weight on my shoulders with this Hawaii deal. But after our talk, I want to prove him wrong. I'm not fucking up. The past few deals were a fluke.

"Not a damn thing," Caleb admits. "I think he's trying to help me out. That, and he thinks I can help keep you on task."

I drive the nail into the shingle, grumbling. "So you get to be a personal watchdog. Great."

Caleb shakes his head and slides the fresh box of nails over to me. "Tony, you're a grown ass man. I'm not going to step in your way of having fun. Hell, I hope I have some fun too. I do have some negotiating experience, so I can help with that at least."

"Oh, yeah?" I ask. "You just said you don't know a thing about negotiations or persuasion."

Caleb nods, getting all the way on the roof and opening a fresh pack of shingles. "I once told a girl she was a demon succubus bitch from hell and she believed it. Got her to put on horns and a little tail and try to suck my soul from me through my cock."

I laugh. "You are so full of shit."

Caleb laughs. "Okay, maybe the horns and tail part is a lie.

The truth is, I was in a rut and Oli offered me a spot with Steele Solutions. I don't want to step on any toes."

"You're fine," I reply, chuckling. "I guess I'll just have to see it as I get my own little Padawan following me around. But you can't start calling me Yoda."

Caleb chuckles. "You're too tall. And not smart enough." He checks out his arms and shoulders. "Well, at least we'll have the tan already, eh?"

"Yeah," I agree, driving another nail, "but I'm starting to feel like fried bacon out here. We need to hurry up. Grab shingles and start laying them out for me?"

Caleb squints against the glaring sun and then begins to lay out the shingles, making sure to overlap them to match the pattern with that of the existing roof. "Looks like we almost got this section done though. If you want, I'll grab the other hammer and start from over there. We can get it done quickly."

"Thank God." One of the reasons I brought Caleb up here today with me is that he's always had this knack for fixing things. I mean, I'm okay. I could do a good job on this patch by myself, but Caleb is a jack of all trades. Fix a wonky computer, tinker with a car, figure out what's causing the toilet to gurgle, all that shit. I like to call him Mr. Fix-it. I would've just hired someone, but Mom doesn't like strangers around the house unless there's no other choice. She's always been that way.

"Good. Cause I'm about ready to pull out the hose and douse our asses," I say, wiping at the sweat on my face before hammering another shingle in.

Caleb grabs a half dozen nails and starts on his end. "Next

time," he says as he drives a nail, "buy or rent a damn nail gun or industrial stapler. You've got the money, you know."

"You boys okay up there?" I hear Mom call below us.

"We're making it!" I call down. "Just a few more minutes and your roof will be like new." I glance over at Caleb, who's driving nails with two swings of his hammer like he's Bob Vila or some shit. "Good point. I'll remember that for next time."

"Finished!" says Caleb a moment later with a sigh after driving his last nail. We both scale down the ladder quickly, glad to be off the roof where the heat was baking off the shingles. They might reflect heat for Mom, but when my happy ass is right on top of them, I'm more than happy to be back on the green grass.

Mom is waiting for us, hands on her hips. Over the years, she's managed to keep herself up and looks even better now that she's finally stopped smoking. Thank God for small miracles. "My, you boys look thirsty. Would you like some lemonade?"

I nod while Caleb speaks up. "I'd love that, Ms. Steele."

She shakes her head, a flush coming to her cheeks as Caleb wipes at the sweat on his brow. "Caleb, you are one tall order, and you're certainly filling out from the beanpole you used to be."

Caleb chuckles, and I think he blushes, but that might be the heat. "Thank you, I guess, Ms. Steele."

"Y'all come on inside," Mom says. "It's much cooler. And Caleb, I could use your help with something in the kitchen."

"Of course, Ms. Steele," Caleb says as he follows Mom inside.

I'm about to head inside after them when the backyard gate bursts open and I hear screaming.

"Uncle Tony! Uncle Tony!"

I turn to see two kids tearing across the grass, my nephew in the lead while his sister, Leah, is right behind him. "Hey, squirts!" I greet them, sweeping Leah up into a hug while Rafe clings to my leg. "Y'all keep growing so fast!"

"Looks like I got here too late," Oli says, walking in with a pretty sweet tool belt around his waist, wearing a tank top.

I wipe the sweat from my forehead with the back of my hand. I can't resist this chance to rag on him. "Yeah, right, I know your game. You timed it just right!"

Oliver scowls at me. "Don't start, Tony."

I laugh. "How's Mindy?"

"Fine. Just at the cafe, training up some new staff. She wants to be sure she'll be able to hand things over when she has to slow down with the new baby."

"I understand that," I reply. "She's really taking care of the place."

Oliver nods, looking up at my repair job and nodding in approval. "Where's Mom?"

"Inside with Caleb," I answer. "Something about tasting her apple pie."

He makes a face. "Jesus, Tony, really?"

I laugh. He thinks I'm half serious. "She needed help with something."

"Okay," Oliver says, scratching his jaw while the kids go over to the tire swing that we put up for their visits to Grandma's. He watches them for a moment, then crosses his arms over his chest. "Look, about . . . I don't want you to get the wrong idea about the other night."

I shrug. I don't know what else to do. Oliver isn't the type to apologize much, though he usually doesn't have a reason to. "It's no big deal."

Oliver shakes his head. "I just wanted to let you know how serious this is and that I believe in you."

"I know, and thank you. I won't let you down."

Oliver lifts his chin toward the roof. "And I really appreciate your helping Mom."

"Yeah, about that," I reply, "Caleb says if it happens again, it'd be a lot faster and easier if we get a couple of those big industrial staplers."

Oliver reaches into his tool belt and pulls out a stapler, holding it up. "You mean like this one? Don't tell me you hand nailed all those shingles."

"Asshole," I grumble. "And yes, I did."

Oliver chuckles, then stops. "Well, you got it done. Hey, you got all your shit ready for the trip?"

"Gonna pack my bag tonight," I say. "I'll be ready for the ride to the airport."

The back door to the house opens and Mom comes out with Caleb, who's carrying a big glass of lemonade in each hand. "Oh, great, now I gotta go back and enjoy the AC again to get more glasses."

I laugh as Caleb hands me one of the glasses and offers the other to Oli. "Nah, I'm good."

"Phew, now I don't have to hide the vodka in it," Caleb jokes. Mom, on the other hand, has ignored the three of us to go over and hug her grandchildren, who are super excited to see her. Caleb chuckles. "She always do that?"

"Ignore us?" I ask, and Caleb nods. "Yep. One time, I damn near bled to death in the kitchen because she was so busy playing peekaboo with Leah."

"Oh, stop," Oli says, laughing. "You nicked your finger with a knife. You didn't even need stitches."

"Yeah, but I got salt and lemon juice in the cut," I add. "You know how much that shit stings?"

We all laugh, but then I make a serious face. "Hey."

"Yeah?" Oliver asks.

I look across at Rafe and Leah, who is laughing her head off as Mom pushes her in the tire swing. "Don't worry about Hawaii. Consider it taken care of."

CHAPTER 5

HANNAH

"*A*-lo-fucking-ha!" Cassie cries excitedly, peering out the window of our plane. Luckily we're flying business class, and I was able to get some much needed sleep in. Either Cassie did too, or her energy has no bounds. "Check that out, Hannah. Have you ever seen anything better?"

I have to admit, it's gorgeous. Peering out from my window, I see nothing but clear skies and sapphire blue waters. I've never really been much of a Pacific girl, preferring the warmer Atlantic and the crystal clear Caribbean, but damn if I might not want to change my opinion. Honolulu itself looks like any other urban city, but surrounding it . . . absolutely amazing. Lush green mountains, tropical forests, and on the horizon, I can even see the majestic brutality of Mauna Loa with its constant eruptions. It takes my breath away. Part of me regrets having to pack my camera in my luggage, but there just wasn't enough space in my carry-on, and the view I have can't be translated to a damn iPhone lens. It's the kind of place where I'd want to live if I ever 'make it'.

"It's gorgeous," I say dreamily. I can see the pale ribbon of beach, and I already want to pull on my bathing suit and try to soak up a few rays. Staying professional is going to be harder than I thought it'd be with that much natural beauty to take up my attention.

"Oh, yeah, can't wait to get down there and show Hawaii what Cassie White is all about!" Cassie says excitedly.

I groan, rubbing at my temples. "You keep saying stupid shit like that, and they might be calling for an evacuation. First time they called one that didn't involve a volcano."

Cassie turns and wiggles her tongue. "Oh, come on! We're gonna have so much fun!"

I scowl. "We're here to make this deal. I'm not saying you can't have some fun too. I might do a little sightseeing myself. But getting this job done is our priority."

Cassie snorts, flipping her hand dismissively. "Come on, pull the barbed butt plug out of your ass. I'm just trying to be in a good mood. We're not in the office anymore. This Wesley guy? He's gonna be giving us the property for free when I'm done with him. Just watch. We'll have the rest of the time to party and have fun. I'm going to find a man with a nice long-board for me to surf on!"

I stare at her, unmoved. "You go in like that, and we're going to be flying home—and our first stop will be the unemployment office."

Luckily, that quiets her. The plane shakes as some cross-winds shake us, and I swallow. I hate landings, but at least I get a blissful nine minutes of relative quiet as our plane makes one more turn and comes in for a landing. We get off the plane and grab our bags, catching a cab to take us to our hotel. I have to hand it to Myra. She booked us in a nice place, not one of the big touristy resorts but instead a beach-side spot that's normally used for family getaways, honeymoons, and stuff like that.

"We've arrived!" Cassie says cheerfully, throwing her arms out as if to hug the whole island as we step out of our cab.

I shake my head as I pay the cab and we make our way down the path to the hotel entrance.

Cassie's wearing heels, which might have looked sexy as fuck on the tiles of the Honolulu airport, but they just look out of place and clumsy on the gravel paths of the hotel. I'm glad I decided to go with some platform sandals instead, still sexy but I'm not tripping over every crack in the damn walkway.

"Just a sec," I say, taking out my phone. I just can't help it. "Strike a pose for me!" Cassie does, and I roll my eyes. "One that you don't mind being put on Facebook!"

"Spoilsport," she says, but she still looks cute and fun as I snap a shot with my phone before letting her take one for me.

We enter the hotel lobby, where I see the restaurant off to the side. My stomach grumbles at the sight, but I take a moment to give the desk staff our bags, telling them we want to eat before we check in.

Cassie is grumbling slightly behind me about sand in her heels, but I ignore her as we approach the hostess, a pretty Hawaiian lady who smiles at us with dimples that rival Cassie's. "Aloha, how many?"

"Just us two."

The lady checks her seating chart, and while she does, Cassie nudges me. "Hey, check that dude out. He's hot as fuck and he's staring at you!"

"Uh-uh," I comment, refusing to look. "I don't need any distractions. Besides, they're all the same from Honolulu to Hackensack."

Cassie shakes me so violently I almost pop her. "Will you just look? The one on the left."

Scowling, I turn my head. His back is to me now, so all I see is his frame. He's standing with another guy who's smaller, but still built well. He's wearing a tropical shirt and cargo shorts and he's covered in sweat. I can see his back muscles through his shirt, and I find myself lowering my shades to get a good look. The sweat clings to his shirt and seems to define every ridge and nook down his back. My eyes fix on his ass, and I can't help it, I gulp.

Despite myself, I bite my lower lip. Damn, he has buns that are begging for a little love bite. "You're right. He's a studmuffin, at least from what I see."

"What did I tell you?" Cassie whispers. "His friend's pretty cute too."

"I can't see his face but his backside is a sight," I agree. "But I'm on a mission, and he's not it."

The hostess leads us to our table on an outer patio over-looking the ocean. As we sit down, I catch another glance of Studmuffin as he walks with his friend toward their bunga-low. But the angle is bad again, so I can only see his back.

We go about our light lunch, my eyes still amazed at the sight of the ocean pounding the beach in front of us.

After we're done, we head back into the lobby to retrieve our luggage, check in, and then make our way up to our room.

"You know, Cassie, you might be right," I say as we get off the elevator. "I'm sorry, I don't mean to be such a downer. If I lighten up a little, this trip might end up being amazing after all."

Cassie grins, slapping me on my ass. "That's the spirit!"

I smile at her as we walk down the hall and make it to our room. But my smile quickly fades when I swing the door open and step inside. The room is nice enough, the flooring made of red Spanish tile with white walls and a vaulted ceiling covered in a woven bamboo, adding a touch of natural coolness.

I like everything about it except for one problem.

"There's just one Queen bed. There must be some mistake . . ." I mutter, shaking my head.

"Oh, it's not that bad," Cassie says, walking around and exploring the room before doing a little twirl. "Haven't you ever had a sleepover before?"

I roll my eyes, heading over to the room's phone. "Quiet, Cassie," I growl as I dial the operator.

"Yes?" answers a woman's voice.

I quickly tell her our problem. "Is this some sort of a mix-up? Our room only has one Queen bed, and we don't even have a sofa!"

"One moment," the woman says softly after asking for our room number, and I hear typing in the background. "I'm very sorry, Miss Fowler, but it appears that's correct. You were booked a standard room. But if you would like to upgrade . . ."

"Never mind," I say. "Thank you for your help."

I hang up, grab my cell, and dial Myra, who picks up on the second ring. "Hello?"

"There's one bed!"

"Excuse me?" Myra asks. "Hannah?"

I tell her about our room and how I'd be uncomfortable sharing a bed with Cassie. Meanwhile, Cassie seems unbothered, peering out the window with a sunny smile on her face.

"Hmm" Myra says. "I'll see what I can do."

I sigh with relief. "Thank you, Myra—"

I hear someone enter her office. I can hear talking in the background. "But you might have to make do for tonight," she says quickly. "Gotta go!"

Click. I stare at my phone, not sure if I want to scream or throw my phone into the Pacific. A whole night in a bed with Cass? I might end up killing her by morning. And there's no way I'm sleeping on the floor.

"What did she say?" Cassie says, appearing cheerful despite my irritation, but she's cut off as my phone rings.

"What?" I snap, but not meaning to. If it's Myra, maybe I'll just lose my job earlier than expected.

"You turn into a crab already? Geez!" Roxy complains, chuckling. "I'm just calling to check to see if you landed safely and this is the kind of reception I get?"

I take a deep breath, blowing out a lock of hair from my face.

It's hot, and I look around for the air conditioner. "Sorry. I'm just a little annoyed."

I tell her about my room situation, and Roxy whistles at the end, laughing. "Well, didn't you say you wanted to be a lesbian? Now's your chance!"

"Do you want to die sooner than you expected?" I growl. She's supposed to be supporting me, not making things worse. "Because you are totally not helping."

Roxy laughs. "What? You said it!" She's being ridiculous, but I can't help but smile. "Are you still playing this nun shtick and pretending you're gonna be celibate for the rest of your life? I thought you would have found a man you'd like to bone already. I fully expected to not get answered because you'd be in full-on Fowler Power mode."

I smile again at the old joke. She Rox'd them, and I've got Fowler Power. "You're damn right. Just call me Mother Mary. I ain't giving up nothing."

Roxy laughs. "Remember what I told you before you left about being sexually repressed? You're going to leave there itching for a cum shower!"

"You know what? I think we've about exhausted all the possibilities of this conversation."

"Don't go chasing waterfalls," Roxy sings with faux emotion, "please stick to the balls and dicks that you're used to . . ."

I can't help it, I snicker. "Okay, I'm hanging up now."

"Chill, babe, I was just playing."

"I would say you're going to hell, but that would be a cruel thing for your baby."

"No way," Roxy protests in my ear. "I'm an angel, remember? Just ask my husband."

"Yeah, yeah," I grumble, feeling a little better. I walk over to my bag, pick it up, and take it over to the bed. I pull out the outfit that I want to wear for the meeting with Mr. Mobber later. It's more conservative than I'd like, but I want to look good for my meeting.

"So, how's the island?" Roxy asks. "I mean, besides the room?"

I sigh dreamily, my irritation momentarily forgotten. "It's beautiful. You would love it here. You and Jake should take a vacation here sometime."

"We've talked about it before. For now, you just enjoy yourself."

"I will, I promise," I reply, but before Roxy can say anything, there's a slam of a door in the background. "Sounds like you've gotta go."

"Yeah, Sophie just came in. I'll call you tomorrow or something. Love you."

"Love you too, Rox," I say, and we hang up.

"Okay," I say to Cassie. "Let's get ready and go get that contract. And pray Myra has a new room for us by the time we're back."

CHAPTER 6

HANNAH

*O*n the way out of the hotel, there's no sign of the two hot guys we saw in the lobby earlier. In a way, I'm glad because I want to keep my mind on meeting Mr. Mobber. First impressions are important.

I've dressed for the weather, a colorful flowered blouse with a blue skirt. Wesley's instructions were that he wanted us to meet him dressed casually, and while this is more along the lines of business casual, I'm not going to do anything to fuck up my first impression by ignoring him. I check, and Cassie's dressed similarly, casual without being trashy.

Our cab driver is great, his smile nearly as broad as his massive chest. "Aloha. Hop in, ladies! You got yourself the best cabbie in town. I'll get you where you need in no time."

Cassie grins at the giant man, and immediately, she's talking his head off. We start, and for the next twenty minutes, we're treated to a spiel worthy of a tour guide as our driver points out the local spots.

We drive through a few tourist hot spots before we start to climb higher. The road wraps around a small mountain before dropping back down a little again, and I see a lagoon surrounded by what has to be paradise on earth. "Oh, my."

"Wow, this is enormous," Cassie echoes.

I can only nod my agreement. The road curves as we pass a pineapple grove surrounded by coconut palms. The land is huge, and it seems bigger than even the stats that Myra gave me. Part of it is the hill. It cuts us off from the relative urban setting of Honolulu, and the other natural hills, bathed in the warmth of the sun, give the whole property a secluded, special feeling. I can see why it's a hot commodity.

The cab pulls up in front of the main gate, which I realize is just a line of banana trees. There's a small gate, but that's it. I can see a house in the distance, but I can't believe it's for real. We both climb out of the vehicle and pay the man before he drives off.

"What the . . .?" I say in wonder, shielding my eyes from the glow of the sun and staring at the thing in the distance. Even at a hundred yards away, it's huge.

"That thing looks like something out of Gilligan's Island," Cassie remarks.

As we come up the path, I see what she means. The whole house looks like a giant multi-floored thatched roof hut made of bamboo, but like no other hut I've ever seen before. "How the hell did he pull off the construction? Shouldn't the whole damn thing just collapse under that much weight?"

Cassie opens her mouth to answer, but before she can, we're interrupted. "Hello," a beautiful female voice says softly. "Are you Hannah Fowler?" We both spin to see a petite Hawaiian woman smiling at us. She's wearing a tank top with a flow-ered skirt and a large flower in her hair.

"I am," I say with a nod. "Are you Mr. Mobber's assistant?"

"Something like that. I'm Alani," she says with a nod, smiling softly. "And this is?"

She gestures gracefully to Cassie, and I'm charmed by her movements.

"This is my business partner, Cassie White."

Alani smiles. "Nice to meet you, Cassie."

"Aloha," Cassie says, but I have to cringe as her natural twang turns the greeting into some sort of parody of itself.

Alani, however, seems amused, and she chuckles softly. It's like everything this woman says or does is soft and graceful. "If you would come this way, Wesley's been expecting you."

"Are we late?" I ask, checking my watch as Alani leads us down the path. Past the banana trees, there's a well-groomed lawn and rows of other bushes and trees that I'm sure are some sort of other small orchard. "What's that?"

She looks where I'm pointing. "Oh, that's Wesley's almond and macadamia grove. He does love his nuts."

I stop and see huts in the distance off to the side and point. "Outbuildings?"

Alani chuckles. "No, that is my village. Wesley allows us to live off the land provided we work some here, too. We helped build this house."

"I see," even if I totally don't. Isn't sharecropping illegal? What the hell is going on here?

"There is much for you to learn about this land, and the special nature it has with my village," Alani says. "I hope that you listen to what Wesley has to say and respect his words. It is . . . important."

I note her words and follow her the rest of the way up the path. Huge pillars of native hardwoods rise out of the ground, creating the framework that the bamboo sides work between, and the whole thing is suspended a little way off the ground, probably in case of flooding. The windows glow with light, and I can see rolled up mats of probably woven bamboo that can be lowered over the windows to serve as shades or maybe even shutters of some sort.

"Wow, this is . . . different," Cassie says politely, although I know what she's thinking, that Wesley is exactly as described —different.

"Thank you," Alani says. "This is Wesley's pride and joy, and my brother's too. He designed the water recycling system, and there is very little wasted water here."

She opens the front door, and inside, I'm amazed again. Everything is airy, light, and open, with breezes trickling through the wide open windows. "Wow, this is a fantastic house," I whisper. "I didn't expect this."

"You're just in time," Alani says. "Wesley is meeting with the other two guests."

"Other two guests?" I ask. "I was under the impression that we had a meeting with Wesley to discuss the property. Was there some mix-up?"

"No, no. Come." Her face is a mystery, and I give Cassie a worried glance, but she just shrugs. She's right. Roll with it.

Alani leads us through the house to a room with two large double doors. She taps on the door once before pushing it open, the doors sweeping back on silent hinges to reveal a huge central room. The floors are lined in woven mats, and all around are carved images, I'm guessing Hawaiian idols or something, with the center of the room dominated by a huge fireplace built of volcanic rock.

Three men are inside, one with some kind of bird perched on his shoulder. That's Mr. Mobber. It has to be. "Wesley, Miss Hannah and her associate, Cassie."

"Thank you," Wesley says, and the two men with Wesley turn around.

My jaw drops as I see the dark hair, green eyes, and memories from the night of Roxy's wedding come flooding back. "What is going on here?"

Tony

IT'S SHOW TIME.

"You ready?" I say, turning away from the bedroom mirror and straightening my outfit.

I've opted for a blue blazer and khaki slacks, while Caleb chooses a tropical weight light gray suit. I figured we'd dress nice for the meeting—first impressions and all.

Caleb straightens his cufflinks and flashes a cocky grin. "Does it look like I'm ready?"

I grin and grab our keys while Caleb double checks his bag, and we head down to the lobby. On the way, I send a text to Oli.

Going to meet with Mr. Mobber now. Game face on.

He replies quickly, even though it's gotta be late at night for him now.

I have faith in u.

We jump in the rented SUV and pull off, both of us quiet as we follow the car navigation to Mobber's property. Coming over the hill, I'm shocked as I take it all in. The place looks totally self-sufficient—solar panels, windmills, and agriculture for days.

We pull up to the house, stopping at the gate. A beautiful Hawaiian woman seems to materialize out of nowhere, knocking quietly on my window.

"Are you Anthony Steele? she asks. I nod, and she breaks out into a smile. "Great, Wesley's been expecting you. My name's Alani."

She opens the gate on the driveway and we pull through, pausing as she climbs in the rear seat. "I'm Caleb," Caleb says as she gives him a polite smile. "It's a pleasure to meet you."

She smiles and orders me to pull around to the back to park.

"Are you his secretary?" Caleb asks, and I can tell he's attracted to her.

Alani smiles, chuckling as she shakes her head. "No. I'm his wife."

Caleb and I exchange glances, and he mutters under his breath, "Shit, my bad."

We pull around the house, park, and get out. "You have a beautiful home, Mrs. Mobber."

"Please, just Alani. Wesley and I rarely stand on formality," she says, leading us into the house. We follow her through the rather primitive looking kitchen before Alani guides us to two massive double doors. "He's in here."

The double doors open into an immense room, and I see a man, deeply tanned, wearing cutoff camo pants and a green tank top. His hair hangs down his back in large braids, and his eyes are closed behind the orange sunglasses he's wearing. He's sitting on a large woven mat in the classic lotus meditation position, murmuring something to himself. If I didn't know better, I'd say he's either trying to conjure up a nature spirit or Wesley Mobber is a Buddhist.

So much for dressing to impress.

"Wesley?" Alani says, and he opens his eyes, a slightly snaggle-toothed grin coming to his lean face. He raises his arms. They're nearly skeletal thin but corded in wiry muscle as he rolls back and, in a nifty move worthy of any ninja movie, he kip-ups to his feet in one smooth motion. He snaps his left hand, and out of the shadows above us there's a squawk, and a large colorful parrot or something settles on his shoulder.

"Anthony Steele!" he says, bouncing on his feet with an almost manic energy. With all the hopping, I have no fucking clue how the parrot stays on his shoulder without digging in its claws, but it does, and after a moment, he stops, walking forward and offering his hand. "Long days and pleasant nights!"

"Uh . . ." I reply, trying to figure out where the hell this man came from besides a mushroom patch. "Yes, Tony Steele. Nice to meet you."

"Tony Steele . . . well, I hope you can show me your armor at some point," Wesley says, not shaking hands but slapping palms. Up close, he's got a scent to him, and I crinkle my nose. Whatever this guy's smoking, it sure as hell isn't on any DEA-approved list. "My man! Who's your soul bro with you?"

"Caleb, sir. I'm Tony's associate, learning the ropes a little," Caleb says. Wesley smirks at the use of the term sir but shakes Caleb's hand.

"Well, I wasn't expecting another, but that's fine. We got plenty of pineapple juice and more. Alani, can we get some refreshment for our guests?"

She leaves, and Wesley looks over our clothing disapprovingly, clucking his tongue. "You shouldn't have worn something so formal. It will just get dirty. I did say casual, right? Or did I say business casual? Hell, I guess it won't matter tonight. We'll adjust," he mutters before waving it off. "No matter, you'll do nicely for the games."

"Games?" I ask, confused. "What games?"

Wesley ignores my question, grinning widely. "So, you guys enjoy the flight over? If you'd checked, your flight went right over the property."

"Yeah, it was easy," I say, and Caleb nods.

Wesley clasps his hands behind his back and gives us a look. "And the property? Beautiful place, isn't it?"

"It's a sight to behold. Love the self-sufficiency of it," I say, relaxing a little and adding in some praise that I think would speak to Mobber. Despite a little awkwardness, he doesn't seem too eccentric, maybe just a little weird. I don't know what the previous prospective buyers were talking about and wonder if Oli's info is messed up. Then again, most people don't keep a damn parrot on their shoulder.

"Who is this?" I ask, nodding at the bird perched on his shoulder.

"Hmm?" Wesley asks. He sees my look and chuckles. "Oh, this is High Chief Moani Momilani, or just Mo Mo for short," he says. "My lovable parrot, been with me twenty years. I take her with me almost everywhere I go." He looks at the bird on his shoulder. "Mo Mo, can you say hello?"

I swear the bird squawks, "Fuck you and the horse you rode in on!"

Wesley chuckles, slightly embarrassed. "Um, she sometimes repeats the last bad thing she hears. My wife and I had an argument this morning . . . and Mo Mo thinks Alani speaks the gospel."

Caleb and I laugh. "Girl power crosses species lines, I see."

"Exactly. So, Tony . . . when was the last time you masturbated?" Wesley asks.

Caleb and I exchange identical looks. *What the everloving fuck?*

I struggle to answer. What the fuck do you say to that? "Uh, well . . ."

"It's all about virility," Wesley explains, looking as if he wants to take my balls out and inspect them for good measure. "I want to make sure you're young and healthy. You don't happen to know your sperm count, do you?"

I shake my head. Okay, change of diagnosis. This dude is fucking certifiable.

Still, I'm here to close a deal. "I take care of myself," I manage to say. I'm glad I don't have that drink in my hand. I might have spat it out by now. Meanwhile, Caleb's trying not to laugh his ass off while I try to formulate answers.

"No offense, Mr. Mobber, but we are here about business," I say, changing the subject before he asks me to pull it out and give him a demonstration. "Your property is uniquely beautiful. I understand you chose my family to be the one to purchase it. I'd love to have the opportunity to discuss what you see your estate as and what we'd like to do with the land if you do agree to sell it to us. My brother and I had a few ideas that I'd be more than happy to explain . . ."

Wesley shakes his head, clucking his tongue repeatedly. "I'm sorry, but we can't talk about that until our other guest arrives."

I frown. I didn't know anyone else would be a part of the meeting. I don't think Oliver did either. This isn't the sort of thing that he'd overlook telling me. "Uh, what guest?"

Before Wesley can answer, the door springs open and my breath catches in my throat as I see the beautiful face looking at me.

"What is going on here?" gasps a voice I haven't heard in over a year, but it sounds like honey in my ear.

There, standing in the doorway, are Hannah and a small brunette at her side with Alani standing behind them. Even after all this time, she looks demure but sexy as fuck in her flower printed blouse, her skirt showing legs that go on for days. Just like on the night of Roxy's wedding, her big luminous eyes seem to call to me with their softness.

Wesley chuckles at our shocked faces, and I can hear his grin in his voice. "Those guests."

CHAPTER 7

"*W*hat the hell is going on here?" I demand in disbelief, my heart hammering in my chest. Both Anthony and his friend look shocked, so at least this is a surprise for them too.

Wesley Mobber, who has a strange half braid, half dreadlocked rat's nest for hair and a bird perched on his shoulder, looks amused.

It's been a year. One very long year. And Tony looks just as good as he did the night I first met him.

"Hannah!" Wesley says cheerfully, waving us over. "Come in!" He claps his hands as he sees Cassie. "How fortunate, never a coincidence is there? The fates deemed you to bring a friend too, so everything will be fair, both teams in balance. I'm Wesley. So very pleased to meet you." Wesley looks back and forth between Tony and his friend, then back to me and Cassie. "Yes, this is perfect, truly divine."

My mind whirls. I haven't felt like this since that night Roxy took me to Club Jasmine. I downed enough Little Mermaids that I'm surprised I wasn't singing *Under the Sea* by the end of the night.

Tony recovers from his momentary shock, clenching his jaw and scowling at Wesley in barely disguised anger. When he turns away, I get a good look at his ass, and I can't help it, I bite my lip.

That looks like the same ass on that guy in the lobby.

"What is going on, Wesley?" Tony demands.

"My wife, Alani, was a gracious hostess, I hope," Wesley says, ignoring Tony for a moment and smiling at his wife.

"Of course," I say as I try to quickly regain my composure, "but wait a minute—why are they here?" I might be able to speak clearly, but that's about it. I've got a thousand questions running through my mind right now. "I thought this was supposed to be just us."

Wesley chuckles. "Your handlers didn't tell you?" He looks at Tony, who bristles at the word 'handlers'. I don't like it either. I'm a woman, not a pet. "Either of you?"

We all shake our heads, and Wesley's grin widens. "Well, your companies intrigued me the most. I have to admit, I sent your handlers instructions that I wanted you two. I could envision the cosmos working through your spirits, and that your meridians are approaching a crucial juncture in your lives. I had to know if there was a congruence of your energies or if karma is simply moving us along in the river of fate and we're just temporarily sharing a vessel."

What the fuck is this man saying? He's speaking English, but I have no idea what I'm hearing. I turn to Cassie, my eyes wide. "Did you know anything about this?"

"No," Cassie whispers. "I—"

"Shut your trap!" The bird on Wesley's shoulder squawks.

"Hush, Mo Mo," Wesley chides gently. "Be kind to our guests."

The situation is already so insane that we all seem to ignore the talking bird telling Cassie to shut up, because that's the least odd thing happening here.

Cassie places her hands over her mouth, whispering to me, "This man is fucking nuts, and so is that damn bird."

I nod. "Makes you look normal."

Cassie scowls, looking slightly pouty. "Hey! I resent that!"

"We weren't interested in splitting the property. Why are we both here?" Tony asks just as I open my mouth to ask the same question. The realization sweeps over me, and it all clicks. Oliver. He's an investor. The man's got more money than he knows what to do with. And Roxy mentioned something about Tony working for his brother. It was just passed-along gossip . . .

Wesley giggles, clapping his hands together like he's got us right where he wants us. "Yes, I have my reasons for wanting to sell my hideaway, or as some people call it, the Blue Lagoon. There are duties and responsibilities that come with the property, and to be quite honest, I'm not up to the job anymore. It is time for the legacy to move into another's hands, as it has for generations before me and will continue to do after me. But I'm not going to sell this property to just anyone. Like I said, those duties are important to me. Don't worry, though. This isn't going to be a bidding war. The money isn't what's important to me."

"What's it going to be, then?" Anthony asks, his voice dropping to an intense growl. "Flip of a coin?"

"But," Mobber continues, ignoring Anthony's interruption, "what we truly desire isn't bought with money. And this estate will go to the person who shows me that they are in touch with what they most deeply desire. Honest in that desire, both to themselves and to others."

He grins when he's done with his little speech, seemingly switching from a loopy philosopher to a clear-eyed businessman in an instant. "So, Caleb, Tony, Hannah, Cassie, if you want my property… you will compete for it."

Am I secretly on a gameshow or something? Where's the camera? A tight smile forms on my face as we stand there in shock. "If you'll excuse me for just one moment."

I turn and leave the room, my fake smile morphing into a scowl as soon as I'm in the hallway. Cassie follows me, her mouth immediately running with a million questions.

"Hannah, what are you going to do? I mean, is it legal for him to do this, and like, what does he mean?"

"Please, Cassie, I can't think," I growl, placing my hand on my forehead and groaning. Seeing Tony here is definitely a curve ball and I don't know what to do about it yet.

"And what's with Tony?" Cassie demands, ignoring my request for her to be quiet. "You know him?"

I sigh, seeing his handsome face flash in front of my eyes. "Unfortunately, yes," I say, giving her a shortened version of what happened on Roxy's wedding day. I pull out my phone, dialing Myra without giving her a chance to respond. All she's going to tell me is how I overreacted and how I should've let him rock my world anyway.

"Come on, Myra, please pick up," I beg.

"Hello?" Myra doesn't sound pleased that I'm calling her so soon. But this couldn't be avoided.

"You didn't tell me this guy was a certifiable nut," I whisper harshly. "I won't even go into how he looks or how he speaks, but he's talking about some sort of *Hunger Games* or something!"

"You're making no sense, Hannah."

I tell her everything, from the moment we were dropped off right up until I called her, leaving out no details. "Now, this wannabe pirate son of a bitch wants us to compete to win the property! Compete against my best friend's brother-in-law!"

Myra hums, her voice at least sounding concerned. "Oh, dear. When he said to send you, I expected some hijinks, but nothing like this."

"Yeah," I growl, not ready to discuss Myra's little deception yet. "What do I do?"

"Do what he says. What else is there to do? We can't afford for you to just walk away. You're already there. See it through. Figure it out."

"Figure it—"

Myra cuts me off. "I have the utmost faith in you. Whatever he's planning, you have the skills and professionalism to win him over and land this contract. I've taught you everything I know, so show me you're capable of this, Hannah. Show me and show yourself."

Click.

"Hannah?" asks Cassie, who's been staring at me this whole time. "What's happening?"

"Get ready. This could get dirty."

"THE FIRST CHALLENGE SHALL BE A CLASSIC, A GAME OF TUG-of-war," Wesley says.

We're on the beach that makes up the edge of his property, the sun going down over the water and turning the whole area a blazing orange that would normally make me want to stop and take pictures if it weren't for the intensity and insanity of what I'm doing. I've taken off my sandals and taken off all my jewelry, Cassie doing the same. With us are three Hawaiians, while on the other side of Wesley and Alani are Tony, Caleb, and three others. My team is four women and one man, a giant with hands the size of a frying pan and an amused smirk on his broad, copper colored face. He's about as wide as he is tall, but solid, and I'm sure could probably throw me all the way back to the mainland if he wanted. He calls himself Iz.

Tony and Caleb's team, however, is all men, each of them strong-looking, though nowhere near the size of Iz. All of them are shirtless, wearing various shorts while Tony and Caleb have stripped off their dress shirts and rolled up the legs of their pants. Tony's body glistens in the orange light, and I want to beat him so damn badly. That attraction I had to him before is creeping in on me, and it pisses me off.

"Now, just so we don't have any mix-ups," Alani says in her soft voice, "we have these for you."

She walks toward us, strips of red cloth in her hands. They're headbands, and I tie mine around my forehead, Cassie choosing to wear hers loosely around her neck. I look over and see that Tony's been given blue, which he wraps around his upper arm just above the swell of his bicep. I force myself not to stare, and I find myself ripping my eyes away every time he looks my way, angry at myself for looking at all.

"Now that we have that, teams take your positions," Wesley directs, gesturing to either side of the giant rope.

We get on our side, with me at the front and Cassie right behind. I glance and make sure Iz is all the way in the back as our anchor. I look and see that Tony and Caleb are at the front of theirs. He smirks, and as the teams get their grips, the shit talking begins.

"Why the sour face?" Tony asks me, his lip curling in a dismissive sneer. God, he's so handsome. "At least wait until we beat you. Don't worry, I won't make it hurt too much. The real pain will be when the humiliation hits later."

He's trying to bait me, even as part of my mind wants to explore the ideas of him making it hurt and just how he'd like to humiliate me. I lock that part of my brain away, refusing to say anything. Instead, I lift my nose to the sky, sniffing as I tighten my grip on the rope, digging my feet into the sand.

He chuckles, trying to set me off edge. "Whatcha think, Caleb?"

"Too easy," says Caleb, flexing his muscles. He winks at Cassie, blowing her a kiss. "Honey, you and I should have drinks after this. I'll make it quick."

"You're going down, asshole!" Cassie yells, yanking the rope.

"Going down on asshole!" Mo Mo squawks from Wesley's

shoulder, and I wonder if he's got the perviest bird in the world or if it's just me.

"Chill, Cassie," I tell her. "Don't let them rustle your jimmies. We still have to be professional here."

"I don't like to lose," Cassie growls. She's totally in competition spirit now. Somewhere inside the bubbly, friendly chatterbox is a fighter, and I'm glad it's there.

"Are we ready?" Wesley says, checking that everyone's in position. I look back and see that not only has Iz taken a grip, but he's wrapped the tail end of the rope around his enormous hips. I doubt a truck could pull him right now.

I dig my feet in and nod, unable to take my eyes off Tony, his chest and arms rippling under his tanned, sweaty skin. "Well then, on your mark, get set . . . GO!"

I expect it to be a stalemate, but almost immediately, Tony's team acts as one, jerking hard, and I'm nearly sent sprawling, sliding through the sand and almost across the line.

"FIGHT, BITCHES!" Cassie screams, and I find my footing, digging in. Iz seems to take the lead, grunting loudly, and we jerk back in time with his grunts, regaining a precious little bit of ground.

Growling and grunting, I dig my feet into the sand, tugging with all my might. I want to win this. I lock eyes with Tony as I tug and pull with all I've got. He smirks at me, sweat glistening on his ripped upper body that looks like it's been carved out of rose marble in the sunset light. My eyes can't help themselves drifting down to his abs . . .

I slide forward, my attention slipping as we lose a few inches. *Get ahold of yourself, Hannah!*

I dig in, my feet churning deep furrows in the sand, past the loose surface stuff and digging into the wetter underlayer. It feels like forever, but every time we start to gain some traction, I swear Tony laughs and my eyes are pulled back to him, watching as his hands tighten more on the rope, his muscles flexing as he pulls just a little bit harder.

The end seems to come in an instant. Iz grunts again, and we go to jerk the rope, but as soon as we finish, Tony's team explodes backward. I'm jerked out of the near-foot-deep hole that I've been digging with my feet, tumbling forward onto the loose sand. I fall at Tony's feet, my hair soaked with sweat as I look down at his ankles, my breath heaving and my heart pounding. My hands are on fire, but the humiliation burns my face more as I look up, seeing Tony looking down at me with an expression of both triumph and desire on his face.

"Hmm, already on your knees for me." *Where you belong.*

His words sting even more. A tug of war with five guys against four girls and one guy? It's unfair, even if Iz is the size of a truck. I feel my disappointment snap into anger and explode. "The teams were unfair and you fucking know it!"

Tony smirks and turns away as Caleb grabs him around the shoulders, pounding him on the back. "Good fucking job, man!"

They're cheering at my expense. I want to jump on his back and claw him and . . . my blood heats as my chest heaves, thinking about what else I want to do with him once I get my hands on his body.

"Assholes," Cassie growls, out of breath too. "I'm only a hundred and ten pounds!"

Wesley doesn't seem amused or sharing in the victory. Instead, there's a large frown on his face. "A draw!" he yells.

Tony and Caleb stop their gloating, turning to stare at him. "What?"

Wesley gestures at me, looking at Tony. "You and your friend gloat as if you won, but who really won here? Tony, you raise your hands in victory at the expense of your opponent literally on her knees before you. You both fought in anger and for your own destructive purposes. The true winner is the rope, who ebbs and flows with life, untethered by desires and the strings by which we tie ourselves down, but simply exists in its space and goes with the flow of the forces surrounding it."

"Dude," Caleb protests, "I don't even know what you just said, but that's bullshit!"

"Caleb, bullshit is the seed of life," Wesley retorts. "It serves as the fertilizer that enriches the very ground you walk on, the nutrients that plants use to feed you. So many people say eat shit and die. I say, eat shit and live."

We all look at each other like we're all on an acid trip, and Willy Wonka here just took the left turn to Kooksville. "So . . . what's this mean?" I ask finally.

"Let this be your lesson," Wesley says. "Look deeper than the surface if you wish to impress and win. This is not a competition of objectivity and rules, but of subjectivity and spirit. Your second challenge starts at the house in thirty minutes, during dinner. Alani and I will be there to explain the rules."

Wesley walks off with the Hawaiians, two members of Tony's team supporting Iz as he coughs and rumbles. I hope he's okay. He fought his ass off for us. Mo Mo circles the group as they walk away, and in moments, it's just the four of us on the beach.

Tony stares at me for a moment and opens his mouth to say something, but I turn away, not wanting to give him any chance to gloat.

"Fuck, it sucks we lost," Cassie gasps, still breathing heavily. Her hands are on her hips as she's trying to recover. "I really wanted to wipe that smirk off that cocky bastard, Caleb's, face."

I look back, watching Tony disappear into the shadows cast by the trees on the way back to the house. I want to be mad, to keep my competitive edge, but the only thoughts running through my mind are how his muscles rippled as he pulled that rope.

I bite my lip and glare daggers into Anthony. "Don't worry," I growl to Cassie. "We'll win the next one."

CHAPTER 8

ANTHONY

"We smoked 'em!" Caleb exults as we're ushered back in the house. "They didn't stand a chance."

Of course they didn't, I think. They were right. The teams weren't fair. And from the sound of it, Wesley made it that way to see how we'd react. A test we sorely failed.

The sun is almost all the way down, the lights are starting to turn on around us, and I feel drained. Caleb is still buzzing in victory mode though, and he looks like he could go party the night away if he had the chance. I'm surprised. He's usually laid back. Now, though, his eyes are alive and he's pumped.

Before I reply, the skin prickles on my neck and I look behind me. The girls are coming through the main door, whispering to each other and scowling at me.

I swallow, thinking about how sexy Hannah looked grunting and growling, her competitive spirit refusing to let her go down without a fight. It makes me fucking want her thinking about it. I knew she was a fighter. Goddammit, why did I fuck it up before? I bet she's feisty in bed.

Caleb scratches his jaw, noticing me looking at her. "What's up with this Hannah chick?"

"What do you mean?"

"It seems like you two have history. How do you know her?"

"We met once," I admit evasively. I'm still in shock that she's here. What are the fucking odds?

"Why are you being coy?" Caleb asks. "That's not like you. You're more likely to tell me all the details right down to her preferred cut of panties."

"Because there's nothing to say," I say shortly. "I met her at a wedding a year ago."

Caleb shakes his head. "Do you know how ridiculous you sound right now? You can almost choke on the tension between you two."

"What do you want from me? You know me. I ran my mouth and went a little too far. But she's still a hothead," I mutter, my eyes fixed on her, and I instinctively lick my lips without realizing it.

"Dude, are we going to have a problem here?"

I ignore him. I don't want to play twenty questions right now. Luckily, one of the staff comes to lead us down a hallway, sweat still beading down my body. "Hey, didn't they say we were eating dinner?" I ask. I've worked up a fucking appetite. My stomach growls as if to accentuate the point.

Caleb chuckles darkly. "I wouldn't get too excited. Who knows what the fuck this dude's going to have us eating."

We fall in directly behind the girls as we're led into a large dining room that looks natural and rustic. The large windows give a breathtaking panoramic view of the gorgeous orchards and grounds of the property. The tables are unusual, more Japanese in style, and there are no chairs. I guess we're expected to sit on the floor.

"I hope they have enough to go around," Cassie says impishly as if she has any idea what they're serving. I see Caleb open his mouth to make a reply, but I bump him on the shoulder. I don't need any big sticks of meat jokes right now, even if Cassie did set herself up with that comment.

Alani motions us through the dining room to another, smaller room that has a table covered with a bunch of hand-woven palm frond baskets that are empty. She gives us a small smile and disappears.

Wesley stands at the head of the table, grinning. The damn bird of his is still perched on his shoulder, and I wonder if it shits on it too. It's almost always there. It sure as hell can't be sanitary.

"What's this?" Hannah asks suspiciously while I look around. I'm not exactly prepared to eat. I'm still shirtless, and I need to wash all this fucking sand off me.

"Challenge number two," Wesley says, spreading his hands out, indicating the empty baskets. "To truly appreciate Mother Nature's bounty, you must be in touch with her gifts. Making dinner for everyone. In fact, to honor your team-mate, you will eat only what they prepare, although I will sample all the dishes for judging. There are some ingredients in the kitchen, all sourced from the land here. You will also have access to the garden, the grove, and whatever else you need. You'll have a time limit, though."

I let out a groan. I could fuck up a microwave dinner. We have no chance in hell.

Hannah and Cassie, on the other hand, immediately start whispering with each other, starting their game plan. Caleb looks at me miserably, and I can see he's in the same position I am. Between the two of us, we may starve because I don't think either of us can make anything edible. I turn to Wesley, shaking my head. "This isn't fair," I protest. "Caleb and I couldn't cook a pizza even if you spotted us a crust, sauce, and an Italian grandmother."

"What's the problem? A few too many protein shakes and drive-thrus?" Cassie taunts, and Hannah smirks. Maybe that's why Hannah brought her. Cassie talks a good game.

Wesley smiles, holding up a hand before anyone can reply. "Tony, I didn't say the teams yet. As you saw earlier, things are not always what they seem and what you think you're being evaluated on is not always my focus. You and Hannah will be one team. Cassie and Caleb the other."

"What?" Hannah almost shrieks, looking absolutely mortified. "Tony and I can't be on the same team!"

"Why not?"

Hannah looks flustered, but is obviously trying to tame her reaction. "Be...because we're supposed to be competing against them!"

Wesley smiles serenely. I swear that this guy is into Zen or something. "It matters not. Your dishes will be judged individually, and I thought I've made it clear it's not only about winning. You need to show that you are capable of helping people, even those you don't like."

She looks like she's going to protest but then stops. "All right.

I'm sure he could use a lesson on how to make it hot and spicy." She flashes me a charming smile that floors me. Oh, this is going to be fun.

Her smile is convincing, but I remind myself that it might be part of her plan. She's not going to flip the switch that quickly. It's going to take work before I have her eating out of my hand. But that smile . . . damn, she's good.

Hannah turns, bending over slightly, and whispers something in Cassie's ear. Cassie nods and walks over to Caleb. "Hey, beefcake, you know how to make shrimp on a barbie? If not, I'm sure we can roast some wieners over an open flame."

Caleb gulps and gives me a look I totally understand. Yep, they can't be trusted.

Hannah comes up beside me and pokes me in the ribs. "Hey, partner," she purrs in my ear. "Don't worry. I'll show you all about cooking. I know how to make everything mouth-watering."

My cock twitches in my pants at her words. Fuck, I don't stand a chance. "Watch yourself," I warn her, trying not to let on to the desire raging through my veins.

She grins impishly, biting her lip before turning to Wesley. "I can't wait to start, but can we clean up a little bit first?"

Wesley nods. "Of course. Meet me in the kitchen in twenty minutes. Someone will show you where you can clean up."

"Thanks."

The devious grin she flashes me as she leaves the room with Cassie seems to say *Game On.*

Twenty minutes later, wearing a fresh tank top and some borrowed board shorts, I can't help but laugh as Caleb and Cassie come in. "Dude . . . you're wearing pink!"

"Don't fucking start," Caleb grumbles. He's got on a pink tank top that says *Cowabunga!* "This is her idea of team spirit. And it was easier to give in than to argue. Can we just get this over with?"

Wesley chuckles and leads us into the kitchen. The prep area's been laid out with all sorts of ingredients, and I feel like I just walked into a cable TV cooking show. There's fish, pork, chicken, all sorts of fruits . . . I can't even begin to identify them all. Meanwhile, Hannah looks like she's in heaven.

"How much time do we have?" she asks.

"Ninety minutes," Wesley says, tapping a clock on the wall. "Starting . . . now."

We head over to the table, and right away, I can tell Hannah's done this before. She goes through the ingredients slowly, thoughtfully deciding on her selections before putting them in her little basket. The whole time, she's talking quietly to herself, and in fewer than three minutes, she has what she wants.

All I've got is some coconut and a mango in my basket. "Okay, let's get you set up," she says, and I bristle and reach for the shrimp, knocking her hand aside.

"Hey, watch it!"

"Just trying to be helpful," I say, and Hannah bites back a reply before smiling. "I was thinking Cassie had a good idea. Shrimp?"

84

"With?"

"I dunno," I reply, shrugging. "Let's see what happens."

Back at our bench, Hannah starts cutting up pineapple into bite-sized bits. Then she douses it in some sort of dark sauce.

"Soy?"

"Balsamic vinegar. It's a slaw. Have you cleaned your shrimp?"

"Uh, what?" I ask helplessly.

"You do know you should take out the poop chute, right?" Hannah asks, and I shake my head in mild disgust, causing her to let out a sigh. "Here, let me show you . . ." She gives me a quick lesson on how to peel and devein shrimp and I'm shocked at how much work goes into it.

"What now?" I ask. "Barbeque?"

"Not unless you want them to have no flavor," Hannah says. "Soak it in soy sauce for five minutes, and while you do that, grab that garlic paste and the coconut."

Hannah abandons her side of the bench to bust open a coconut. She quickly shreds the fresh coconut before mixing it with the garlic paste. "Okay, take out your shrimp and . . ." I listen to her orders intensely, following them one by one.

"Guac," Hannah says when we're done with the skewering and cooking, running up front with two big avocados. "Squeeze of lime, salt, and a chopped up tomato. Mix, done."

I nod, getting it done quickly. When it's finished, I dip a finger in to taste. I'm not sure, so I hold it out to Hannah. "Try?"

She hesitates, and for a moment, I think she'll refuse. But

then she wraps her sweet lips around my finger and I'm forced to hold in a groan as my dick becomes rock hard in my shorts. At first, I thought it was genuine, then she makes a show of it, fluttering her eyes and swirling her tongue around my finger like it's my cock.

"Two minutes," Wesley says, reminding us and shaking me back to reality. Hannah grins devilishly at me as I pull my finger out of her mouth and I'm speechless.

Shoving down my lust, I hurry to finish up. "Five, four, three, two, one . . . that's it, hands up, step away!"

I throw my hands up and step back, amazed that I actually put together a dinner, and look over at Hannah, who's smiling at me. I know I shouldn't trust her, but it almost looks real.

We carry our dishes into the other room, where Alani has laid out placemats on the floor, ringing the central area. "Now . . . as a show of respect to your fellow competitor," Wesley says, sitting down easily behind one of the placemats, "you will feed your partner the first bite."

I sit down and Hannah is directed to sit next to me. We place our dishes in the middle, waiting to figure out what he's talking about.

"Watch," Wesley says, using his fingers to pick up one of the shrimp I prepared, and he feeds it to his wife. It's a sweetly sensual moment that I feel a bit voyeuristic watching. He smiles at Alani, then looks at the rest of us. "Just the first bite. Then eat up!"

I glance at Hannah, who gulps, while Caleb and Cassie seem to chuckle. I guess their cooking got along pretty good.

I turn to Hannah, and she picks up her plate, smiling at me.

There's a mischievous spark in her eyes, but I can't for the life of me figure out what she has up her sleeve. "Tuna and halibut ceviche."

She takes a chip to scoop up the fish mix she made, feeding it to me. As I bite down, the delicious seasoning assaults my taste buds.

"Holy shit," I manage, devouring it. "You're talented."

"Thank you," Hannah says, letting me feed her the other part of what we made, a lettuce cup with guacamole. There's a little left on her plump lip afterward, and when her tongue flicks out to lick it off sensuously, I feel a tingle start in the crotch of my shorts. Fuck, I wish this weren't just a game.

With the formality of feeding of each other completed, we start dinner. I'm not allowed to eat anything I prepared, but each bite of Hannah's meal is delicious. I wonder what Caleb and Cassie made, and more importantly if it's better than our dishes since they seem to be chowing down happily. The more I eat, the more Hannah smiles, and I start to wonder if she's really enjoying this. I can't get a read on her.

"A delicious meal," Wesley says, getting up and going over to the side table and coming back with a teapot. "Now, a little tea to wash it all down."

He pours the tea into cups made of bamboo and brings us all a cup. I toast Hannah, who's still smiling. Maybe it's her game face, maybe it's real, but my heart is speeding up and I feel warm. The tea doesn't help, and I shift around, realizing that for some reason, I've got major fucking wood.

"Problem, Tony?" Hannah asks innocently as Wesley sips his tea. "Shh, let's find out who won."

"Of course," Wesley says. "You can guess that the keys for this competition were not just flavor and presentation, but being the cook who best highlighted and respected the natural state of the ingredients. For it is in the natural state . . ."

I try to listen, but my dick is throbbing so hard I'm forced to adjust myself in my shorts.

God, I haven't popped wood this painful since I was going through puberty, I think to myself. I feel like I'm going to explode out of my shorts . . . or fuck, maybe *in* them, right here at dinner.

I look over and see Hannah stifle a smirk. Then it hits me. Hannah. She fucking put something in the food.

"So, Hannah, it was quickly obvious that you are tonight's winner," Wesley says. "But don't get overconfident. There's more tomorrow. You'll be staying here tonight as my guests. Alani can show you your rooms. We'll get started first thing in the morning."

"What—" Hannah begins to complain but stops short at Wes's sigh. "Let me guess. You insist?"

Wesley nods with a tight smile. "Enjoy your evening."

He leaves, and Cassie grumbles about having to stay the night, but Alani doesn't seem to hear her.

Hannah doesn't seem as upset. She's probably still reveling in what she's done to me. As we get up from our seats to follow Alani out of the room, I reach out and pull Hannah in close. Her eyes go wide as I press myself against her side, letting her feel how hard I am. "What the hell did you put in that food?" I demand.

She grins and pulls free, going over to her side of the table, where she tosses me a bottle. "Something to give you a little kick. Some people claim it doesn't work." She looks down at the huge fucking bulge in my shorts, then back up at me. "Looks like they're wrong."

She walks away with a huge smile on her face as I squint at the label. There's some Chinese writing, then in small letters underneath, it says Horny Goat Weed.

Turning my gaze around, I watch as she triumphantly struts down the hall, leaving me wishing I could give her a good dicking until this shit wears off.

"FUCK, MAN," I GROAN, TURNING OVER IN MY BED, MY COCK straining against my shorts. It's been an hour since Alani showed us to our room, and I still have a raging hard-on. "I knew she was up to something."

I grit my teeth as another pulse jolts my dick. Those sweet smiles, the way she sucked on my finger. Good God, she was playing me the whole time.

"Dude, why don't you just go rub one out?" Caleb says in the single bed across from me. Wes made sure we were accommodated in a small room equipped with two beds. It's not as nice as our suite back at the hotel, but at least it's clean with a view of the ocean.

"Fuck that," I growl. "Then she would've won." *When she needs to be taking care of the situation she caused, maybe on her knees.*

"Well it's a whole lot better than sitting there groaning for the next however long." Caleb laughs.

"You're right," I say as an idea suddenly occurs to me. "Which is why I'm going to do something about it."

I roll out of bed, grab my phone, and head for the door.

He gives me a look, probably wondering what I'm doing but not wanting to ask as I walk out of the room. The hallway is mostly dark, just pale moonlight illuminating my footsteps as I find a corner, dialing Oliver's number. I need to give him an update.

"Hello?" he answers after several rings, sounding groggy.

"Oli, what are you doing?" I whisper.

"Trying to sleep. It's like . . . why the fuck are you whispering?"

"Listen, I've got to tell you something. It's about this deal."

I hear Oliver curse under his breath, and then some fumbling, but moments later, he's back, sounding clearer. "What's going on?"

"You're not going to believe this shit," I say before I tell him everything—about Wes, Hannah, and the competition. The only thing I leave out is the hard-on raging in my shorts.

"Hannah?" he asks in disbelief when I finish. "Really? That makes this a little more complicated," Oliver says.

"What do you mean, more complicated? What do you want me to do, walk away?" I ask, but even as I say it, I don't want to. That'll probably mean I won't see Hannah again for another year. Besides, she fucked with me, and I want revenge. There's no way I'm going to let her get away with this.

"No, we can't do that," Oliver says, relieving me. "You said he wants you guys to compete? You can't help that. Just do what he says. Don't play dirty. Be fair."

Don't play dirty. Too late for that, I think.

"Gotcha," I tell him anyway. "And Oli?"

"Yeah?"

"Do me a favor. Get me Hannah's cell number?"

Oliver sounds confused. "Why do you . . . never mind, hold on. I'm sure Mindy has it around here somewhere." I hear him go away and come back a moment later.

He gives me the number, and I repeat it back to him. "Thanks, Bro."

I hang up and rush to the bathroom, turning on the lights, and whip out my throbbing dick, getting a good angle for a picture of it. When I've got a good shot, I attach a text message. *Congrats, you won today. Tomorrow is my turn.*

I hit *Send*, thinking about how hot she's going to get when she sees it. I know it's going to make her pussy wet. I can tell she still wants to fuck me, but I don't want to go overboard like before and piss her off.

Just thinking about it causes me to let out a tortured moan. I reach down, wrapping my hand around my shaft. It's nowhere near as sexy as Hannah's lips when she sucked on my finger, but my brain fills in the details as I replace my finger with my cock, imagining it sliding between Hannah's lips, the way her tongue caressed my skin . . . she'd feel so good licking and sucking on my cock.

I explode, blowing my load all over the shower stall. After I'm done, I rinse the mess down the drain quickly and leave the bathroom with a smile on my face.

I wish I could see her face when she opens that text.

CHAPTER 9

HANNAH

"*J*can't believe he's making us stay here," Cassie complains, lying back on her small bed and sticking her legs straight up into the air. "He's like the insane guy from *Back to the Future*," she says. "Fucking nut job."

We're in a medium-size room in the middle of the house. There are two beds, not the greatest but beats being in that room at the hotel with one bed. And it has a nice view of the outside, and I can see the moonlight glimmering against the beautiful waters.

"I was pissed at first," I say, sitting on my bed and smiling, "but after I thought about how I would have to either sleep in a bed with you or on the floor, I'm kind of glad we're staying here tonight. Besides, I feel so good after my win. And the way I left Tony . . . that was icing on the cake."

"Oh, please," Cassie grunts, squeezing her thighs together. "You're just glad to be near Tony. You want him to ice your cake, don't you?"

"Hell, no!" I say sharply, so much so that I'm not sure who I'm trying to convince. An impish smile comes back to my face as I think about the torture Tony is going through . . . but damn, did that bulge look big.

"You surprised me tonight, that was an evil stunt you pulled," Cassie says, chuckling deviously. "But hey, I loved it. They deserve it for gloating after beating a bunch of girls in tug-of-war. You should've told me and let me slip some to Caleb, though. All his 'aww, shucks' charm doesn't hide the fact that he's full of himself too. I can't believe I got him to wear that pink tank top for *team solidarity*. I told him we were the C-team! Mental note, I guess my Cassie Charmer bit works on him."

I smile evilly, agreeing. I can't believe he fell for my sweet act. He was so into cleaning those damn shrimp that he didn't notice a thing. "Hey, Cass?"

"Ugh . . ." she groans, sounding as if she's trying to pass gas, her legs still tied together and stuck high in the air.

I can't take it anymore. I have to know what the fuck she's doing. "Okay, just what the hell are you doing over there? Trying to lay an egg?"

Cassie grunts again and then laughs. "Actually, I'm using a yoni egg at the moment."

Huh? "Do I want to know what that is?"

Cassie turns her slightly flushed face to me in shock, staring. "You don't know what a yoni egg is? It's a stone that women use to strengthen their vaginal muscles. You've never heard of it?"

"You're exercising your pussy right next to me? Cassie, I just can't with you."

"What?" Cassie protests. "Don't knock it 'till you try it. Give it two weeks, and I bet you could make Tony—"

I shake my head, interrupting her. "Let me just stop you there. I told you, I'm not interested in Tony."

My phone buzzes and I pick it up. It's late, but I figure it's probably Roxy texting, checking in on me.

My smile disappears and my heart skips a beat, my throat going dry as I see the text first.

Congrats, you won today. Tomorrow is my turn.

Then I see the image, and my jaw drops. A big, hard, delicious cock fills my phone's screen.

That fucker. My mouth is watering just looking at it. How the hell did he get my number?

"Hannah?" Cassie asks when I've gone quiet, staring at the screen, lowering her legs and sitting up in bed. "What is it?"

"Nothing," I whisper, trying to keep my cheeks from becoming too flushed. But I can't tear my eyes away. They're glued to the screen and I'm pretty sure my eyes are as wide as saucers.

"It's something. You should see your face right now," Cassie says, squirming. "Show me!"

I snap my eyes away from the picture, desire burning my blood. "It's a . . . it's a dick pic. He sent me his dick." My breath is raspy, and I squeeze my thighs together from the sudden pulsing sensation. The bastard! I can't get the image out of my head. And even worse . . . I want it.

Tomorrow is his turn? What about right fucking now?

"He did not! Oh, my God, let me see!" Cassie pleads.

"No," I snap, shutting off my phone and holding it to my chest. I want that picture all to myself. "I'm gonna try to get some sleep."

Cassie gives me a look. "Yeah, you're not interested in him at all . . ." she says with a knowing smirk.

THE NEXT MORNING, I FEEL MORE REFRESHED, AND thankfully, Tony's cock has only flashed in my mind a couple of times. Okay, maybe a couple of dozen times if I'm honest with myself. But the dreams were pretty spectacular, leaving me aching between my legs this morning and wondering how close they are to the real thing. He's so going to get it.

There's a knock at our door. It's Alani, holding some clothes in her hands. "Good morning, ladies. Wesley wanted you to wear this for today's challenge."

"What is that?" Cassie asks over a yawn and stretched arms. I don't know how much sleep she got, but I hope her pussy is satisfied with the workout. Mine could sure use one from a certain someone . . .

Goddammit, did I really just think that?

"Clothing for Hawaiian dancing." She steps forward and lays a small pile on each of our beds. A red and white floral print wrap-around skirt is paired with a simple white bandeau top, a shell and woven necklace, and matching bands, four of them. I guess they're for our ankles and wrists. "Please get dressed. Your breakfast is waiting for you downstairs, and then I will show you the way to the beach."

With a respectful nod, Alani disappears just as quietly as she entered, while Cassie looks uncertainly at her clothing.

"Hawaiian dancing? Couldn't we just shake our ass a little and call it a day?"

I shrug and reach for the skirt, thinking about how I'm going to face Tony. I can't let him know how much he turned me on. Maybe I'll play it off, act like I never got the text.

We get dressed quickly and head downstairs for a breakfast of fruits and some oatmeal. There's no sign of Tony or Caleb, which I'm grateful for. I could use a few more minutes to figure out how I'm going to face him and to get my head right for the competition.

After breakfast, we hit the beach. As we walk up, I see Wesley, along with Tony and Caleb and a Hawaiian man waiting for us. Wesley looks his normal self, but Tony and Caleb . . . they're dressed in barely-there thigh-length loin-cloths, shelled necklaces, and nothing else. Half of Tony's face is covered in black tribal designs, and his abs are already glistening with sweat.

My breath quickens as my heart rate speeds up, my stomach churning with desire. I'm trying not to think about how hot Tony looks, but all I keep seeing is his perfect cock in front of my eyes.

Remember why you're here! A voice of warning at the back of my mind snaps.

With effort, I tear my eyes away from him, but not before seeing the cocky smile he flashes at me.

Fuck, he knows.

With Mo Mo perched on his shoulder, Wesley is brimming with excitement as usual, clasping his hands together. "Morning, ladies!"

"Morning, ladies!" Mo Mo repeats, and I'm surprised she didn't call us bitches or something.

"Good morning," We reply, stopping in the shade of a palm tree. Thank God for SPF 50, but I'm not going to bake my ass today unless I have to.

"Hope you slept well," Tony says, drawing my attention back to him. He's got a slight smirk on his face, as if he knows my dreams were filled with one thing. And his eyes say he knows I liked it, too.

"Nothing big happened. How'd you sleep?" I shoot back, giving him an airy smile. "I know those spices yesterday were hot. I hope your bed wasn't too . . . hard for you."

He mutters something under his breath and I grin. I can give as good as I take.

"So today's challenge is traditional dancing," Wesley says. "Just as the food we eat is a thanks to the bounty of nature, dancing is a way to express our thanks to the health that the earth has bestowed upon us. While there are many different dances to choose from, I have asked Pete here to help the boys, while Alani has volunteered to teach you ladies."

I feel confidence surge through me. Maybe I can't dance like Roxy, but I can move. "Don't worry," I tell Cassie. "I had the best damn teacher ever. I got this. You can sit back and chill."

"Hey!" she protests. "I've got some moves. Just because you're a big booty ho don't mean I can't drop it like it's hot!"

"Big booty ho!" Mo Mo squawks, and I glare at her, gritting my teeth. I could so kill that damn bird.

Where's Mr. Felix when I need him? I wonder, thinking about my cat I left back home in Roxy's care.

Ignoring her, I blow Tony a kiss. "Say hello to your second loss," I say, shaking my hips.

Tony smirks, glancing down. "I have something to shake too, but it's all in the front."

My face burns scarlet at his words.

"WE ARE NOT CLUB DANCING," ALANI SAYS FIRST AS SHE LINES me and Cassie up. "This is refined, the product of a thousand years of my culture. Please treat it respectfully."

We're under another palm tree in the main yard, the ground smooth so that we can dance in our bare feet. Across the yard, under another tree, Tony and Caleb are doing the same.

Tony sees me looking and stands up from his half-squat. "Don't worry, you'll see more than enough later!"

"You mean we won't see nearly half of what we want!" Cassie taunts back, holding her hands up about three inches apart. Alani tuts, and Cassie grins. "Sorry, I'll be good."

As we work, I show off by adding just a little bit of extra pop to my moves, more for Tony's benefit than for actual hula practice. I don't know if it's worth it, though, as Alani notices what I'm doing. "You're supposed to represent the ocean waves and the beat of your heart," she says reproachfully. "I told you we're not doing that type of dancing."

Tony, on the other hand, starts really awkwardly with stomping, chest beating, thigh slapping, along with all the grunts and yells. During a water break, I laugh so hard, watching him stumble. As awkward as he is initially, I'm surprised when, after Pete tells him it's a big display of masculinity and power, Tony really gets into it. I realize he's doing really well.

Meanwhile, I quickly find Caleb and Cassie dropping behind. I don't know what Caleb's issue is, but Cassie just can't help breaking all the rules. "Pop it, pop it!" she yells at one point, dropping it low and shaking the little bit she's got. "Drop it, drop it!"

"No, no, no!" Alani says, sounding truly pissed off. "That's not how you do it! Hula is not about dropping it low and shaking your ass! It's about celebrating life!"

"Whaddya mean?" Cassie asks, strutting and snapping her fingers. "I'm giving you life! Unlike the cavemen over there!"

Bless her heart.

"Practice is over. Time to bring you together," Alani finally says, and I'm nervous as she waves the boys over. "Your dance will be a recreation of an old Hawaiian legend."

The legend's pretty simple, really. A warrior and a girl meet and fall in love, warrior leaves to fight but returns, and they live together as warrior and bride forever on their island. Alani and Pete demonstrate for us, and it's a beautiful seven- or eight-minute performance. When they finish, she turns to us, smiling. "Your turn."

Cassie and Caleb soon drop out, too hopeless for Alani and Pete to even try helping them any further. They sit off to the side, tossing comments as Tony and I find ourselves working together yet again.

My body flushes as I feel more and more of myself pour into the dance. Tony's every movement pulls at me, and I feel him being drawn to me as well as I dance for him. It's the secret I remember Roxy telling me once. Regardless of whom you're performing for, in that instant, don't worry about the crowd, focus on making it real. Even if only for ten minutes.

"Break!" Wesley says suddenly, and I realize he's been watching us the whole time again. "Ten minutes, rest and have some juice, and then we'll do a final performance."

"I should add some extra . . . spice to your juice," Tony says, his chest glittering with perspiration as he pours me a glass. "I wouldn't want you to tire out."

"I've got more than enough left," I tease, and I can't stop my eyes from tracing a drop of sweat down his chest.

The final dance is done on the beach in front of the whole house staff, the waves acting as a crashing backdrop as we dance. I feel my pulse pounding and a clenching desire between my thighs as Tony dances, pounding his powerful chest and roaring with a primal ferocity. I'm so into the performance that I feel my mind starting to think like the warrior bride even, and I see Tony as a suitor, not my competition.

I feel like he's my warrior. That he'd protect me, give me strong children, everything I could want.

When the last beats of the drum fade away and I'm in his arms, I can feel him pressing against my ass, and I can't help but melt into him. I stumble slightly as I step back, quickly regaining my composure as I hear the applause of the crowd.

"Well done, both of you!" Wesley says, lifting his hands up. "You have honored the tale of the two young lovers."

"Young lovers! Young lovers!" Mo Mo repeats, and I have to blush. I glance at Tony, who gives me a smile, both of us laughing at the bird's antics.

"However," Wesley says, "There was one of you who was just a little bit more authentic. The effort, the passion put into every movement, they spoke not only to the legend, but also to the soul of Hawaii. So . . . Tony, congratulations."

"What?" Cassie gasps, and I feel the same. "No way!"

"Hannah did great, but her dancing felt forced," Wesley explains, and I kick myself for putting in that hip pop that I swore would work. So it wasn't pure Hawaiian. But neither is Spam, and they love that shit here. "Also, Tony's growth from this morning to what we just saw was impressive."

"I understand," I reply, feeling slightly chagrined.

"I hope so," Wesley says. "You must understand, these islands were born tens of thousands of years ago. Generations of Hawaiians have lived, loved, and died here. It is from these people's legacy that we are able to enjoy the richness and bounty of what this special place offers us today. It's important to respect the past."

I feel a tear come to my eye, understanding what Wesley means. My whole dance, I wasn't thinking about honoring anything. I just wanted to get another one over on Tony. I wanted to tease him, to entice him, and while it probably worked, I lost.

"Well now, it was a fun morning. Let's have some lunch," Wesley says after a moment. He leads us back toward the house, where we find a picnic set up on the grass underneath the almond trees. As the gentle scent of almonds fills the air, we dig in.

"This is delicious," I say gratefully as I relish the thin, grilled fish. "Wow."

"So, what brought you to your line of work?" Wesley asks Tony and me. "I'm curious."

"My brother," Tony says almost immediately. "After he came back to town and started his own company, I really thought about what he offered me. I could have gone with him. I could have gone and apprenticed under my dad. But Oliver . . . well, he offered me more freedom. And more respect."

"Freedom to dance?" I tease, and Tony smirks.

"Freedom to be my own man," he replies. "What about you? Last I heard, you were working with Roxy."

Wesley's eyes gleam, and I shrug. "Franklin Consolidated was just a stepping stone for us both. I always worked hard, but ultimately, I was just going through the motions. Roxy gave me an extra little inspiration when she left. The job wasn't bad, but I didn't love it. I traveled, made a go of it as a photographer, and bounced around a little . . . it was tough. I felt like I was facing one of two issues. Either I did what I loved and starved, or I did what I hated and made a decent living. Now I'm with Aurora Holdings, and while it's still not my end game, I enjoy it, and I can still do my photography when I'm out at beautiful places like this."

"There is more to life than money," Wesley replies sagely. "I know that sounds silly coming from a man with money, but I didn't make money to pursue the things I enjoy. I pursued the things I love, and the money found me."

"So what do you pursue now?" I ask, not ready to go that far in depth with him. To hear more about his own struggles, though . . . maybe that's what I need right now to help figure out what makes him tick and what he wants out of this contract deal.

"You'll see after lunch," Wesley says. "For now, eat up."

I glance over at Tony, who's cleaned off his face paint and is still eating his food. I can't stop myself from looking at him, but I try to hide it. I swore to myself I wouldn't say anything, but I want to let him have it over the text last night. I just don't want to say anything in front of Wesley.

The rest of lunch is pleasant, even with the little jokes and flirtatious jibes coming constantly from Caleb and Cassie. I swear, those two are going to end up either killing each other or fucking behind a palm tree at some point before this is all over. I glance at Tony again, and the idea of fucking him behind a palm tree has my fingers trembling as I finish eating.

"Wow, that was delicious," Tony says, licking the last bit of tea off his lips and filling my mind with ideas of what else he can do with that tongue. "Is dinner going to be this good?"

"That's going to be totally up to you," Wesley says, standing up and dusting off his shorts. "You're going to have to catch your own dinner."

CHAPTER 10

ANTHONY

*T*he afternoon is beautiful, with the ocean glittering and large, puffy clouds in the sky occasionally breaking up the glaring sun. I can't help but have a feeling that this land is doing more than just tanning my skin, like I'm being soaked in more than sweat and UV rays.

Wesley smiles at me as if reading my mind. Saying nothing, he turns left as we reach a section of beach that's tidal pools and volcanic rock, leading us toward an area where the waves are huge and gigantic spumes of mist splash into the air as they crash.

As we cut inland and around the rocks, I can feel Hannah's eyes boring into my back. Her struggles of finding her way keep running through my head. I dealt with the same thing for years, and it felt good catching a glimpse of the real her, not just an act to win. It drew me to her for more than just her luscious curves and sexy smile.

Thinking of the dance . . . the way she moved and brushed her body against me. Fuck. I want her. More than that, dancing together brought out something in me that I didn't know I had.

I shake my head, trying to clear it. I made a promise and I need to re-focus. Besides, she might want to fuck me, but she hates my guts.

But what if she doesn't? a voice at the back of my mind asks. *What if it's an act?*

Questions swirl in my mind as we make our way along. When we reach the far side of the rocks, there's a man waiting for us with a rack of gear.

"Bowfishing," Wesley says, taking out an unstrung bow. "Have any of you ever tried it?"

"Does bobbing for apples count?" Cassie asks. "What about bobbing for—"

"Shh!" Hannah growls, smacking Cassie in the shoulder.

I hide a grin. During their down time from dancing, Cassie's gone all in on the competition. Wearing her bandana around her head, she's even painted her face, and somewhere, she got a feather that she's wearing in her hair like some sort of Sioux Indian. I don't know if it's offensive to the Hawaiians or not, but I like her spirit.

Wesley chuckles and ignores her. He seems to be more interested in Hannah and me. "The plan is simple. Jay, here, is going to give you a quick lesson on how to use the bow, and you'll have a little practice time. Then you're going to work in teams, catching shore crabs for bait. You bait the water, aim, fire, and voila, dinner is served."

When he's done explaining, I feel a little anxious. I've fished before, but it was nothing like this. I usually just cast a line, sit there drinking a beer, and if a trout hops on my line, it's great. If not, I grab dinner from the store. Apparently, it's more complicated to fish for parrotfish in the ocean than brown trout from the lake.

Jay takes over, handing us all a sturdy looking bow. "This is a recurve bow," he says, showing us each of the parts. After showing us how to string it, he checks each one. "They're simple, and they're effective, but the ones you have are not that strong." We all listen to him explain. "Come over here," he says when he's done. "I have some targets set up."

Shooting the bow is actually fun, and I find myself enjoying hitting the small balloon targets more often than not. I get frustrated, though, as Jay spends most of his time helping Cassie and Hannah.

"No, no, you're holding your riser too tightly. Relax your grip," he says softly to Hannah. He steps behind her and lifts his arms to mimic her stance and covers her hands with his own. "That's it."

I can't help but feel a slight twinge of jealousy. Sure, let *him* put his hands on you . . .

"It's a bow, not a cock," I tease. "Just a light touch is all it needs." Hannah's next shot goes wild, making her growl. I laugh, earning a fierce scowl.

Jay gives us further instruction, and after we get practice in, we're sent down to the tidal pools in the lava rocks with buckets to find bait.

Cassie, for all her fierce appearance, squeals and drops a crab back into the pools. "That crab—it tried to pinch me!" she wails. "Why can't we just use worms or something as bait?"

"I got a big juicy worm you can catch, baby," Caleb taunts her with a laugh.

"I hope you get a nice double set of claws to the balls!" Cassie shoots back. "Too bad it won't give us much bait!"

Caleb winks at me, enjoying the chaos he's causing. I know he's not an asshole like that. He's trying to sow discord. But I give him a little nudge. "Like football, man. A little trash is fine, but don't get a damn penalty thrown on us, okay?"

Wesley's giving us a little space to learn, but he can still probably hear enough. Caleb nods, and right then, Wesley blows a small whistle. "It's time!"

Jay and Wesley lead us to a cove among the rocks where the waves aren't too bad and we've got decent footing. "Remember, the waves come in sets. You want to try and shoot during the calm between the sets."

Jay starts chumming the water, and soon, there are ripples between the waves. Fish. I nock an arrow, pull back just like Jay showed us, sight, and fire . . . hitting not a damn thing.

"Whooo, nice one there, Robin Hood!" Hannah teases, raising her own bow and firing, but she gets the same result.

"You were saying?" I ask, and Hannah grumbles in reply. For the next twenty minutes, we all hit jack shit, Cassie struggling the worst. I can see what it is, honestly. She doesn't have the patience that the rest of us do, and instead of slowly relaxing her fingers and pulling through like Jay taught us, she's 'yanking and shanking', as he called it.

Finally, just as I wonder if we're going to end up eating nothing but bananas, Caleb gets the first fish, a near-perfect shot on a parrotfish that he pulls out of the water and brandishes over his head.

Just when I'm about to gloat, Hannah releases an arrow that strikes home. She struggles and needs Jay's help to pull it out, but when she does, my mouth goes dry. The fish is fucking huge, easily two feet long and almost as wide. "What the hell is that?

"Roi!" Wesley says enthusiastically. "It's a kind of grouper. Good catch, but it's inedible. Too much poisoning of the waters."

I keep shooting, aiming just for the bigger fish but hitting nothing. Hannah hits another small fish, and now the girls have two to our one.

"Five minutes," Wesley says, but I let it all fall aside as I see something that makes my heart speed up.

I nock my arrow and pull back, knowing I won't have another chance, and I hope the damn line holds. I let fly and feel the jerk in my hands as I hit. The line starts to fly off my reel, and I struggle as Caleb rushes over, helping support me. It's not like rod fishing. There's no bend of the rod to work with. Jay sees what's going on, rushing down to the water with a spear, and with a mighty thrust, he hits home.

"What the hell is it?" Cassie asks, and I'm glad for Jay and Caleb's help as they pull the giant fish up onto the sand.

"A reef shark," Wesley says wonderingly. "A Galapagos reef shark."

Hannah and Cassie try desperately to get another shot in, but Wesley soon calls time. Jay runs off to get some helpers, who carry the six-foot-long shark toward the main house along with the rest of the catch.

"Please wash up. I'll announce the winner at dinner," Wesley says. The four of us head back up to the main house, the girls quiet while Caleb is ecstatic. I say little, happy about my certain win, but I keep stealing looks over at Hannah.

Watching her shoot the bow, it was sexy as hell. She had a total Wonder Woman vibe going, except for the wrong color hair. *Face it, you got lucky.* If that reef shark hadn't been there, I'd have lost.

Dinner is delicious, if anticlimactic. And it feels nice to wear something besides that hip wrap again as we gather on the beach for something akin to a luau. Wesley stands up as the roasted fish is brought in, shark fin soup being the centerpiece. "Today, I hope you learned a vital lesson. In the circle of life, we must respect and take only what we need. The ocean is a bountiful provider, but it's not a Golden Corral."

"Today, we were lucky," Wesley continues. "One doesn't simply harvest a reef shark with a bow, so that makes the winner pretty obvious. The current tally is Anthony and Caleb two, Hannah and Cassie one."

Two to one so far. I should feel good, but looking at the dejection on Hannah's face, a big part of me is uncomfortable, winning at her expense. But my family needs this. Hannah said she's working for Aurora, but it doesn't ring a bell. I'm sure it's some big multinational or something. Knowing them, they'd slash and burn the land around here and put up some sort of damn theme park.

"Oh, by the way," Wesley says, getting up on his feet and pulling my attention away from Hannah's beautiful yet dejected face, "I've decided that you'll be my guests for the rest of the week as well. Like today, it will make it easier without your having to transit back and forth."

We all kind of look at each other, knowing there's no point

in trying to argue against it. That is, except for Cassie. "But what about our stuff?" she asks.

"We'll have it taken care of," Wesley says. "If you give Alani your keys, your bags will be delivered by tomorrow morning. And don't look so down," Wesley adds as he notices we aren't too thrilled about this but just aren't saying anything. "I think you all know as much as I do that this visit will change your life, regardless of the winner."

"Big booty ho!" Mo Mo says again out of nowhere. I'm sure Hannah is ready to take a broom to that damn bird.

"If you wake up with a dead bird in the morning," Hannah growls, "don't be mad at me."

Wesley chuckles. "It's getting late. Let's get back."

On the walk back, I think about it and realize that despite the stakes, we're probably all secretly enjoying this. This place is a hell of a lot more fun than any hotel. It's growing on me.

As we walk toward the main house, I feel Hannah fall into step with me. The way through the trees is somewhat narrow, and more than once, I feel her arm rub against me. The trees are lovely, dark, and mysterious with just hints of pale moonlight filtering through them, and in the half light, I glance over at her. She's more than just sexy. She's angelic, vulnerable, and more. I clear my throat, looking ahead, and Caleb and Cassie have already stalked back to the main house, and we're almost alone.

"You looked good out there today," I say quietly. "I got lucky."

Her lips part in surprise as if she wasn't expecting a compliment. "T-thank you. But you won both games."

"The dancing was just Wes's opinion," I say, stopping. She

stops, and everyone moves further ahead. "Please don't slap me again, but . . ." I add quickly, "The way you moved your hips . . . that was fucking hot."

She laughs, this time not taken aback. "It might've been Wes's opinion, but I can't help but agree with him. You felt like my big fierce warrior, just home from battle." After a moment, she sighs, stepping off the path. I follow her, wondering where she's going. Finally, when the lights from the main house are just glimmers between the trees, she turns to me again. "You know, I wanted to tell you this for a long time after Roxy's wedding . . . I'm sorry, I overreacted. We were getting pretty hot and heavy and you were just going with it."

I step closer, close enough that I can feel the warmth of her body even in the tropical night. Fuck, I want her. "The only thing you should be sorry for is leaving me with a raging hard-on last night."

"Oh?" Hannah says, taking a half-step back. She bumps into a huge rock taller than I am, and somehow, the light from the moon is just right. I can see her face. She's grinning, but at the same time, I think she's turned on, too. "And sending me that picture was okay? You know, that's a crime in some states."

"Is it? Isn't that only if the picture isn't wanted?"

I step closer, so close that I can feel her trembling breath on my cheek, and she can't help but bite her lip. "I–I—" she stutters, at a loss for words.

I press my hard body up against her, feeling the soft resistance of her breasts, and she doesn't fight it but instead moans lightly. I shift my hips, and I know she can feel the hardness of my cock press into the space below her belly button. "Tell me, Hannah. Did you want it? What did you feel when I sent you the pic?"

"Oh, fuck . . ." I hear her moan under her breath.

"You left me hanging," I growl, leaning down and whispering in her ear. I can feel her body almost vibrate, and unconsciously, she puts a hand on my hip. She wants me as much as I want her. "All fucking night. I had to jack off thinking about how wet your pussy got when you saw it, wondering if you were touching yourself. It got me through the night, but your dancing, and watching you be all sexy and powerful with the bow . . ."

"It's hard for me again," Hannah whispers, and I feel the heat growing between her legs. "I can feel it."

"Good," I say, stroking her hair and leaning in. "I want you to feel something else too." I close the last inch, my lips crushing hers in a searing, passionate kiss. Hannah doesn't resist, her hand on my hip wrapping around to grab my ass and pull me into her. I knew she wanted this as much as me. Our tongues twist and taste each other, and I bring my hand up, squeezing her breast through her top and pinching her nipple lightly. "Trust me, you don't need any secret tricks to make me hard. You do that just by being yourself."

"And you make me—" Hannah says, but I cut off her words with another searing kiss, knowing exactly what I'm doing to her. She lifts her leg, wrapping it around mine, and I can feel the heat from her pussy press against my hip. I slide down, pressing the bulge of my cock directly against her, and she moans thickly in my ear. "You feel so fucking good."

"And it's all yours," I growl before I grab her ass, squeezing and kneading it as she bites my lip she's so turned on. I slide my hand up her skirt and inside the back of her panties,

113

feeling the firm, silky soft skin of her ass. It's the best ass I've ever felt, and I massage it, Hannah moaning in my ear as I use my free hand to push my shorts down. My cock springs free, and Hannah gasps as she feels it rub against her inner thigh. I run my hand around to pull her panties to the side, feeling the sopping wet heat from her pussy as I do. "You're going to be all mine, too."

She moans, but at the same time, she pushes me away, a choked sob in her throat. "Wait! We can't do this. I'm sorry . . ." My jaw drops open in shock, and before I can reply, she runs off into the night, back toward the path.

My balls are aching, and my cock throbs as it bobs straight out in front of me. But my grin is tight and spreading on my face. Run . . . for now, Hannah. The competition is just getting heated, and the stakes are a lot higher than just this property.

CHAPTER 11

"What's up with you?" Cassie asks after I get to our room. She's changed clothes, wearing a little set of pajamas. "You haven't said a word since walking in."

I sit down on my bed, avoiding her gaze. I'm still burning up from when Tony pressed up against me. I could feel that big, hard, throbbing . . . a sigh nearly escapes my lips as goosebumps prick my flesh.

I almost let him have me right then and there, pressed against that rock and my pussy begging to have him. At the last minute, I was able to summon strength from the depths of my gut, but even now, I want to go find him again and ask him to fuck me raw.

"Hannah?" Cassie presses.

"Nothing," I reply. "Just exhausted. All of this is taking it out of me."

"You're telling me." Cassie snorts in agreement. "My back

feels like I just went through the CrossFit games after that shit with the bow. Why can't Wesley be a normal human being and just sell his property to the highest bidder? No, he wants us to play *Hunger Games*."

I laugh. "It is ridiculous."

Cassie bites her lip. "But I'd be lying to you if I said I wasn't having fun. Maybe it's all the reality TV I watch, but this is exciting."

I go quiet at her words. I am too, and it's starting to distract me from my goal. Not because of the games, but because of Tony. I don't want to tell Cassie that though. I'll never hear the end of it. I've got to buckle down and get us back on the right path, Myra is counting on us. "I'm having fun too," I admit, "but let's not let it distract us from why we're here. At the end of the day, we still have a job to take care of and people are depending on us."

"Right, and I have every intention of kicking Caleb's teeth in. He needs his ass whooped." Cassie growls, and I can't help but try to hold in a laugh. She's so full of shit. Yeah, she might want to beat him, but there's no real malice in her words. It's like she sees him as a rival or something.

I chuckle. "That's the spirit." I yawn, stretching. I lay back in the bed and turn on my side. "But it's time to catch some Zs. The crackpot is going to have us doing God knows what in the morning. Goodnight, Cass. May the odds be ever in our favor."

"'Night, Han. May you have sweet dreams of Tony."

I ignore her and try to snuggle against my pillow. I hear Cass's bed creak as she gets settled in. For a moment, it's silent and all I can hear are the creatures of the night singing outside. Suddenly, their symphony is broken by a buzzing sound coming from Cassie's side of the room.

I turn on my side and look across the room. Maybe some sort of giant blood sucking night bug has come through the window. "What the hell is that?" I demand, but then I see what Cassie has in her hand from the moonlight, and I blush in outrage. "Cass!"

Cassie looks guilty, hurriedly putting the vibrator back in her bag. "I was just making sure it worked. I wasn't using it!"

"Ugh, I just can't with you! Go the fuck to bed!"

"All right, all right," she complains.

We both settle back in, and within minutes, Cassie is softly snoring. For the next twenty minutes, I toss and turn, trying to focus on going to sleep, but all I can think about is Tony. About how his cock would've felt sliding inside me.

"Fuck," I mutter. "Get out of my head." But the more I try to fight it, the more I think about it. I need some fresh air, I think.

Shaking in need, I get up from the bed, quietly walking across the floor and outside. I suck in a deep breath of the fresh tropical air. It's a beautiful night. The moon illuminates the land and the ocean, with glints from the water and dappled bits of moon sparkling the land and making it look like I'm looking over a field of pearls. Everything is so majestic and pure. It's the closest I've ever seen to heaven. I go back to my room and root in my bags. I find my camera and pull it out, so moved by what I see that I have to record it somehow.

Wesley is such a kook, but in a way, I can see why he always spouts the naturalist stuff. The land is gorgeous. It feels sacred and I want to cherish it.

I walk over to the palm tree near the house and lean against it, sucking in another breath of air as I take in the gorgeous scenery.

"Trying to cool off?" asks a deep voice in the shadows. I let out a strangled cry and drop my camera.

"Shit!" I cry out, picking it up and checking it quickly. It doesn't look like there's any damage. I turn to see Tony standing to my right. He's still got on his shorts from earlier, but he changed into a tank top, his muscles rippling in the soft moonlight.

"What are you doing out here?" I whisper loudly. Just when I had something else on my mind, my body remembers what it felt like being pressed against his, and I start to heat up once again. "You almost bought me a new camera!"

He chuckles. "I could ask you the same thing."

"I was just going back inside," I reply, but he steps in front of me. I start moving around him, but I freeze when he reaches out to grab my arm.

"Wait." I stare at him, not moving an inch. I'm like a bird frozen in the glare of a viper . . . but something tells me he's not a snake. "Stay. I'm not going to do anything you don't want."

That's the problem. I want you so fucking bad.

"It's beautiful out here," he says, making me relax.

"Yeah," I agree, my eyes drawn back to the waters. It's absolutely gorgeous. I put my camera strap over my shoulder, keeping it safe. "It's a paradise."

Tony sighs, then shakes his head. "You know, I've done evaluations and research on all sorts of places, but never something like this. I don't think anyone can say they're prepared for this place."

"I know what you mean. It's the first one where I don't know if I'm evaluating as a professional or for myself. Not that I could afford something like this."

"I know. Hey, come walk with me," Tony says, holding out his hand. "I promise, just a walk."

My heart pounds in my chest. This is so dangerous in so many ways. Finally, I take his hand, and I'm thrilled at the warmth and strength in his grip. Walking together, we make our way down to the shore, walking just inside the high tide line where the sand is still compact. The waves crash on the beach in the moonlight, and it's just gorgeous. Tony is quiet at first, just taking it in, then he clears his throat. "So . . . are you going to tell me what happened after the wedding?"

I hesitate on going this deep with him. But I can't hide the fact that our social circles are intertwined. I take a deep breath. "Life happened."

"That's not very specific," Tony says.

"Well, after seeing Roxy, I just wanted more out of life than an empty apartment. I tried finding a guy of my own, but dating . . . well, it didn't go so well. I tried photography, but I had to give it up when the choice was pictures or the light bill. Then I found my new job, and now I'm on this big mission to take this land, and in direct competition with you."

Tony chuckles. "Do you really want to win this thing?"

I nod, letting go of his hand to pick up a rock and throw it into the waves. "It's not about just wanting to win. Our department needs to show some signs of life."

He looks me over silently for a long time, and I turn back to him. In the ghostly moonlight, I see a softness in his eyes. "And if you don't come away with the deal?"

"Then I'm told we're most likely going to be looking for new jobs," I say shortly.

Tony squats down and picks up a rock, tossing it into the waves along with me. He's so elegant that I hurriedly snap a few shots, wanting to catch him just as he is in the moonlight. "I wouldn't want to see that happen."

He sounds sincere, but I have to remember he's a charmer. I knew that from the moment I met him. I lower my camera, curious. "And what would you want to see happen?"

Tony throws another rock before turning and stepping closer. This close, I can barely see him because of the shadows of the night, but I can hear it in his voice. "A girl like you deserves every happiness in the world." He leans in, and I take a step back, but I can't escape when his lips press into mine again. It's not fierce, but sensually sweet, and he tastes delicious. I let myself melt into him for a moment before we pull back.

"I should probably get to bed. We have an early morning," I manage.

His eyes gleam with amusement as he nods, seeming to say he'll let me go . . . for now.

Tony nods. "Yeah, but I think I'll stay out here a little longer. Sweet dreams."

"You too," I reply, turning and heading back toward the

house. It feels like my legs weigh a thousand pounds as I move away from him.

Tony

WATCHING HANNAH WALK AWAY, SHE'S LIKE A GODDESS, HER hips swaying in the moonlight before the shadows from the trees swallow her. My body is throbbing from head to toe, lust pounding in my veins. I want her so badly.

What stops me from chasing her down to take what we both know she wants to give me was the look in her eyes. I think about what she said and it haunts me. I'm out here for the same reason she is. But the intensity of what she said, what she will lose if she can't ink this deal . . . that hits me hard.

I don't want that for Hannah. But at the same time, I know Oliver is depending on me and trusts me. I have the future of our family in my hands, and I have to make this work. I have to win.

I pick up a rock and throw it into the ocean, watching it splash in the inky black water. I feel torn, conflicted. I want Hannah, and for some strange reason, I feel compelled to try to give her everything her heart desires. On the other hand, there's my family, and my responsibilities and duties to them.

I pick up another rock and throw it harder this time. For an instant, it's a dark speck against the silver of the moon, and I keep my eyes there, hoping for guidance, for answers.

But there aren't any, just the crash of the waves and the crash of the questions in my head.

CHAPTER 12

HANNAH

I wake up with a moan, my eyes fluttering open as I hear bells going off from somewhere in the house. My back feels like iron rods have been shoved up my ass from the physical activity yesterday. My muscles cry out at even the thought of having to do more work. Dancing is one thing, but the Hawaiian dancing used muscles I didn't know I had, never mind the hundreds of pulls on the bow string.

"Someone kill me now," I groan, not wanting to get up. It doesn't help that I didn't get a good night's sleep. I spent all night tossing and turning, my dreams of Tony interrupting me every time I started to drift off.

He seemed like a presumptive ass at the wedding, but maybe I had him wrong. Yesterday, he was the perfect blend of cocky flirting and seemingly honest intensity to pierce past all my defenses. And the way I opened up to him and he kissed me . . .

Ugh.

It's exactly what I said I wasn't going to do, get drawn into another guy. Especially one like Tony, whom I have both history with and am competing against. If we lose this and by some miracle the division doesn't shut down, Myra will fire me in a hot minute if she finds out my mind may have been on Tony's affections and not the task at hand.

I have to keep my eye on the prize. Besides, who knows if his intentions are genuine? He could be playing me like I did him at first.

"Morning, sleepyhead," Cassie says cheerfully from her bed. Hair crazy and sticking out in all directions, she sits up, stretching before she lets loose with a jaw-cracking yawn. "Have some good dreams? I heard you over there grunting in your sleep . . . I think your exact words were 'ooh, fuck me, Tony, fuck me! Make me your big booty ho!'"

I snort, my worry immediately disappearing at those last words. She's just fucking with me. "Never gonna happen," I lie. "I'm just sore."

"Tell me about it. I never thought shaking my ass could make me this sore," Cassie grumbles. She lets loose another yawn and rolls out of bed, bending over to touch her toes and unleashing another series of firecracker pops. "But you know what? I'm kinda glad Wesley wants to hold us hostage. Everyone here is growing on me."

She said as much last night. I feel the same way. "I'm beginning to think—"

There's a gentle knock at our door, and Alani comes in with our laundry from last night. "Good morning, ladies. I thought you could put these away. I also have things that—" Alani starts forward but trips over Cassie's bags, which she left near the door. The bags tumble to the floor, and a large object thunks as it rolls across the floor.

"I don't know her!" I deadpan to Alani immediately when I see a big vibrator roll across the floor. "I swear, I was practically forced to bring her along!"

"Oh, please!" Cassie half yells, rushing over to pick it up. "This is Hannah's. She forced me to put it in my bags because she gets embarrassed. Why didn't you just leave it at home then, hmm?"

"Stop lying!" I hiss, "before that damn bird hears you!"

Alani laughs, not paying us any mind. "Breakfast is ready and waiting, then Wesley wants you to meet up for the next challenge."

I get dressed quickly, something comfortable, just shorts and a tank top with a pair of those water shoe things that Alani gave us. I grab my camera, just in case, and I'm ready. Looking up, I see Cassie's dressed the same, except that her top is slightly tighter and she has her red bandana around her wrist this time. "Let's go kick ass."

After a quick breakfast, Alani leads us across the main road and through the jungle to the base of the large hill that dominates the terrain behind Wesley's estate. As we do, I hear falling water, and we emerge from our trail to an absolute paradise. The water plunges down the side of the mountain, breaking up on outcropping rocks along the way to fall into a pool that's so deep it looks black as I stare into the depths, even though it's crystal clear. Broadleaf trees and bushes surround the oasis, and with my thoughts so obsessed with Tony, all I can think of is a romantic moonlight interlude with him here. Especially on the edge of the pool, where there's a natural shelf that would be just right for him to fuck me . . .

Dammit, get your head right!

I grunt at my own advice. I need to start coming up with a game plan to win. They're ahead and there's no prize for second here.

Wesley, Caleb, and Tony are waiting for us at the foot of the waterfall, and as we approach, it feels amazing, a light shower of mist cooling the air. As usual, Mo Mo is perched on Wes's shoulders, earning a glare from me.

I hope Tony's not trying to tease me. It's working even if he isn't. He's shirtless and wearing the shorts that he had on last night, the ones that do little to hide what's underneath. I can't help it—I start to stare at him unconsciously.

He gives me a smile and my skin flushes, realizing I'm looking at him like he's a juicy piece of meat. To throw him off, I raise my camera and snap a trio of pictures of him against the backdrop of the waterfall, the whole time promising myself they're just for gamesmanship and not personal gratification.

"Good morning," Wesley says. "To be ready to take over my estate, you will need to challenge your strength, but most importantly, your spirit. Your next challenge is a hike up the mountain, to the top of the falls. At the top, there's a type of blue rose that grows nowhere else in Hawaii. I planted it there myself when Alani and I married. You will retrieve a single flower each."

"Ugh, okay. Just let me stretch my legs for the ass kicking I'm about to give you boys," Cassie says.

Tony smirks, and I feel another flutter in my chest. "When you're ready."

Cassie grumbles but gives Wesley a nod, who drops his hand. "Go."

The path is clear and well-marked, and we start marching up the mountainside. As we do, I'm enveloped in the wonderful beauty of the forest, listening as small creatures move from tree to tree. It's not scary, but enchanting, and I love the feeling of the dappled sun on my shoulders. There's a small stream that mirrors the path, and part of me wants to just sit down on a nearby rock and relish the peace and quiet all around me.

I can't though. We need a win here, no matter what. Looking ahead, I see Tony, his muscles in his back, ass, and legs rippling as he strides ahead, slowly gaining distance on me. I want to ignore what the sight of his clenching glutes does to me as I think of how he could drive his huge cock deep inside me, but it's difficult when he's right in front of me.

"Shit, this is rough," Cassie says, wiping at her sweaty fore-head. She's trying her best, but already, the guys are way ahead of us. It's not her fault she's short and their strides are making more of a difference. "I don't know how we can possibly win this damn thing, not unless they are too color blind to figure out what a blue rose looks like."

"I'm already thinking out a plan," I rasp. "You gotta be ready."

"What? What kind of plan?"

I whisper quickly to Cassie. "I'm thinking about pretending to be hurt—"

"OW!" Cassie cries, her ankle twisting as she falls to the ground. "It hurts! Fuck my ass, it hurts!"

I kneel down next to her, trying to move her ankle, and she screams louder. "Damn it, Cassie, I wanted a fake fall, not a real one!"

"It was an accident!" Cassie says, but even as she does, I hear movement on the trail. The guys are coming back, and below us, I hear Wesley hurrying up to our position.

"Hurts!" Mo Mo repeats, squeaking and beating its wings when Wesley arrives. "Fuck my ass, it hurts!"

"Are you all right?" I say, ignoring the squawking bird. I feel bad for Cassie, and I feel even worse knowing this was just what I'd planned to pretend had happened. That would have been fucking low.

"What happened?" Tony asks as the guys come back, both of them sweating. Tony looks at the whimpering Cassie with concern.

"She fell and twisted her ankle," I say, feeling guilty that I'm just a tiny bit jealous of the worry in his face. Seriously, why the hell should I feel that way?

"Let me see." Wesley says with concern. Cassie whimpers as he checks her ankle. "You've got a sprain. It doesn't look so bad, but you should probably stay off it."

Tony and Caleb reach down, helping Cassie to her feet. "I think I can make it," she says bravely, attempting to walk, but with every step, she winces a little bit. Finally, she looks up, tears in her eyes. "I'm sorry, but I don't think I can make the hike."

Wesley looks disappointed, but he nods. "Don't worry, it happens."

"What do we do? Do we all go back down?" Tony asks, looking at me and Wesley.

"Just go on without me," Cassie tells him. "I'll go down slowly. I'll be fine."

"No, I'll take you down," Caleb says. "But don't get too used to it." With little effort, Caleb picks Cassie up and tosses her onto his back like a backpack.

Cassie grins, running her hands over Caleb's arms and shoulders. "Ooh, I need this for the rest of our stay! Let's go, horsey!" she says, kicking him lightly in the ass with her good foot. "Giddyup!"

"Don't make me drop you," Caleb threatens. "And for your information, I'm no horse, even if I am built like one from the waist down."

"I will join you for the rest of the way up the mountain," Wes says, cutting in as we watch Caleb and Cassie make their way back. "Let's resume, shall we?"

We start up the trail again, and I find myself focusing on the scenery. I have to. Tony starts striding ahead more and more, and even as I push harder, my legs and my lungs burn. Still, even as it hurts, I'm swept away by the beauty as we climb higher and higher, emerging at the top to find a clear plateau that is windswept and clear. Tony's ahead of me, but I still stop, what little breath I have left taken away. "It's like I'm on top of the world," I whisper, looking up at the clear sky, the green grass all around me, and the ocean off in the distance. "It's the most beautiful thing I've ever seen."

Wesley clears his throat, and I hurry, reaching the rose bush just as Tony clips a single flower off and hands it to Wesley.

Wesley turns to me, and I bite my lip before shaking my head. "No offense, but we're all here. I might as well leave the flower on the bush. They're beautiful and I don't want to clip them."

Wesley nods. "I'm going to head back down and check on

Cassie. You two stay if you want. If you're not back by lunch, I'll come and find you. I'll announce the winner then."

He leaves, and Tony and I look at each other, not sure what to say. The land is beautiful, and eventually, we just walk together into the shaded forest that borders the clearing. Following the sound of more water, we find another mountain pool, where we sit down, soaking our bare feet. "I wonder if Caleb is still alive?" I say, breaking the silence, "Or has Cassie killed him by now?"

"Oh, she's not that bad, is she? She's got spirit. How did you find her, anyway?"

"I don't know," I reply, laughing. "My boss hired her, and until this, I've never really known her outside work. What about Caleb?"

"We were friends when we were kids, and my brother hired him," Tony confides. "I've been having some bad luck, and Oliver thought Caleb could . . . well, he could help me turn things around."

The more I see, the more I like Tony. He's not perfect, even if his body is, and it makes him even more attractive. He's trying to be a good man, which is so sexy to me. Gulping, looking to change the subject, I look around the little pool we've found. "Have you noticed, it seems like every time you find what you swear is the most beautiful sight you've ever seen, you turn the corner and there's something that tops it? This place takes my breath away."

Tony nods, looking around the clearing. "The waterfall's smaller than down below, but I like the way it bubbles as it hits the pool. It kind of looks like someone pouring champagne."

I giggle, laughing. "Please don't say like one of those cheesy ass champagne fountains of glasses like you see at parties."

Tony laughs, shaking his head. "No. It just looks like someone is pouring champagne into a glass."

I look over, amazed at the poetry in his thoughts. "Wow, you really surprise me."

"Well, be prepared for another surprise," Tony says before he suddenly pushes me back. I go tumbling into the pool, which is a lot cooler at the bottom that at the top. Thankfully, it's not that deep, and I come up sputtering.

"You son of a bitch!" I yell at him, even as I start laughing. "Why the hell did you do that?"

He laughs, jumping into the water near me, disappearing. The bubbling water makes it hard to see, and when he doesn't resurface, I spin around, looking. "Tony?"

With a splash, Tony pops up behind me, grabbing me around the waist. I push away, laughing. "Asshole!"

"What?"

"You know what!" I laugh, splashing him with water. He splashes me back, and within seconds, we're having a pretty epic water fight, both of us soaked to the skin as we tread water. Eventually, we tire and drift to the shallow end of the pool. I see a dark space behind the waterfall and look. "Hey, what's that?"

"Looks like a cave," Tony says, sliding up next to me. "Wanna look?"

"Why not?" I reply, smirking. We walk through the waterfall to find the entrance to a small cave. Leading the way, I crawl through, amazed at what I see. "Wow . . ."

"What?" Tony says as he comes in behind me, his voice failing as he looks around. The cave looks like it's encrusted in diamonds, and through small holes in the roof, we can see each one gleaming with every color of the rainbow.

"Are those?" I whisper, reaching out to touch one.

"Probably quartz," Tony says, then chuckles. "Well hello, One-Eyed Willy."

"What?" I ask, thinking he's making a dick joke, but the look on his face tells me he's not. "What do you mean?"

"This cave . . . it's like a miniature of that one in the old movie, *The Goonies*. It's a treasure cave."

"You're a Goonie," I tease, and Tony laughs. He reaches out, taking me by the wrist and pulling me close.

"And you're a treasure," he says softly, looking in my eyes.

Tony gives me a look that has my body burning again despite the chill in the cave, and I swallow. "Tony . . . why'd you start working for your brother?"

Tony blinks, then shrugs. "After Mom and Dad broke up, Dad took Oli with him, and I went with Mom. Oli was groomed to take over the family company while I was just a back-up plan. They had their falling out, and Oli came home. I was glad, but at the same time, I sorta resented him for that."

"Resented your brother?" I ask, surprised. "Why?"

"He was always the superstar," Tony says with a touch of bitterness. "To try to stand out, I basically turned into a party boy. I wanted Dad's attention, but then when Oli left, for so long, I couldn't understand why, even after he told me. Then when he came to me for help, needing me to watch over

Mom while he went on a trip with his future wife, we kind of patched things up. He's not the asshole I thought he was. So when he offered me a spot, I took it, mainly to learn what made him tick. He's my brother, and for a long while, I felt like I didn't even know him. And, I mean, he makes money like I eat sandwiches. He's always been there and I haven't. I swear, Mom started smoking because of me and my fucking up."

"It seems like you turned things around though," I say, and Tony laughs.

"Like I said, I've had some bad luck on the last few gigs we've gotten into. This job? I wanted to prove that it was just that, bad luck, and not me slipping back into old habits of being careless. I'm sorry that you're the one here competing against me."

"Why?" I ask, and Tony pulls me closer, wrapping an arm around my waist. "Tony . . ."

"Because ever since I saw you at that wedding, you've been at the back of my mind. I've had a chain of failed relationships, and sure, my carelessness may have played a part in that. But I want to believe that it was because they weren't you. You're the woman I really want."

He lowers his lips, and as his lips touch mine, nothing else matters. Who's going to win or lose doesn't matter.

Instead, I kiss him back, enchanted in the glow of the crystals that surround us.

CHAPTER 13

TONY

The first touch of Hannah's lips sends a shock through my body like I've never felt before. We're in a cavern that looks like it was carved out by nature for just this moment. The way the crystals glitter with a rainbow of light plays across her skin as I pull her close, her wet tank top peeling away from her skin as we tug at each other's clothes. Lifting up, I kiss her skin, the refreshing taste of the spring water cool and electric on my tongue.

Hannah leans her head back, and I kiss and suck on her throat, crushing her to my body as I relish the feeling of her breasts pushed against my chest. For all of her strength, she feels fragile, like a hummingbird under my fingers as I cup her ass and grind against her, my desire growing with every beat of my heart, my cock straining inside my shorts. The cave floor outside the small pool at the entrance is smooth and water-worn, and as we sink to the cool stone floor, it feels natural to kneel together, kissing and tasting each other's skin as I strip off her tank top and bra, bending down to nibble at her breasts.

Hannah moans when my tongue wraps around her right nipple, running her fingers through my hair as she gets lost in the pleasure. I suck harder, savoring the hard tip between my lips, running my tongue around and around until she's gasping. Grinning, I switch to the other side while laying her back, sucking on her breast while tugging and pinching the just abandoned nipple.

"Fuck, that feels so . . ." Hannah moans before her words are lost in the whimpers and cries of pleasure. I feast on her body, stroking my hands over every inch of her stomach and legs, exploring with my touch. Her whimpers are music to my ears as our bodies press together. Sliding her shorts and panties down her legs, I feel like I'm on the verge of something life changing.

"You're beautiful," I murmur in the dim light of the cave as I look at Hannah's body. I mean it, too. Each curve is just the right size, every mark in just the right place to make her even more beautiful than the inch before it.

Hannah bites her lip, smiling at me. "Do you have protection?"

I blink, stunned, and hunt in the pocket of my shorts. My wallet is soaked, but I haven't been carrying much cash recently anyway, and I'm glad that putting my wallet in my shorts is as natural as combing my hair in the morning. Pulling it open, I see inside the inner pocket a condom, still sealed in its foil wrapper. I pull it out with a triumphant smile, like I just discovered El Dorado or something. "We're in luck!"

Hannah laughs and stretches out, her breath catching as I push my shorts down and my cock springs free. She blinks, reaching out with her hand to wrap her fingers around my stiff, throbbing dick like she's never seen anything like it before. I wrap my hand around hers and help her stroke me, showing her that the long, thick length is for real.

"That's it, feel me," I whisper as I lie down, cupping Hannah's pussy and massaging her with my fingers. I rub her clit lightly with my palm, my hand tickled lightly by the trimmed dusting of hair she keeps. Moaning, she strokes my cock with a feather-light touch. Rubbing her pussy lips in small circles, I get my fingers wet before sliding two fingers inside her, finding the ridge inside her that makes her body jerk with the lightest of touches. "So that's what you like . . ."

"Please, don't stop," Hannah whispers as I rub her clit and the spot inside her, kissing and sucking on her neck. Her body starts to tremble, and her fingers grow tighter on my cock as she starts to lose control, almost painfully tight as she grows closer. "Tony . . . Tony . . ."

"Come for me, Hannah," I whisper in her ear, licking the curve of the pink shell. "Show me how much you want my cock."

Her hips jerk, and her back arches as she starts to come, her stomach tightening before she moans deep in her chest, her pussy squeezing my fingers. I kiss her strongly, pulling my fingers out and sliding the condom down my aching cock before turning her over. "Wait . . . I need a minute . . ."

"You're on my time now," I growl, lifting her hips and rubbing my cock all around her pussy, giving her at least a few seconds of respite. Hannah doesn't protest, moaning instead as the broad, thick head of my cock rubs over her clit and I pull back, lining myself up. I'm tempted to slam inside in one deep, quick thrust. I want her so fucking badly, but something makes me pull back at the last second, instead going in slowly. I shiver as every tight, wet inch of Hannah's pussy wraps around my cock, our bodies joining as one. Her blonde hair hangs in strings as I pull her back onto me, groaning at the feel of her. "You're worth a year's wait."

"Couldn't have said it better myself," Hannah moans as I pull back and thrust again, this time harder, taking her and claiming her as mine. She gasps, squeezing her pussy around my cock as I start pumping in and out of her. My hands hold her waist tightly, not letting her move as I take her, speeding up before slowing down and pleasuring her with long, slow strokes. I grind deep inside her, letting her feel me stretch her body in ways she's never felt, and she shivers, whispering my name blindly, reaching back for me. I let go of her waist to grab her wrists, holding on as I start stroking in and out again.

I don't know how much time passes. The magic atmosphere of the cave seems to make time stop as I thrust in again and again, our moans and words blurred and echoing off the walls. All I know is that my cock feels harder, longer, and fuller than it's ever been in my life. Sweat trickles down my chest and over the ridges of my stomach muscles as I begin to pound her, Hannah's ass smacking with every hard thrust. Her body shakes as we go faster and faster, so hard that I can feel the impact of our hips with every thrilling stroke of my throbbing cock deep inside her. "Hannah . . ."

"Yes, Tony! Yes!" Hannah cries, her pussy squeezing my cock again, pushing me over the edge. I pull her tight, thrusting hard one last time as I come, filling the condom as her body shakes and she cries out, our screams of orgasm harmonizing and filling the cave.

I pull Hannah up, my cock still inside her as I pant, overcome with the feeling of what we've done. And no matter what, I can't let this be the only time. I have to have her again.

MY HAND IS SPLAYED ACROSS HANNAH'S LOWER BACK WHEN WE return to Wesley's bamboo mansion. After our session at the falls, we went to the bank to dry out and talk before beginning the trek down. Wesley still hadn't come, and our stomachs drove us as much as the desire to spend more time with just the two of us.

I'm not sure what it was, but it was like the floodgates opened with Hannah afterward. She talked to me like I was an old friend, telling me about her life, dreams, and goals in general. I swear I was hanging on to her every word on our descent, enchanted by how we're both similar and complimentarily different.

"I really enjoyed our . . . time together," she tells me quietly as we cross the main yard toward the huge wooden doors. "It was . . . more than I expected."

"Thank you," I say, taking her hand and kissing it, garnering a blush. "I enjoyed it, too."

We walk into the living room and see Cassie chilling in a makeshift hammock, her ankle bandaged and hanging off the side. She doesn't look bothered at all, leafing through a Hawaiian tourism magazine and humming *No Scrubs*. Or at least that's what I think the song is.

"Cass, how are you feeling?" Hannah asks with concern, pulling away from me to go to her side.

"Oh, so now you two come back," Cassie says teasingly, looking up from her magazine and fixing us with a fake scowl. "Got any Trojans left in your pocket?" she asks me in an accusatory tone. "I could hear you two all the way down here."

I chuckle, shaking my head at her ridiculousness. She's right, but there's no fucking way she heard, and I'm not a kiss and tell kind of guy, at least not with Hannah. Hannah's face goes red. "Seriously, how's your ankle?"

Cassie brushes away her worry with a gesture. "It's nothing, a little bruise. Alani fixed me up good. Said if I don't put any pressure on it for the next few hours, I should be fine by tomorrow. She even hooked me up with this and all the tropical drinks I can enjoy. It's like Vegas and Honolulu wrapped up in one."

Hannah sighs in relief. "Thank God."

Hannah looks around. "Where's Caleb?" she asks suspiciously.

As if summoned by the question, Caleb appears in the doorway carrying a stack of wood, Wesley coming in behind him. "Right here," he says, walking over to the side of the room and then lowering the wood to the floor with a grunt. "Though I think my ears are bleeding from being yapped at the whole time down. I think I'm going deaf," he says as he grabs one ear and wiggles it, giving Cassie an amused glare.

Cassie sticks her tongue out at him. "Oh, shut up, you know you love me. Find me some grapes and maybe I'll let you feed them to me, cabana boy."

Caleb snorts. "Oh, I'll feed you something all right, but it won't be grapes. I knew I should've abandoned you."

Meanwhile, Wesley gives us an evaluating look, sizing us up

and seeing us all eager to see who 'won'. "It's a tie. You each get one point."

Disappointment flows across Hannah's face while Cassie whines, "Aw man, that sucks! But I'll take it. It's better than a loss."

Hannah glares at her. "You'd really complain when I did all the work?"

Cassie nods. "Being carried down the mountain by this sweaty, muscly jerk was a pain in the ass. Literally. He kept bouncing me. I think he just liked feeling my tits rub against his back."

"Okay, screw abandoning you. I should've dropped you on your head," Caleb retorts.

I have to laugh at the shenanigans. Caleb and Cassie are intent on needling each other, and the longer it goes on, the longer I can see that they're engaged in a game of one-upmanship.

"So tell me about the hike," Wesley says, peering at us with interest. "What was your favorite part?"

Hannah looks at me and blushes fiercely. We both know damn well what our favorite part was. And just remembering exploring her body makes my blood run hot. Being inside her in that beautiful sacred space was what dreams are made of.

"I–I, uh, er . . ." Hannah mumbles, at a loss for words, her face flaming.

"And that's exactly how she sounded while she was up there with her arms around Anthony," Cassie accuses. "I uh, er arrrrgh gargle . . . cookie monster."

Caleb busts out laughing, but I pretend not to notice, clearing my throat and recounting our finding the cave and everything else—minus the hot sex, of course.

Wesley is silent when I'm done, digesting my words. Finally, he speaks. "So you both experienced the remarkableness of nature. What was the most beautiful?"

"Hannah was." I'm shocked as the words leave my lips of their own volition and silence fills the room. Hannah is staring at me in open-mouthed shock.

Shit, that was supposed to be in my head. I can't believe I just said that.

My admission doesn't seem to shock Wesley, though, and he smiles at me. "Maybe the magic of the land has found a home in you, after all." He studies me quietly, and for some reason, I feel uncomfortable in his peaceful gaze. After a moment, he looks at us all. "Go rest, and change into something more relaxing." Bowing his head, he leaves the room, and I'm left with Hannah's still shocked but touched eyes, Cassie's mischievous smirk, and Caleb's accusatory glare.

Great. Now everybody fucking knows what happened up there.

CHAPTER 14

HANNAH

"**W**hat happened?" Cassie demands as we go back to our room so I can change out of my damp clothes. I'm grateful for Caleb's help again with getting her up the stairs. He's actually a gentleman when it counts and didn't mind carrying her. It saved me at least ten seconds of questions.

That time's over now as she hops over to the bed on one leg, plopping down with a sigh. "And don't tell me nothing either! You had a smile as wide as my ass when you walked through the door!"

That's not very wide, but heaven is what happened, I think as I remember our passionate encounter. It's been over an hour and goosebumps are still all over my body.

I laugh, shaking my head, though I know the glow I'm exuding has to be a huge red flag. "Nothing happened," I lie. "Sure, we flirted, but it was all part of the game. The only fucking that went on was with Tony's head."

I pull off my soggy shirt and toss it in the bin, feeling sore as hell from the hike and the mind-blowing sex. And the crazy part is, I still want more. Two times? As good as it felt with Tony, I'd have been willing to let him make me come twenty times.

Cassie looks like she doesn't believe me, and I understand. I wouldn't believe it either. "How's your ankle feeling?" I ask, trying to change the subject. I'm a terrible liar.

Cassie scowls. "Oh, hell no, Miss I'm The Most Beautiful Thing Tony Saw Today, don't try to change the subject!" She leans forward and sniffs like she's a bloodhound. "I can practically smell him all over you. You dirty little slut, you."

"That's probably your upper lip you're smelling," I say offhandedly, taking off my pants. "Maybe someone got a pain relieving hot beef injection from Caleb on the way back?"

"Oh, hell no! Don't make me go get Mo Mo!" she threatens. "You know she and I aren't messing around!"

I laugh. "You're a total nut."

"And you're a—"

Cassie's cut off by the ringtone on my cell, and I pick it up to see who it is. It's Myra. Oh, now she wants an update?

Anxiety twists my stomach as I answer the call.

"How's the competition coming along?" Myra asks. Before I can answer, she drones on. "Everyone's getting antsy. They're worried about securing the property. After running the numbers, they say this thing is too huge to lose. Please tell me you girls have got this thing in the bag!" The panic in her voice causes my heart rate to speed up, and I admonish myself for letting my focus slip, even if I do want to do it all over again.

My mouth runs dry and I suddenly feel a huge weight on my shoulders. I part my lips to reply before closing them, unsure of what to say. Myra will flip out if I tell her things aren't going too well. Even worse if I tell her I slept with Tony. "Good," I say finally, trying to inject enthusiasm in my voice with sweat beading my brow. "We're doing awesome!" I give her a quick rundown of what Wesley has us doing, not letting on that we're still two points down after this morning and I have no idea how many games Wesley has left in his little bag of party favors.

"Thank God!" Myra exclaims, her voice awash with relief. "I knew I could count on you! What did he say when you presented our offer? Any idea of when he'll make a decision?"

"Well, he took our offer and the contract paperwork, but didn't let me discuss it with him. Just said he'd read over it. I'm not sure on his deadline, but it can't last much beyond the end of the week," I tell her. "But he hasn't told us everything. He seems to like to spring things on us unexpectedly. Like I said, things are looking good and we're doing our best, but it's going to be close."

"I don't care about close, I care about you closing this deal! Make sure he reads the offer thoroughly, go over it with him personally if you can."

I nod, wishing I felt more confident than I sound. "We've got things under control here! Listen, I gotta go, I'll talk with you tomorrow." I hang up the phone, not knowing how to feel. I just lied to my boss and I feel conflicted and confused. Tony needs this, too, just for more personal reasons.

"I can't believe you just did that," Cassie says, looking at me like I've committed a cardinal sin. "You totally lied to her!"

"I didn't know what else to do," I say. "What should I have

done? Tell her the truth, that we're down with who knows how many chances left?"

"But there's a chance we're gonna lose. How's she gonna react then, if we don't pull this off? How can we win when you're sleeping with the enemy?"

Her words cause my skin to prick. Is that what I'm doing? *Sleeping with the enemy . . .*

Well, when the enemy can make me feel like he does . . . damn it, I'll gladly sleep with him.

"I am not!" I object, my cheeks turning red. Technically, I'm not lying. We haven't slept together yet. "Besides, Wesley doesn't seem like he's going to go strictly by the numbers anyway. I think my passing up the blue flower today is what salvaged us a point. We definitely need to be at our best for the challenges, and that means not fraternizing with Tony and Caleb. I've got to find a way to discuss the actual offer with him too. We need to figure out how to direct this deal back to the business of selling, not just the games, even if they are fun. We're not on vacation here!"

There's a now familiar soft knock at the door. It's Alani. "My husband wants to see you in the main room in fifteen minutes."

We nod, and she leaves, closing the door gently behind her. I sigh and change clothes quickly, pulling on dry underwear, some new shorts, and a t-shirt. I also put on the Nikes I packed, knowing with Wesley, I need to be prepared for anything.

I like it here, but always being in the dark is starting to feel less like an adventure and more like a joke on us," Cassie grumbles, rolling over and pulling on socks and shoes. She stands up, wincing but eventually nodding. "Just make sure I don't faceplant. Knowing my luck, we're going to be doing a three-legged race over a crocodile infested lagoon."

We go down to the main room, and once again, I'm struck by how peaceful Wesley's home is. There are mats laid out in rows, and the breeze is trickling through the windows, cooling the room and making it seem even airier. Wes smiles when he sees us and applauds Cassie as she limps in, a determined set to her eyes. "Come in, free spirits of our wonderful world. I must seem like such a bad host, making you always arrive second."

I smile, looking around the place until my eyes meet Tony's. Like a flash, the connection we had at the waterfall is back, and it's like I'm looking inside his mind. It's so strong I almost feel like we have telepathy. I remind myself of the conversation I just had with Myra and tear my eyes away as Wesley continues.

"I understand you're sore and tired. So this afternoon, I've decided to lead all of you in some guided meditation. Before you start to worry about your ankle Cassie, the practice is not meant to stress your body, but to help it reconnect with the restorative powers of nature, and the healing power within yourself. We all share a connection, just like how each of the Hawaiian Islands share a common base underneath the waters of the Pacific. This isn't a challenge, just something for us to do as one."

He goes over to the mat at the front of the room and spreads his hands, indicating for us to sit. I glance at Cassie, who nods, and we all arrange ourselves on the mats. As we do, I notice that Tony and I are seated next to each other, with Cassie and Caleb on our outsides. I feel heat creep up my neck as Tony glances over, and I hurriedly work on taking off my shoes and socks. "Is Mo Mo going to be joining us?" I have to ask as I undo my knot. "I saw yoga with baby goats on YouTube. Adorable, but um, don't get me wrong, but she isn't as quite as cute as a baby goat."

Wesley smiles and shoos Mo Mo away. "No, she won't be joining us today." She leaves his shoulder and flies over to a stand in the corner, where I see there's a small cup of seeds for her. "She'll be preoccupied for a while."

I sit down cross-legged, swallowing as I force myself to keep my eyes on Wesley and not on Tony, and put my hands on my knees. I've been to a few yoga classes before. I want to be respectful to Wesley even if this isn't a challenge. I realize with a start that even more than Wesley, I want to be respectful to this place, which with every breath means more and more to me.

"Now, imagine yourself as a pure ball of energy, and think about how everything around you is also energy. Reach out with your mind and look for that connection with the air, the water, the trees, and the earth itself around you."

Wesley takes a deep breath, a soft smile coming to his face. "Please, everyone, concentrate. Feel the earth, the wind, the water, and the sun around you. Feel the network of threads creating a web containing all that exists. The sun warms the earth, making the plants which we and the animals eat, giving us energy which we return to the earth."

I try to focus on Wesley's words, but the only energy I can think of is Tony's. My mind flashes back to the magical glow in the small cavern and how his hands caused my body to come alive. I imagine his hands caressing my body now, making me feel like a new person. Forget becoming one with nature. I'm becoming one with Tony.

"Hannah," a voice says, followed by an annoying squawk.

"Big booty ho!"

I barely hear either voice, my mind on Tony and how his cock felt in my hand, and how he felt with his fingers inside me . . .

But I'm forced to open my eyes when Cassie complains loudly, "Okay, I can't concentrate with Cookie Monster moaning and groaning over here!"

"Cookie Monster!" Mo Mo squawks.

Heat burns my cheeks. I'm so embarrassed. I had no idea I was moaning.

I clear my throat, trying not to look at him. Then everyone will know who I was moaning about. "Sorry," I say. "I, uh, thought we were supposed to be ohm'ing. I was really getting into it."

"Oh, you were into it, all right," Cassie mutters.

"Quiet, ladies," Wesley scolds us, irritation in his voice. "Close your eyes and focus. Concentrate."

Looking at Wesley, I can see he's trying to do something genuine here. Sucking in a deep breath, I close my eyes and try my hardest to concentrate. I listen as Wesley has us focus inward, trying to shut off our minds. It's hard, though, and Cassie grumbles. "It's like a convention going on in my head."

"Then like a convention hall, try to focus on one voice," Wesley says quietly. "I want you all to focus on your dreams, your future. Build in your mind that one image, the thing you want most in your future."

I take a deep breath, breathing along with Wesley as I try to focus. But still . . . "It's all so staticky."

"That's because you're trying to force it," Wesley says. "Don't think. Feel. Let it go, let it flow over you."

I try again, and as the minutes pass, I'm aware of a growing presence next to me. Tony. In my mind, I don't see myself winning the competition. I don't see myself living in a penthouse or driving a fancy car. Or with millions of dollars. I see . . . Tony. I see him, a few laugh lines in his face, a little bit of softness to his chiseled abs, but a look in his eyes that still burns with more warmth and love than I've ever seen in my entire life. "Oh, my God."

"That's good," Wesley says, clapping his hands lightly. "Now, I won't ask you to reveal what you saw in your mind. Just reflect, and I'll see you in a few hours. I hope you feel more refreshed. This evening will be more recovery for you."

He gets up quietly and leaves, the four of us following behind him. I don't say anything, forcing myself to look down and not face the question that's tearing through my brain. How am I supposed to win this competition when I'm starting to have feelings for my opponent?

CHAPTER 15

ANTHONY

fter we finish the meditation session, my body feels relaxed even as my mind whirls. I've spent the last thirty minutes trying to clear my thoughts, to let it happen, like Wesley said. Instead, the whole time, my thoughts keep going to Hannah. Feeling her presence next to me, I had to stop myself from reaching out to take her hand. So while my body is ready for whatever we're going to do next, my mind is a jumble of thoughts, most of them about how much I want Hannah. I kept feeling the pulse of our hearts as we were in the lagoon, how she looked in the sunlight both before we went in the cave and after. Most of all, I remember how she felt, how soft her skin was, how her eyes widened the first time I slipped my fingers inside her. I remember what my orgasm felt like, and how I wished there wasn't a condom to get in the damn way. I'm surprised I'm not tenting my shorts like a teenage Boy Scout at this point.

"Meet outside after dinner," Wesley says, getting to his feet. "I'm going to be introducing you to the clearing house before bed."

"The clearing house?" Hannah asks, getting her shoes on. She glances at me, and I can see the way her t-shirt molds perfectly to her body, my mouth going dry again in an instant. "What are we clearing?"

"You'll be clearing yourselves," Wesley replies. "It's special to me. It's a place meant for the cleansing of both mind and body."

"Wash your ass!" Mo Mo screeches, although for a moment there, I thought the bird said *watch your ass*. Good advice either way.

Wesley leaves with a smile, ignoring Caleb, who keeps trying to stammer another question. Cassie follows him out, saying something about how she's glad she doesn't have to listen to Cookie Monster anymore.

Hannah shakes her head, and after a glance my way, she leaves the room.

I want to follow her, but I control the urge.

"Any idea what the fuck he's talking about?" Caleb asks as we leave and go back to our room. "Any company I've ever worked for, he'd be out on his ass after failing a piss test, I'm sure of it. And the bird thing is just . . . shiver me timbers," Caleb jokes as he covers an eye with his hand as a makeshift patch.

I laugh at him. "Actually, in some ways, I like the bird. It gives him character."

"I don't know," Caleb counters. "Cindy Crawford having a mole gives her character. The Rock having a bionic eyebrow gives him character. Wesley Mobber having a foul-mouthed parrot that uses his shoulder as a perch for most of the day just means he's probably got a lot of parrot shit in that hair of his."

We both laugh. "I know you think he's—"

The ringing of my phone interrupts my thought, but seeing that it's Oliver, I answer. In the background, I can hear babies crying and Mindy singing to them, trying to calm them down. While she's not bad, Roxy definitely inherited the singing genes in the family. "Hey, what's the progress?"

"Consider it handled," I say simply. Oliver doesn't need to know about what Hannah and I got up to. I had enough problems dealing with Caleb's looks during our break. "We're winning his games, but he hasn't said how many there are."

"That's good fucking news!" he exults. I can hear Mindy saying something to him, and he chuckles. "Sorry, honey, you're right."

"What is she saying?" I ask, smirking.

"She's not happy," he says. "With both my language, and also . . . she's been talking to Roxy about all of this. She thinks someone's going to get hurt with Hannah being practically family and friend."

"Then what do you want to do?"

"Just do your best, but be fair. We'll figure something out to make it right if you win," Oliver says. "Call me if anything changes. I've got to go give Mindy a hand."

Oliver says farewell, and after he hangs up, I let out a sigh. Mindy's right—someone could get hurt.

"What was that for?" Caleb asks. "Never, in all my life, have I seen someone so sad to be winning. I would've thought you'd be ecstatic."

If it were anyone besides Hannah, I would be happy. But the thrill of winning and competition is starting to fade away, replaced by a need to see Hannah smile, to hear her softly call my name as I kiss every inch of her body. It's being replaced with a need to have her with me, to make her mine.

I can't tell Caleb that, though. He wouldn't understand. "I just want this to be over. Hopefully, this cleansing or whatever we're doing works. I need a total mind wipe and the meditation wasn't working one bit. I kept focusing on how my little toe was falling asleep."

Caleb chuckles. "Yeah, I know what you mean. Me, I'm hoping it's like those bathhouses, some nice girls who know how to give a great lomilomi massage and a very happy ending."

I can't help it, I laugh. "You're a pervert, you know that?"

"I'm just kidding, man. You know I'm not like that."

Dinner is, for the first time since we got here, very quiet. I try to keep my eyes off Hannah while we eat, but it's impossible, especially as she starts giving me glances too. My body is tingling, my cock growing in my shorts and a burning ball of something I'm not ready to acknowledge in my gut.

After a quick washing up, we meet outside. The sun is setting, and I'm reminded just how late sunsets are in summer. The girls changed during their prep time, both of them wearing bikini tops and light skirts, while Caleb and I are wearing tropical weight shirts and cargo shorts. Just the sight of Hannah has my blood boiling and my mouth watering. She snaps a few photos of Cassie striking a pose in the sunset, but the one being photographed should be her.

"Follow me," Wesley says, heading off in the twilight. The girls stay in front this time, close to Wesley while Caleb and I hang in the back. Caleb is enjoying the evening breeze while I'm trying not to spend the whole walk staring at Hannah's ass. We turn at the road, wrapping around past the village and up the side of what I think is the same mountain we climbed this morning, just the other side. As we get closer, I see what looks like a Japanese style bath house, except that the roof is thatched. "Welcome to the clearing house."

Wesley leads us up a stone path, and as we get closer, I can smell the unmistakable scent of volcanic waters. It's not the stench of Sulphur, but the rich mineral scent of something else. "Hot springs?"

"Very good," Wesley says with a small smile. We reach the front door, which slides open to reveal a beautifully organic wood-paneled room, and the scent coming from them is rich and heady. It's like a small, beautifully decorated spa, with flowers growing in pots and bonsai trees in alcoves along the walls. There are two curtains, and down the halls for each, I see what looks like rooms for massage tables and more. Sadly for Caleb, I don't see any cute spa attendants.

"Alani named this place for me when it was built," Wesley says, turning to us with a smile. "To her, it became a place of purification, of cleansing and cleaning. So she named it after the ancient temple near Holualoa. So, welcome to Pu'uhonua. this will give you a chance to clear your body of toxins and a chance to cleanse your spirit as well. Enjoy the cleansing offered freely by the baths, let it wash away your worries and open your mind and heart to a path pure in its creation from the very waters that spring from deep within the island. Through the curtains, you'll find changing areas, towels, and showers. It's tradition that you shower first, then go to the steam rooms naked."

"Naked?" Hannah gulps, and Wesley nods. She gives me a look, then nods.

"What about lomilomi?" Caleb asks, and Wesley chuckles. "What? I could use a rubdown after hauling Cassie's butt down the hill. She weighs a ton!" he exaggerates.

"That can be arranged. I know Alani's sister is quite skilled," Wesley says. "But I hear she's a little . . . forceful."

Now it's Caleb's turn to gulp, and I have to snicker. Wesley chuckles, too, and points. "Now, ladies to this hallway, and men to this one."

I give Hannah a look. She bites her lip as she looks at me. We both know what we want, but with everyone else here, there's nothing that we can do about it. Instead, I follow Caleb through the blue curtain and into the changing area, which is already warm as I strip down.

The two of us walk through the connecting door to the shower room, which is a lot hotter than the changing room. "Fuck, it's hot," Caleb says, already red-faced and sweating. "If the shower room's like this, what the fuck is the steam room supposed to be like?"

"We're about to find out," I say as we finish a quick rinse and head to the steam room, which isn't as bad as I thought it would be. It's nowhere near as humid. We settle in on the fragrant wooden lounge chairs that are there for us, and I sigh, feeling my muscles start to unknot, and for a few long minutes, we're silent. It smells like apples, of all things.

Finally, Caleb breaks the silence. "So what are you thinking about all this? What did Oli say this morning?

"He's as surprised as we are about the whole thing. He's a pro though, said to do my best, be honest and fair, and of course, he's expecting me to win Wes over. It's just…" I let out a big sigh.

Caleb gives me a side-eye. "You're a good guy, Tony. You've had a couple of bad deals lately, but you always do your best. When he brought me on for this, he told me that he's proud of you, how far you've come and how fast you're learning. I think you might be a little distracted right now though. Not that I blame you."

I sputter, "I'm not…I'm not distracted." as I push a hand through my hair, knowing that I'm lying to myself as much as I am to Caleb.

"Really? So I've been meaning to ask, what went down up there on the hike after we left?"

"A better question would be to ask if you enjoyed carrying Cassie back?" I ask, evading the question.

Caleb grunts and shifts around a little. "That girl is lucky I didn't drop her and keep on my merry way. Dude, she's got a mouth on her."

I laugh, enjoying the feeling. I haven't been laughing enough recently. "Are you saying you're not attracted to her?"

Caleb shakes his head, chuckling. "She's cute. But our banter just feels like it comes from a different place than that, like there's no real sexual tension attached. She thinks she can get away with shit just because she's got that young and innocent look about her. If I were really into her, I'd bend her over my knee and spank her."

Caleb goes quiet for a moment when I don't respond, then sighs. "Fuck, it's so hot in here. I can't handle this sauna shit. I'm gonna find out what these recovery gardens are. You gonna hang out in here a while longer?"

He stares at me as I climb to my feet and head back toward the shower area. "Where are you going? The recovery gardens or whatever he called them are the other way."

I shake my head, opening the sliding door. "I have to go take care of something first. I'll be there soon."

I step through, closing the door. I hear him mutter something but the closing door obscures it. Wrapping a towel around my waist, I head to the other hallway. I find the girl's sauna room. Their space is laid out a little different from ours. I knock on the wood door. There's a sharp cry of surprise, and Cassie, her face covered in some sort of green goop, sticks her head out. "What the hell are you doing here?"

"There's someone who is expecting you in the recovery gardens," I lie, jerking my thumb over my shoulder. "Something about his back needing a massage for carrying you."

Cassie stares at me, ignoring the fact that I'm in just a towel. "Seriously? I wouldn't touch him if he was the last dick on earth."

I snort, giving her a smile. "Yeah, well, it's not the last one on earth, but I'm sure he's willing to give you a nice massage in return as a thank you."

Her eyes flash. Caleb's going to kill me, but this is more than worth it. "Well, since you put it that way, I guess I can go keep him company. As long as I get mine first."

Cassie's head disappears back into the room, and I hear her

talking. "I'm going to go rock someone's world to the point he'll want to be my love slave. Oh, and you've got a visitor."

Cassie comes out a moment later, her face freshly scrubbed and a towel wrapped firmly around her upper body, and walks off.

I chuckle, taking a deep breath to calm my nerves before I open the door. As I reach for the handle, I hear Cassie on the other side talking loudly to Caleb. "Yeah, I'm back. I hear you're ready to give me a massage, but no funny business . . ."

I shake my head—she is a trip—then I walk in. My breath stops in my throat as I see Hannah, sitting on one of the wooden lounge chairs, no spa mask but her body also wrapped in a towel. I guess they both decided to ignore Wesley's rules. Hannah's legs look long and beautiful as she sits up, my cock hardening underneath my own towel as I imagine what treasures lie underneath. Her skin's flushed, and her eyes are wide as she sees me. "What are you doing here?"

"Tell Cassie sorry, but I had to lie to get her out of here. I came to serve you."

"Serve me?" she says suspiciously. "And just what does that mean?"

I look around, seeing a bottle of coconut oil lotion, and pick it up. It's more than just coconut, but all I can say is that it smells heavenly, and I can only imagine Hannah smelling the same way. "Yeah. I thought you could use a little spa treatment."

Hannah bites her lip, looking at me uncertainly. "But—"

"Just relax," I reply. "I promise, it's just what you need."

She hesitates a moment but gets up, going to the connecting door to the relaxation garden, where I see a body-length woven mat on the ground and high walls that separate us from the rest of the world. She lies down on her stomach, and I kneel down next to her, undoing the towel. The soft lantern light of the garden makes her skin glow as I really get my first look at her naked body. The earlier encounter was so shadowed.

I open my mouth in amazement but shut it as I get some lotion on my hands and start rubbing down her back. With each sweep of my fingers and thumbs, it feels like I'm sewing. Instead of cloth, I'm stitching myself to Hannah, not to her body but something deeper, something scary it's so intense.

She moans softly as my hands reach the amazingly soft skin on the back of her thighs, her ass quivering and her knees parting a little. My eyes catch just a glimmer between her thighs, and I want to rush, but I hold back. "So, where'd you learn to use a bow?"

"What?" Hannah asks, her voice thick as I rub her inner thighs. "Oh, you mean the bowfishing? I learned a little at Girl Scout camp, but that was when I was twelve."

She sighs softly as I edge closer, moaning as I pull back to start massaging her ass. The scent of her arousal fills the air as I knead and squeeze her ass, my thumb working toward the middle, and she wiggles her hips lightly, another deep moan coming from her. My cock throbs. It's raging hard as I think of what I want to do to her. Suddenly, she slides over and pops up on her knees, totally naked. "My turn."

I gulp, taking in the glorious sight of her glistening body, my cock oozing precum as I look at her. "I didn't get your front yet."

"I insist," she says, her voice full of desire. "Lie down and let me return the favor. I'll get your front."

I chuckle. "Fine, have it your way. But you know what you're going to find."

I lie down, undoing the towel around my waist, and Hannah's eyes go wide as she takes me in. Still, even as her breasts heave up and down from breathing harder, she kneels down and pours some lotion into her hands.

She starts on my shoulders, rubbing them with sensual strokes as her breasts dangle just out of reach above my lips as she works the knots out of my muscles. It's erotic torture as she finds tight spots in my muscles I didn't even know I had. "Don't tell me you learned this in Girl Scouts."

"No," Hannah teases as she runs her hands up and down my body. I suck in a breath. Her soft touch feels amazing. She reaches out, wrapping a hand around my hard cock before smiling and bending down. "And I definitely didn't learn this at Girl Scouts."

Her tongue strokes me from tip to base. I've never felt anything like it before as the soft massaging texture of her tongue sends shockwaves up my body. She teases me, giving my cock little butterfly kisses before licking the head like an ice cream cone, and I growl. "You're such a tease."

"You didn't say the magic word yet," Hannah teases me, licking my cock again. It's too much, and I reach out, grabbing her calf and pulling her toward me. Hannah fights me for a moment before I pull her hips over my chest. It's not perfect, but I'm able to bend my head enough to stick out my tongue, running the tip along the wet lips of her pussy, and she freezes. "Oh, fuck."

She pushes herself back toward my eager lips and tongue so I can reach her better, and I suck on her pussy before my tongue slides inside her. Hannah cries out, then buries my cock deep into her mouth.

Every stroke of my tongue is mirrored by hers and every stroke of my hands on her hips and ass makes her bob up and down on my cock, her fingernails scratching at my thighs as we go faster and faster.

I reach around, grabbing her ass to pull her tighter against me, and as I do, my fingers slide deeper, the tip of my right middle finger stopping as it presses against her asshole. Hannah freezes, pulling her lips from my cock. "Tony . . . please . . ."

I notice she must like it, and I start to massage her ass with my finger as my tongue circles her clit. Hannah's moans are of pure, unbridled lust, and she grinds her hips on my mouth, riding my face as I take her. When I feel she's ready, I slide my middle finger into her while sucking her clit, nibbling on it. I can hear her screams muffled as she gobbles my cock, sucking me like her life depends on it.

Her mouth is voracious, sucking me hard, her tongue a whirlwind around my shaft. I flick my tongue faster in reply, and I can feel her pressing herself down harder on my face. From deep in her throat, she starts humming, the vibrations driving me wild, and her ass clenches tighter.

My balls ache, growing tight as she takes me all the way down, sending me rocketing toward my orgasm. I suck harder on her clit, stifled moans coming out as I do. My cock is throbbing so hard it hurts, and I can't hold back any longer. I only last a second later, thick squirts of my seed shooting into Hannah's mouth. She moans and sucks hungrily, her pussy soaking my face as she comes right along with me. It feels like she's sucking my soul out of my cock, and I moan in pleasure as it keeps going, almost feeling like it'll never end.

When it's finally over, we lie there, Hannah's pussy just an inch from my face as I gasp, trying to slow my heartbeat. Slowly, I withdraw my finger and Hannah turns around, snuggling against me and resting her head on my chest. She licks her lips then kisses me tenderly. "I thought you had a talented cock, but your tongue and mouth . . . you're a god."

"You're not too bad yourself," I say, kissing her back. "And tasty."

"You're the tastiest muffin I've ever had," Hannah jokes, and when I give her a raised eyebrow, she shakes her head. "Never mind, just a joke. So . . ."

"Hannah, I know we're supposed to be fighting for the property, but that doesn't mean we have to be enemies, does it?" I ask, and Hannah shakes her head.

"I guess not," she says guardedly. "Then again, you're in the lead."

"Hannah, I—" I start to say, but suddenly, there's a yell and a laugh from the other side of the massage house. I can hear Caleb yelling.

"Get the fuck back here, that was so wrong!"

There's a laugh and the sound of Cassie running. "Gotta catch me first!"

I look at Hannah, and we both laugh nervously. If we can hear them, they may have heard us. We get up and shower quickly before I retreat to the men's side to get dressed.

Caleb's soaking wet when I get in. Apparently, Cassie thought a bucketful of cold water was a funny prank. But he says nothing as he gets dressed.

Before we were interrupted, I wanted to tell Hannah that to me, none of this is important anymore. That more than 'winning' this contract, I want her. I want to tell her that I'm scared that I'm going to win one and lose the other.

And no matter what, I don't want to lose her.

CHAPTER 16

HANNAH

"*R*ise and shine, sleepyhead," Cassie says. "Time to go mount that epic comeback!"

It's been two days since the hike, and each day, we've had two games. Yesterday, we managed to get back within one point after we raced jet skis around the bay and I just edged out Tony. He and Caleb swear it was because I had a weight advantage, but it doesn't matter. Now, I'm scared. We're down one point, and by my guess, this might be the last day. Next to the last day at most. Either way, I know our time here is coming to an end.

"Ugh," I groan. "I don't want to get up. My ass is still throbbing from that damn jet ski."

"Come on, we're running behind for breakfast. No time to worry about your aching ass. We need to take care of business today so we can win this. I think we have a pretty good chance. Wesley's backing off on the purely physical challenges," Cassie says.

Rolling out of bed, I quickly get some clothes on. I give my teeth the thirty-second brushing treatment and head down-stairs with Cassie to the dining area, where we find the guys walking in with us. Wesley, of course, already has Mo Mo on his shoulder, and I swear if that fucking parrot says anything about my ass, I'm going to strangle her.

I take a seat, my eyes immediately meeting Tony's as soon as I sit. He's dressed the same way we all are, in a t-shirt and cargo shorts, as if we're trying to be ready for anything Wes throws at us.

He gives me a smile, just like he always does, but it feels different. When Tony and I first met, his smiles were arro-gant, those of a man who knew he was King of the Moun-tain. Now, they seem genuine, like he's happy to see me. I've tried to keep my guard up just a little bit. I can't be sure he isn't just using me, but he doesn't strike me as that kind of man. "How'd you sleep?"

I spent half the night wishing you were next to me, and the other half dreaming you were, I want to say before replying. "Well, I think I'm finally getting acclimated. How about you?"

"We slept great," Caleb answers for him, grinning like a shark. "Can't be much longer before we win."

Caleb's boast makes my head spin, although I don't know if it's because of the possibility he's right or the fact that regardless of who wins, our time here is coming to a close. If I win, Cassie and I go back and someone from Aurora will take over the next phase of whatever is going to happen. If I lose . . . I'll probably never see this place again. Hell, who knows if or when I'll even see Tony again? And that hurts worse.

"There's two team challenges left," Wesley announces as the staff brings in breakfast. "You are going on an adventure controlled by lines. Latitudinal and longitudinal, that is. You are going on a scavenger hunt. Both teams will be given a list of locations around the grounds. You will be provided with two backpacks per team, one with your supplies and one empty to collect your items. Both teams will have the same list. You can choose to work together or alone. After finding all the items, you will need to assemble a puzzle to complete the task. So teamwork may help you, or it may mean your opponent finishes the puzzle before you. Choose wisely and let your heart be your guide."

We all look at each other. This being a more analytical game, I feel like Cassie and I have a good chance. It's been a long time . . . but map reading was one of my strongest skills in Girl Scouts.

My mind is telling me to beat the hell out of Tony, but my heart is saying to work with him. I don't know what to do. I feel like I don't know if I can trust him or if this is a foolish combination of hormones, stress, and the location. He could be the ultimate player, playing me like a fiddle. It's just one big clusterfuck of uncertainty.

After breakfast, we go to the back of the house, where our bags have been laid out on the steps, two in blue and two in red. I look at Tony and make a decision. "Let's work together as a team? At least until we get the puzzle pieces."

"What are you doing?" Cassie whispers, grabbing me by the arm as Tony immediately looks relieved. "Caleb needs his ticket punched!"

"Are you going to tell me what happened between you two? Since you dumped a bucket of cold water on him, you two have been glaring at each other like you're each other's worst enemy."

Cassie's face turns red. "None of your damn business, thank you very much. But you're the boss, so however you want to do it."

I shrug and pick up one of the red bags. It must be the supply bag because it's packed.

Tony gives me a questioning look, seeing that Cassie might have a problem. "So, team effort?"

"Together," I confirm. Caleb, meanwhile, has a GPS, map, and a piece of paper with coordinates on it. "Whatcha got?"

"Eight digits," Caleb says in frustration. "I thought maps had latitude and longitude. What is this shit?"

I look at his paper and the map and thank my Girl Scout experience. "It's military grid coordinates. Here, let me see . . . okay, the GPS is set for that too."

I show them how to use the map, and Tony takes the lead. I start to follow, but about halfway across the yard, I stop, recognizing that Cassie's not with us. I turn and see that she's still standing with her arms crossed, a pissed off look on her face. I go back, giving her a look. "What?"

"Are you trying to win this or what?" she asks. "You saw it— the guys didn't know what the fuck they were doing. So why are we working with them? I get it, you like Tony, and I won't say shit about it. I like everyone here too, but this is our jobs on the line here! The good looks and tight asses go out the window when I might not be able to feed myself."

I get Cassie's point, and for once, she seems to have more sense than me. Still, that competitive spirit just isn't in me now. "You already know that with Wesley, it's not just about who crosses the finish line first. Besides, the puzzle we're still doing individually. I don't know if there's anything dangerous out here, but if there is, I want them nearby."

That seems to satisfy her, but Tony calls out before she can respond. "Hey, you guys coming? Or do you want to split off?"

"We're coming. Just a little girl talk," I call back.

"All right, you in? Let's do this," I say, offering my fist, which Cassie lightly pounds and gives a little nod, smiling her acceptance of the plan.

The first location is pretty easy to find, and as we walk, we wonder what sort of craziness Wes is up to. "There has to be a twist," I mutter as we find a large banyan tree. The four of us split up, searching until Cassie finds the 'treasure,' two black plastic canisters about the size of cans of soup.

The next treasure is further away and a lot more challenging to get to. We emerge from the woods to see a rocky outcropping, not quite a cliff but damn close. Sticking out about halfway up the wall are a red and a blue flag. Displaying his physical prowess, Caleb scrambles up, retrieving the two canisters.

Even Cassie gives me silent acknowledgement that working together may have been the smart decision. There's no way the two of us could have conquered that rock without ropes or a jetpack.

As the day progresses, I'm shocked at how well we're all working together, moving from location to location. Cassie and Caleb continue their banter, but it's back to the playful vibe they've had since we've been here.

We're stopped dead in our tracks at one of the coordinates,

the smell reaching us before we're even a hundred feet away. "Oh, shit."

"Shit is right," I say as we approach a huge pile of manure. I see the tiny red and blue flags on top, and I wince. "That is like a dinosaur-size pile of shit."

"Oh, fuck no!" Cassie yells. "Good thing we're teamed up. Gentlemen…" she tells them with a wave of her hand, indicating it's all theirs.

"Oh, I'm thinking this is a time for ladies first," Caleb jokes. "Just remember, like Wesley says, eat shit and live!"

Cassie glares at him. "You know, sometimes I just wanna kick your nuts so hard they pop outta your nose. This is one of those times."

Tony and I burst out laughing, causing Caleb to turn red with embarrassment. He doesn't come back and instead opens the boys' supply pack, finding a canteen and taking a big drink of water.

"But seriously, what do we do?" I ask. "This is fucking disgusting."

"We're gonna have to go through it," Tony says. "The flags are right there."

He looks around at the three of us, none of us wanting to have anything to do with it. "Fine. I guess it's time for the real man to put on the big boy pants and get to work. I'll take one for the team."

Tony puts on some big gloves that were in the bag and starts trying to move it out of the way by handfuls. Just when I'm thinking this is going to take all day sifting through handfuls at a time, he lets out a triumph yell, pulling out two canisters.

Holding them out, I can't help but cheer and clap a little as Tony grins. "Nice job!" I say.

"We need to get those fucking things cleaned off a little," Caleb says. "I don't think any of us want to carry a can of shit all the way back."

Tony laughs, pulling his t-shirt off to wipe the canisters clean. He's trying his best not to get any on himself, but he's going to need a damn good shower, that's for sure. "I need another shirt. They're still not clean, and mine's dirty as fuck!"

With a smile, I shrug off my pack and pull off mine, leaving me in my sports bra.

"Here," I say, tossing him my shirt. "I don't know if I want that back though, even if it is washed."

Tony uses my shirt to wipe some more before he's satisfied. "So . . . your shirt off your back. That's pretty serious. Does that mean we're going steady? Wanna hold hands?"

"Fuck off!" I laugh, running away from him. I edge back, dashing forward to grab my backpack and pull it on. "You need a shower before you come near me!"

After a few laughs, we head off. Our last two coordinates are near the beach. One's just off the coast, but there's a problem with that. "Uhm . . . the coordinates are in the water."

Tony shrugs off his pack and takes out some goggles. "Well, I guess that's what these are for." I open our bag and pull out a matching pair.

"Let's divide and conquer, finish this up, and move on. I'll take Miss Motor Mouth while you and Hannah go for a swim," Caleb says. "You could probably use a little rinse anyway."

"Since we're on the subject of mouths, I have one, and only one use for yours," Cassie growls. "I see that look on your face, and it's not that either. Kiss my ass!"

Caleb laughs. "That'll be the day. Come on, slowpoke, let's get ours and get back."

The two run off, and I look at Tony. "What are we waiting for?"

He grins at me, and we hurry to the shore, shucking shoes and putting our goggles on.

"You ready?" he says, excitement in his voice.

Looking into the sparkling waters, I nod. "When you are."

Holding hands, we wade in. The water is darker blue than I thought, and as I struggle downward, I realize that it's a lot deeper than I thought it'd be, too. Though we went in together, I don't see Tony. Panicking, I turn, looking all around. I can barely see below the surface, but Tony comes up a moment later, causing me to sigh with relief. "You okay? I was right there beside you."

"Sorry," I gasp, grabbing onto his body. "I didn't see you go under."

"It's all right,' he says softly. "I'm fine. Let's go down and look together, okay?"

I nod, feeling relaxed in his arms.

Tony smiles and gives me an encouraging kiss. "With me, take five big deep breaths, and then we go under. Hold onto my belt and kick like hell."

We do it together, Tony putting those muscles to use as we sink fast. The water starts to get darker the deeper we go, and I'm starting to think I might need to turn back up when I see the flash of red and blue. It's an old anchor, and attached to it are two tiny canisters on a floating buoy. Tony reaches out and undoes the simple bow knot holding it to the anchor, and the whole thing shoots up, Tony and I right behind it.

Breaking the surface of the water is like being reborn. Sweet air rushes into my lungs and the sun is dazzling bright as Tony and I hold each other. Cassie and Caleb cheer at us from the shore, waving their canisters at us.

"What took you so long?" they yell. "Y'all need a minute?"

Grinning, we swim in, Tony tossing the package to Cassie before pulling me into his arms and giving me a quick kiss on the cheek. I wish we could go further, but there's a time and a place. We've got a challenge to take care of.

We quickly get our shoes on, the four of us heading back to the house. Wesley is waiting for us, and he claps his hands gleefully, jumping a little bit like a kid on Christmas morning. "Ah, I'm so glad to see you all worked together. Very telling and wise of you, but it's time for the puzzle. I have two tables set up just outside the house for you to use. You may begin."

Cassie rushes over to our table, while I exchange a glance with Tony before joining her. Cassie's already gotten three of the canisters open, and we see that it is literally pieces of a puzzle. "Oh, fuck, I suck at puzzles," Cassie grumbles. "Shit!"

"That would be this canister," Caleb says, tossing over their empty metal tin. Cassie squeals and knocks the thing to the ground while Caleb laughs. "And no cheating!"

"No cheating! Big booty ho!" Mo Mo squawks, and it feels like the metal canister is just the right weight to throw, even if I don't hit anything but air.

Taunts and banter go quiet as we all focus. We sort out the edges and get the corners when suddenly, Tony yells, "Yes!"

"What?" I ask, feeling desperate. Did they finish already?

"It's the resort!" Tony says before realizing he may have made a mistake. He glowers and stares at his puzzle while Cassie and I start to see what we're missing. I go quickly, seeing chunks of pieces fall together while Cassie starts to work methodically. Finally, I see the last piece, the flag on the top of the yacht in the water, and slide it home.

"Done!" I yell.

Tony looks up in shock, his fingers holding a piece. Wesley comes over, checks, and nods. "A win for the ladies. The score is tied for tomorrow's finale."

Cassie hugs me, but I see nothing but the disappointment in Tony's eyes as he comes over. He sees our puzzle, then shakes his head. "It's not the same."

"Of course not," Wesley says, chuckling. "I wanted to make sure it was fair, so each team's picture was different. So your comment about it being a resort didn't help the ladies."

"How close were you?" I ask, and Tony shrugs. It doesn't matter. He turns and goes inside, and I walk around to look at Tony's puzzle. One piece is missing . . . it was that close.

Wesley looks at me as I pick up Tony's piece and slip it into place, completing his puzzle. "So, what did you learn today?"

I glance up at him, not ready for another of his speeches. "The property, this place . . . it's special. It's more than beautiful scenery. It's a living, breathing entity. The oceans, the forests, and even the giant pile of cow shit—they're all connected."

"True, but you knew that before the challenge," Wesley says. "What did you learn today?"

I swallow and think about the look in Tony's eyes as I finished. "I learned . . . I learned that sometimes, winning really doesn't feel like winning at all."

"How true," Wesley says. "Go relax. There is a festival in the village tonight, very special. You should see it, and you should be able to prepare for tomorrow's finale. Enjoy it, for tomorrow, you're right—the friendships you've built these past few days may very well be undone."

CHAPTER 17

ANTHONY

"**Y**ou know, man, I can't believe we lost that," Caleb says as I clean up my stubble with a razor. The air in the bathroom is still steamy. I just got out after an incredibly long shower where I scrubbed myself thoroughly. It took me three scrubs and a thorough jet spraying with the shower head over every inch of my body before I finally felt like I was cow shit-free and clean. "I gotta give you props for digging through that shit, though."

"There was a reason I did it," I say, scraping the last spot on my left cheek smooth. "Because I know it will go toward what Wesley thinks of me. I took one for the team."

"I didn't think about it that way," Caleb says, grinning. I hear him slapping his cheeks. He's probably put on a little after-shave. A regular Hai Karate man, Caleb is. God knows why. When I come out of the bathroom, he's already got his button-down shirt on. We're dressing up a little tonight for the festival. "I guess you're right, but there's one problem with that. Wes wasn't there."

"It doesn't seem like much that happens here gets by that man," I tell him. "No way was he going to let the four of us go after that cliffside canister or dive for that last one without someone nearby just in case something went bad. Not to mention, I'm sure he could fucking smell me."

"Well, let's go have some fun. Let it be our rally before we pull off the big win tomorrow!" Caleb says. I can't share in his enthusiasm though. I don't even know what I want anymore. I don't want to let anyone down, but I don't want to do that at Hannah's expense. One thing's for sure—I know I want her. And tonight, I'm going to show her something special.

Caleb notices my silence. "What's the matter, dude? And don't say you're tired because today wasn't even that bad."

"A lot on my mind," I say, putting on some fresh underwear. "Just thinking."

"Fuck that. Your head is not in the game," Caleb says. "You're catching feelings for Hannah, just admit it. We can all see it, man. Is it serious or are y'all just fucking around? Because she's got you tied up inside. Just make sure it's not one-sided and she bolts on you when the dust settles after this competition." When I stay silent, he presses. "Everyone knows what's going on. No shame in it, no use denying it."

"Whether it's true or not, it's no one's business," I reply as I pull on my lightweight slacks.

"You're right, maybe it's not. But I'm your friend and will always tell you the truth, even if you don't want to hear it. Be careful with Hannah. I'm not sure who will end up more hurt here, but it's going to be one or the both of you. And I won't be the one having to explain it if we lose.

I can't argue with his words as I put on my Hawaiian shirt that I leave open at the front. "Don't worry," I say finally, "I don't know what's gonna happen...with Hannah and me or the competition, but I'll be ready come tomorrow. And Caleb, no matter what, I'm glad I didn't come for this alone. Thanks man."

"That's my boy. Now, let's go have some fun. Just remember, tomorrow morning, it's all business."

"All business," I repeat.

As we walk out, I don't know whom I'm lying to—Caleb . . . or myself.

Hannah

"I can't wait to get out there and enjoy the island," Cassie says as she applies eyeliner, making sure she gets just the shape she wants. We're in our bathroom getting ready for tonight's festival, and I'm both excited and leery. Tomorrow's the end, and it's hard thinking that this will be over soon. It's even harder when I think that there can only be one winner. Someone's going home a loser . . . and even with how much I've come to want Tony, I really don't know if I want it to be me. "Don't get me wrong. I've been having fun, slinging arrows, pretending be Yoda and all that, but I'm ready to let loose a little. Enjoy some island eye candy."

Despite being distracted by my thoughts, I chuckle at Cassie's antics as I apply a light shade of lipstick to my lips and then step back to critique my appearance. I have on a beautiful multi-colored Hawaiian dress that I just felt I had to wear. It's so beautiful. I've gone with matching makeup, rainbow colored eye makeup with some glitter and blush over my cheeks. I even have a red flower Cassie found in my hair. Cassie says I look like a pale Hawaiian goddess and I smile. But there's this one damn curl that won't stay and it keeps coming free. "If only this damn curl would just hold."

I finally get it fixed and look at Cassie, who's finished up her own makeup. "You look pretty," I say, smiling at her. Cassie is in a beautiful green and white dress, her dimples shining even more than normal.

"Thank you," she replies before blushing. "You look stunning too, but then again . . ."

"What?" I ask, seeing the look on her face as her voice trails off.

She bites her lip, worry in her eyes. "Please don't get mad at me when I say this, but . . . how far are you willing to go to win this thing?"

I fidget with my hands, suddenly nervous. "I don't know," I say quietly.

I can tell she's afraid to say what she's thinking. "Look, I know something is going on between you and Tony. I think it's kinda sweet, but our jobs . . ." Her voice trails off, and I totally get what she's saying. A pain bites my chest. It hurts to even think about it. "I know I was sent along with you to be your helper, and I know I haven't done a great job at that. I've gotten caught up in the fun and games. Maybe both of us have. But we need to consider the very serious consequences if we're not successful."

Tears spring to my eyes and trickle down my cheeks. It hurts so much to see her like this. It's not the Cassie I've come to know, and I pull her into my arms. Hugging her, I swallow down the lump in my throat. "We're going to win." God, why does this have to be so damn hard? "And you've never hurt our chances. It wouldn't be this close without you."

"Promise?" Cassie asks, and I nod, holding up my right pinky. She smiles bravely and hooks it with her own. "I've never had anyone pinky swear with me before."

"Well, you do now. You know, Cassie, I used to think you were annoying."

"And now?" Cassie asks.

"You're still annoying . . . but you're also a good friend."

She smiles, and we leave our room, heading downstairs. In the living room, the guys are waiting. Tony's shirt pulls my attention to the tanned, muscled skin underneath. I look up into his eyes, and I see he's just as stunned. "Hannah . . ."

Wes is with Alani, and for once, I don't see Mo Mo on his shoulder. The parrot's on her stand in the corner. "You two are almost matching," Wes comments.

I glance and realize Wesley's right. Tony's shirt and my dress have the same pattern. I gulp, looking at Tony. "You look handsome."

"You look absolutely gorgeous," Tony says, grinning. In his eyes, I can see that the connection that I've felt growing between us over the past few days is almost visible in the air between us.

Caleb comes over, taking Cassie by the hand and smiling. "You look cute."

Cassie laughs but blushes too. "You're just saying that to get some brownie points."

Caleb laughs, offering his arm. "Please. I could have you on your knees if I wanted. I don't need brownie points."

Cassie laughs, taking his arm. "Oh, shut up. If anyone is getting on their knees, it's you."

We all laugh. There might be nothing there, but I'm not completely convinced. Tony comes over, extending his hand, and as he comes closer, I can smell a faint cologne. It's tropical, and it feels special.

"Are you ready?" His smile is pearly white, and my mind starts whirling, thinking of all the ways that he could be meaning his question. Am I ready for the festival? Yes. Am I ready for this trip to be over? No. Am I ready to maybe break his heart? Fuck, no, I don't think I ever will be ready for that, not without breaking my own.

He takes my hand, and I hear Cassie and Caleb whispering, probably about us. I smile back and decide that no matter what tomorrow brings, tonight is about one thing. Tony, and what we can have . . . for now.

"Yes. I was born ready to party."

CHAPTER 18

HANNAH

*T*he beat of the Hawaiian drums pounds in tandem with my heartbeat as Tony and I walk onto the festival grounds, trailing the rest of the group.

There are all sorts of colorful tents set up and down the shoreline, each offering some kind of delicacy, the aromas mixing in with the vibrant colors and carried on the warm winds. There are even game booths further on down where people are gathered around, shouting and engaged in fierce competition.

I suck in a deep breath as I take everything in, my eyes feasting on the explosion of culture on display. There are groups of women here and there hula dancing, their tanned bodies moving in a seductive, ritualistic manner. As they swirl around each other, the air seems to come alive with a kind of joyous energy, crackling against my skin and causing goosebumps all over.

With the backdrop of the sparkling ocean, the kaleidoscope

of colors, and bright lights, the wild pounding music, dance, and people, I'm almost dizzy with wonder.

"This is beautiful," I half whisper, shaking my head in awe.

"It sure is," Tony agrees. He points. "Look over there." In the center of the village, we can see the recreation of a volcano glowing orange-red and spewing clouds of steam. Some wiseass has even painted a sign in front of it, Mt. Fuka'ayuu.

"A sign?" I ask.

Tony smiles, flashing his beautiful teeth. "Maybe." He reaches out his hand to me. For a moment, I stare at it and then glance ahead, where Cassie and Caleb are razzing each other, blissfully unaware of us. Meanwhile, Wesley and Alani have already walked off and are talking with a group of locals. None of them are paying attention, but even if they were, it seems everyone already knows there's something going on between Tony and me.

Smiling, I take his hand. He squeezes, and my anxiety ebbs. My heart swells in my chest as we walk hand in hand together, slightly trailing Caleb and Cassie.

"You're always talking like I'm not good enough for you," Cassie is complaining just a tad too loudly. "Like, I'm too young, or I'm too short. Like what the hell? Get out of here with that mess. You want to know what I think? I think you're just scared that I would rock your world."

"Don't flatter yourself, darling," Caleb chuckles. "The only thing that would end up being rocked is your mind when I gave you the best orgasm of your life."

"Tell you what, Mr. Hot Shot," Cassie says, placing her hands on her hips. "Let's make a bet. If I can grab a girl faster than you can, you have to bow down and kiss my feet. If I lose, I'll do the same."

Caleb arches an eyebrow and guffaws in disbelief. "You grab a chick?"

Cassie nods. "I'm not ashamed. I'll show you that not only am I hotter than you, but I have more swagger and a bigger set of balls, too."

"You're fucking nuts!" Caleb laughs. "But game on!"

The two quickly disappear off into the crowd, and Tony and I shake our heads, chuckling.

"Since becoming an adult, I've never in my life seen Caleb act this way," Tony remarks. "You'd almost think he was a kid in the candy store."

I shrug helplessly. "What can I say? Cassie is a bad influence." I sigh wistfully as we pass a stand with mouth-watering delicacies on display. "But to tell you the truth, I like having her around. She kind of reminds me of myself a few years back."

Tony chuckles, arching a skeptical eyebrow. "Seriously? I can't imagine you acting like that."

"I was different, sure. But Roxy and I did get into some crazy shit."

Tony appraises me with interest. "So you're telling me there's a wilder version of Hannah locked away somewhere?"

I grin and poke him in the side. "Maybe, so don't fuck with me."

Tony laughs. "Oooh, scary. I'll make a mental note not to cross you."

"Good decision."

Tony can't contain his grin as joy seems to surround us, and he tugs on my arm. He leads me around the festival and we take in the sights. I have to admit, it feels good walking around on his arm in public, like we're a couple. No one here cares, and it just feels so right. For all of my self-talk about not needing a man to be complete, I know that as I put my arm around Tony's waist and he pulls me close around the shoulders, I've never felt more complete in my life.

We stop by several booths to play games, and Tony shows me his competitive spirit that I've come to love, playing aggressively to win. But each time, he gets to the end of the match, only to lose to some local. Finally, in an arm wrestling contest, he triumphs, winning a stuffed animal. A parrot.

I scowl at the parrot in disgust. It even looks like Mo Mo. "I love you for winning this, but . . ."

Tony laughs. "Just think, you got her a boyfriend. She might love you now."

I certainly won't miss being called *big booty ho*, that's for sure.

We come up to a food stall, where they have a whole pig roasting on a spit. Tony tries it, then holds out a sample to me. "Here, it's hot but delicious." I take it into my mouth, and he's right, it's sweet, salty, a little spicy . . . it's the best pork I've ever had. I suck on his finger, lost in the flavor, when Tony chuckles and leans in to whisper in my ear. "Watch it, you're going to make me pop wood out here in front of all of these people."

I chuckle and wipe at my mouth with my pinkie finger. "Sorry, I couldn't help myself."

He grins, motioning over to a group of couples dancing. "Wanna give it a go?"

"You're joking!"

"Hell no, I'm not!" Tony says, pulling me toward the group. A couple of the locals look surprised, but when Tony strips off his shirt and starts dancing, recreating the moves that we did for the competition, they're getting into it. My heart soars so much that I wrap my arms around him, kissing him hard.

"I can't believe we just did that!" I say as we get applause. He's covered in a fine sheen of sweat, but I don't care. He's the sexiest thing I've ever seen as he kisses me back.

"Let's go get a drink. I've worked up a sweat."

We go to a punch bowl stand, grabbing two massive cups. I see that this is the real stuff, not shit from a bottle. Tony makes a joke about keeping the punch in the cup and not in his face this time. It seems like that happened a lifetime ago, as I give him a little sheepish grin. I'm finishing my last drop when Cassie comes by with a girl on her arm. "See? What'd I tell you?"

Caleb, who's just coming up empty handed, looks shocked. "No fucking way."

"Way. Told you, don't doubt me," Cassie boasts, triumphant even though her newfound friend is at least half drunk. "Kalena, say hello."

Cassie's newfound friend giggles and squeezes her cheeks. "Hello. And who wouldn't love her dimples?" she says.

"Well if it weren't for Tony's dancing messing up my game, I would've won," Caleb says, stopping by the water balloon game stand. "His little display has all the girls around here eyeing him."

"Sure. Excuses, excuses," Cassie says, kicking off her sandals and brandishing her petite feet. "But you know what time it is. Don't be a sore loser. Get down on your knees and get to worshipping!"

Cassie's so caught up in her gloating that she doesn't appear to notice Caleb's hand moving behind his back as he moves his lips toward her feet. But with mere inches to go, he shakes his head.

"Kiss 'em real good," Cassie gloats, winking at Kalena. "Don't be afraid of the toe jam."

Caleb hikes his arm higher, opening his mouth.

"Tell me he is not gonna—" I begin to say, but Caleb is fast, throwing the water balloon right into Cassie's chest, where it explodes, soaking her and her friend.

"Boom! Money shot!" he yells, taking off running.

"Motha . . . fuck!" Cassie yells, shoving Kalena to the side and running after him. We both laugh at them as Cassie calls after him, "Get back here, asshole!"

"Someone's gonna end up dead." Tony laughs as Cassie's newfound friend squawks, then shrugs and walks off. "We're so gonna have to patch one of them up."

"Forget them—let's go for a walk," I reply, taking his arm. I grab a water balloon to hold as we pass. It feels cool in my hand to hold, refreshing against the heat. We move away from the main festival, melting into the shadows as we walk. The moon is still high, and while not quite full, it's beautiful as we head down a walking path that connects the village to Wesley's place. "This whole trip has been life changing."

"I know what you mean," Tony says. "I can't believe it's going to end soon."

"I don't want it to," I admit. "Tony . . . I don't want it to end."

We stop, and he pulls me close, kissing me softly. I wrap my arms around his neck, my desire tempered by the mood. He's tender, looking at me with something that shakes me to my core, and I lay my head against his shoulder when we're done. Tony strokes my back, his voice heavy with feeling. "For now, let's just enjoy the night."

"Okay," I reply, feeling a little better. I don't want to ruin the night thinking about it. I want to retreat to a safe place from my feelings, and I look back toward the village. "I wonder if she's caught him by now and beaten his ass."

"I'm pretty sure she's all talk," Tony says with a chuckle. "But still, she's a feisty little thing. I can't picture you being so bold."

"Oh, you wanna bet?" I ask.

"I do," Tony challenges me.

I lob the water balloon I've been carrying in his face. Splat!

"That was for doubting me!" I yell, running for my life.

"You're so dead!" he shouts, laughing.

I pump my legs fast, feeling like a child. Everything drops away, all the worries, all my thoughts about how it's going to end. Instead, there's just this moment, my muscles straining as the air pours in and out of my lungs in laughs and squeals. There's only the moon, and the path, and the laughter as my man comes pelting down the path after me, coming to claim me.

"You're mine!" he yells, stumbling over something in the path before recovering. I pour on the speed. Maybe I can outrun him. Laughing, I push just a little harder.

"You've gotta catch me first!"

CHAPTER 19

"*Y*our ass is mine!" I yell, running her down. She got a head start, and I stumbled once, but I'll catch her. My heart is pounding, my entire body flooded with testosterone and desire.

She's wearing herself out trying to run as fast as she can. I close within a foot and grab her, the two of us falling to the soft ground of the path, Hannah yelling in protest. "Ahh! Get off me!"

"Get off you?" I ask, pinning her to the ground and holding her hands over her head. "You sure that's what you want?"

Hannah's reply is cut off as I kiss her neck, and she moans as I run my hands down her body. I bring my hand up to cup her breast, massaging it through the thin fabric of her top. Her nipple pebbles against my palm, and I stroke it, pulling away to look into her eyes. "Give up?"

"I give up . . ." Hannah moans, putting her arms around my neck.

I get off her, lifting her in my arms. "Come on, I don't want us to be interrupted. There's a little clearing through those trees." I swoop her up into my arms, crossing the tree line into the field and setting her down in the soft grass.

"Tony . . ."

A streak catches our eye, and we turn, watching as shooting stars start to fill the sky. It's beautiful, and as I turn back to Hannah, I remember a childhood ritual. "You know what they say about shooting stars . . . we need to make a wish fast." I watch as Hannah closes her eyes, her lips moving silently. As her eyes open, we lock eyes, and she lies back, opening her arms and offering herself to me.

"Tony, tomorrow is tomorrow. But tonight is ours. Make my wish come true?" she asks with a hopeful look in her eyes. Hannah reaches for the tie on her dress and undoes it, letting the top fall down to reveal her perky tits, her nipples already hard with desire.

I nod, understanding her wish for tonight's magic to carry us through, as if tomorrow won't destroy everything. I reach behind my neck and pull my shirt off, lowering down to meet her halfway in a kiss. The kiss is sweet and tender, with an undercurrent of passion that soon has our tongues wrapping around each other, my hands running up and down her body, working her dress to her feet and then off. She lies before me, her pussy hidden by a tiny scrap of lace. "Fuck, you're beautiful," I tell her as I grab the sides of her panties and lower them.

Lying back down over her, my lips trail down Hannah's throat, sucking and licking her delicious skin. I cup her ass, massaging it and squeezing, her moans of arousal growing as I knead the taut flesh. I trail my lips lower but stop and smile into her hip as I remember something that I saw earlier. I get up, telling her not to move, and Hannah gives me a worried look. "What are you doing?"

"Making perfection even tastier," I joke, walking away for just a few seconds before coming back with what I remembered. "Mango."

The fruit is ripe, and I tear it in my hands, squeezing the fresh juice over her breasts as I kneel down, burying my tongue between them. The taste of her skin with the sweet mango leaves me ravenous, and I suck hard, licking and tasting her skin before I devour her nipple, tugging and biting it, Hannah moaning my name and running her hands through my hair. "Tony . . . for God's sake, Tony, you're amazing."

I growl, switching sides and sliding a hand between Hannah's legs, rubbing her slick lips. She spreads her legs and I slip two fingers inside, pumping them in and out as I lick and suck on her breasts until there's no mango left, just the wonderful texture of her skin under my lips. I rub her clit with my thumb, Hannah's hips jerking as I stroke in and out.

I kiss up to her lips, sharing the last of the mango with her as my fingers speed up, pumping her tight pussy as I stroke her hair and kiss her tenderly. "You're amazing," I whisper to her. "Nobody is like you."

Hannah tries to answer, but her body shakes so much that all she can do is clutch at my back, her fingernails digging into my shoulders. A moan rolls from the depths of her belly, and her pussy clamps down tightly on my fingers as she comes. "Mmm . . ." I moan, licking my fingers clean before sharing them with her. "Sweeter than the mango."

Hannah laughs. "That was amazing. But you still haven't

done what you promised. You still planning to follow through on your claim?"

"What?" I ask, confused for a moment until Hannah rolls over, wiggling her ass at me with a raised eyebrow and a smirk. "You serious?"

"You said my ass was yours . . . here's your chance, studmuffin," she says. "Rare chance. Take advantage."

I don't need any more encouragement, getting behind Hannah and pulling her ass toward me. I reach out with my tongue, coating her asshole with spit while I rub her pussy with my right hand, gathering her juices to add to the sensual massage. I can't believe she's offering this to me. Her sighs turn into joyous moans as I slide in one finger, then another into her ass, slowly stretching her open.

"Tony . . . please, my mouth," she begs, and I understand. I move around, my two fingers still buried in her ass as she turns her head and slides my cock into her mouth, pumping it slowly in and out to get it extra nice and wet for her. I pull out with a loud pop and move behind her. I pull my fingers out and just touch her with the tip of my cock.

"You ready?" I ask softly. As much as I want to plunge in hard, I know she needs to have a chance to prepare, and I wait until she nods to push the head of my cock in slowly. I wait, listening to her breathing as she hitches, then gasps as I slide in further, opening her up. "Fuck, you're tight."

"Or you're big," she teases, her words slurred with lust as I slide more into her. I go slow, small strokes that open up her body as Hannah reaches down, rubbing her pussy with her hand to relax herself until I feel my hips settle against her ass. I growl, reaching down and pulling her up for a shared, lingering kiss. "Take me," she begs.

I kiss her hard in reply, letting her settle back onto the grass before I pull back and thrust in long and deep, my cock filling her until we're both gasping, the tight clench of her ass around my cock making my heart hammer in my chest. I thrust again and again, stretching her and gradually speeding up. It's like some sort of island magic fills us, and sweat glistens in the moonlight while I pound her, crying out words I don't even recognize, just sounds and nonsense, but Hannah seems to understand, the two of us going faster and faster. My hips slap hard against her, and Hannah pushes back, squeezing herself around the throbbing length of my cock and sending chills up my spine.

The world evaporates. I can't feel the grass under my knees, I can't hear the cries of the forest animals or feel the wind on our skin. There's just the growing heat in my belly, the sound of Hannah's cries as I thrust in and out of her, and the beating of our hearts. My cock throbs, and I'm on the edge of coming deep inside of her. But there's something holding me back, and I know what it is. It's my heart. I need to open it up completely to her, all the risks be damned.

Fine. *I don't know if you love me, but I love you*, I say in my head, and even admitting it to myself is enough to push me over. I cry out, coming hard, but I can hear Hannah moaning too. She's coming again, her ass clamping tightly around my cock and drawing out the feeling until it almost aches, and I explode. I've never felt anything like this, filling her ass with blast after blast of my hot come. My fingers are clamped on her waist and my eyes stare at the sky, I've thrown my head back, and all I can see is the last of the meteor shower as the last of me pours into her.

After it's over, we lie there, curled on the grass. I wrap my arms around her, troubled. Falling for her? Hell, I head over heels, already fallen in deep. But she lives a couple of hours away by plane. I remember that much. And she's got a life, a career. I doubt this could have ever been more than just a fling in paradise. But . . .

I care for her. More than any other woman I've ever had in my life, I care for her. She can drive me nuts and she's motivated me to dig through a huge pile of shit, regardless of what I told Caleb. Right now, though, I'd do it all again just to see her smile or to kiss her lips. I've never felt like this before. I'm not sure I'd know what to do even if there weren't all these conflicting issues. But there are issues. Tonight may be perfect, she may be perfect…

But tomorrow . . . it all ends.

"We should go back," Hannah says, fidgeting.

We get dressed, and I let Hannah use my shirt to clean herself before I wipe myself down and pull on my shorts. I don't need a shirt. I reach out, taking her hand, and Hannah clasps it to her chest, kissing my knuckles. "Listen . . . I know tomorrow, we have to fight . . . but tonight is something I'll never forget. Thank you."

"Thank you," I reply softly as we walk back toward the house. We get back, not saying much, even though I want to say more. Instead, I give her a kiss as we enter the house and watch as she goes down the hallway toward her room, my heart and my mind still churning with questions to which I have no answers.

CHAPTER 20

HANNAH

"*Y*ou sure do have a glow about you," Cassie says from the bathroom when I get back to the room. Crackling with energy, she looks like she's down to party another few hours.

I definitely don't blame her. Tonight's been magical. I'm still drowning in the afterglow of being with Tony. Every moment with him was incredible. And I didn't want it to end.

If tomorrow never came, I'd be a happy woman.

"What the hell happened to you?" I ask as my eyes focus on Cassie's face. She looks like a cave woman, with wildly disheveled hair and a torn dress. If not for the grin on her face, I'd be worried.

"Caleb had his way with me," she says, slipping out of her ruined dress and into pajamas.

"No way!" I exclaim in disbelief. I was beginning to think their flirting and taunting was playful, not sexual. Was my radar that far off on them?

"Get your mind out of the gutter," Cassie says as she grabs a brush and starts trying to tame her wild mane. "I mean, he about tickled me to death when I tried to jump kick him in his ass for throwing that water balloon at me. Don't worry, I gave as much as I got. You should see him!"

"Oh." I laugh.

"Yeah. Can you believe it? He's jealous I have more swag than him." She makes a face. "The bastard made me beg him to stop, and I had to because I was laughing so hard I thought I was gonna pee."

Just imagining Cassie screaming at Caleb while he tickles her mercilessly only makes me laugh harder.

Cassie pauses her brushing to fix a murderous scowl on me. "Oh, that's funny to you?"

I only laugh harder. "No," I say anyway, clutching my sides. "Sorry."

"What happened with you? Did you two . . .?" Her voice trails off into silence, and I swear the only sound is my heartbeat.

I could lie. Tell her that nothing happened, and we just enjoyed each other's company. But I don't want to anymore. Nothing that feels that good should be kept secret. Besides, she knows. She just doesn't know any details.

Slowly, I nod my head.

Cassie looks worried as she sets down her brush, staring at me for a long time before replying. "Han, listen . . . I'm glad that you and Tony are into each other. Really, I am. You guys actually make a cute couple." She looks down at the floor, fidgeting with her pajamas before looking back up at me.

"But be careful. Someone could get really hurt here. You know that, right?"

The worry in Cassie's eyes is touching. In my heart, I don't know if I'm lying to her or not as I answer, "I appreciate that. But we agreed that we're both going to just go and give it our all tomorrow. Only one of us can win, and I accept that."

"Okay," Cassie says, swallowing but giving me a smile. "See you in the morning."

If only getting to sleep were that easy. It's hours before I can even close my eyes.

THE SUN GREETS ME THE NEXT MORNING AS I WAKE UP, anxiety tearing at my stomach. I look over at Cassie, who's also up, and we exchange silent glances. There's no need for words. Shit or get off the pot, as my grandpa used to say.

"Ready?" I ask Cassie, and my phone rings. Myra. "Fuck, I can't talk to her right now," I say, shutting it off. "You ready?"

Cassie comes up and hugs me, and I hug her back. "Now I'm ready."

Breakfast is like a library. Everybody's quiet. The stakes are too high for us to disguise it with normal chit chat, and if they're at all like me, they're regretful that this is ending. Tony gives me a smile, but it's not enough to tame my nerves. When we're finished, Alani leads us toward the bath house, turning toward the ocean just before we reach the mountain. We emerge to see . . . "Oh, shit."

"Good morning, teams," Wes says. "Today, we're doing a challenge that is going to be so much fun, admittedly maybe more so for me to watch, but nonetheless. And also, I've decided there will be one more challenge after this. Though that one will only be for Hannah and Tony."

"Just when we think we have the answers, he changes the questions," Caleb mutters, but Wes ignores him, continuing.

"The staff and I have constructed a bit of an obstacle course, and both members of the team have to cross to win. You will start, run to the slide, up the stairs to the top, down the next slide, then run the tires, where you must step at least one foot in each."

I look at the zigzag of tires worriedly, but Tony chuckles. "I remember those. Guess those two-a-days for football were useful."

"Continuing to over/under bars," Wes says, walking us through the course. "You can over or under but you have to alternate, so start strategically. You next belly crawl under the rope netting, and yes, the mud's sort of clean. Next, you have to hop post to post. If you touch down, start over. And then run for the finish line."

It's intimidating. Some of the post jumps look insane, but the guys look confident. "Hey, Cassie," Caleb jokes, "I think that post might just be big enough to satisfy you."

"You mean big enough to shut that mouth of yours," Cassie says, and I have to smile. It helps break the tension. Still, I need this win. I need to get the edge going into whatever this final game is.

"Hey, Hannah?" Tony says, and when I look over, I see him smiling. "You sure your big booty can fit through those bars?"

"Big booty ho!" Mo Mo squawks, and Tony can't help it, he

starts snickering. I have to laugh too. I know exactly why Tony chose the words he did, and I shake my head.

"Just make sure to get on your knees when you have to kiss it after we win!" I tease, blushing as I think of what happened just last night. We get ready, lining up at the start line, and with a clap of Wes's hands, we start.

The first few obstacles are no problem, although the guys are so much more aggressive it's hard to watch. Tony, in particular, nearly breaks the slide as he takes a flying leap from the top, his ass and lower back cracking into the slide about three quarters of the way down, making me wince a little. The guys gain ground on the tires too. They've done this before in football and such, while Cassie and I have to make sure we don't get caught in the rims.

We don't stand a chance. I know it, and they know it. But we continue on anyway. I'm not just going to give up.

"Come on, we need this!" I yell to Cassie, helping her up and over the last bar. Tony stops and looks back, and I see something in his eyes before he dives under the net. When he gets up, he slips and falls, allowing us to close the gap a little.

"Push!" Cassie grunts as we get out, seeing the final obstacle, the jumping posts. Tony and Caleb are more than halfway across, and Caleb takes another big hop, landing on one foot before stretching out and jumping again, clearing the last two logs in the air to land surefooted and make a last dash for the finish line.

"Tony, go!" Caleb yells, but his timing is just a fraction off. Tony stumbles and falls off the log he's aiming for. He walks back to the beginning of the obstacle, and his eyes meet mine again. He starts up the logs while Cassie and I start our own, working together to balance each other as we step from log to log. Tony is jumping, skipping logs, and is nearly at the end when he falls again, having to start over. Caleb screams in frustration, but Tony seems calm as he starts back, and as Cassie and I finish, he's actually behind us.

"Go, go, GO!" I yell to Cassie, who takes off as hard as she can. It's close, and I've never run harder in my life, but we cross the finish line just ahead of Tony, who doesn't look as dejected as he should be for losing.

Caleb, on the other hand, doesn't look pleased. "What the hell, man? You're a former athlete. Coordination is supposed to be your thing."

"I fucked up. I was too winded," Tony says, clapping Caleb on the shoulder. Wesley gives Tony a sly look and Tony looks away. Cassie jumps up and down, hugging me, not believing we pulled it off. Her joy is infectious and I find myself smiling back at her when the guys give us a high-five, Tony saying, and Caleb grumbling, their congratulations.

"Hmmm, it was fun to watch. Perhaps not in the ways I expected, but you all showed great heart today. I'll see you in the main room at three o'clock," he says quietly. "Congratulations."

He leaves, and I look at Tony, who's still red-faced. He gives me a small, chagrined smile, and I shake my head. "You shouldn't have done that."

"Shouldn't have done what?" Tony asks.

I cross my arms, raising an eyebrow. "Winning is good, but sometimes, you lose when you win. I guess some of Wesley's voodoo shit is soaking in." I step closer, looking in his eyes. "I don't want to win like that. Got it?"

Tony smiles, nodding. "Got it."

CHAPTER 21

TONY

"Now for the final challenge," Wesley announces as the four of us gather. "I want you to complete it by tonight and turn it in to me before the night's end."

Regardless of the victory in the obstacle course, I know that if I take this, then I'll win. Wesley says it's the most important of all the 'challenges'.

I don't really know what the hell I was thinking, letting her win the last one. Caleb's still a little annoyed since it was one he knows we should've won. And I think he at least suspects I didn't give it my all.

I look over at Hannah, who's biting her lip and trying to hide her nervousness.

She knew I boned it on purpose. I guess it was the look I had in my eyes. Wesley looks between the both of us, his expression grave. He suspects what I did too, I can tell, but so far, he hasn't said anything. I guess he figures if I want to give up, that's my prerogative.

"The final challenge . . . is an essay. You have both been here for quite a few days and have learned a lot. I want you to tell me what you have learned during your stay and why you should be the winner. You can say anything you want, as long as it's from the heart and honest. Don't share it with anyone, seal it in the envelope, and I'll announce the winner tomorrow."

"An essay?" Cassie gawks.

Wesley nods. "This is for Tony and Hannah only. I want their thoughts and their feelings. If you would please give them their privacy."

"Come on, Cassie," Caleb mutters, walking away. "Let's go."

Cassie lingers for a moment before walking over and giving Hannah a hug, whispering something in her ear. They kiss each other on the cheek and my heart warms at their friendship as she slips away. I don't miss the fear in her eyes at what's to come, and I feel the weight on my shoulders increase. Cassie's under the same guillotine that Hannah is, I'm sure of it. And I like the petite firecracker too, even if she is a pain in the ass.

Wesley sighs when everyone's gone. "You can use the desks over by the windows to write. You'll find pens, papers . . . everything you need. But you absolutely can't communicate with each other. Your words will be yours and yours alone." He gives us a stern look to drive his point home. Now if you'll excuse me, Mo Mo and I will give you some space."

Wesley crosses the room, settling down on one of the mats, crossing his legs in a lotus position before picking up a book. I have no doubt I don't even want to know what it is.

Hannah looks at me, her eyes filled with anxiety. "Are you ready?"

I look across the room, where there are two sets of writing tablets, and nod. "Ready as I'll ever be."

We walk over, but neither of us can sit down yet. I look out the window and see the mango trees, and my mind fills with the images of last night. I keep looking, and I can see the beach through the trees, and the rock where I first kissed her, and the path that leads to the village, and the clearing where I took her last night. I look, and I think . . .

It's a long time before I look down at the blank piece of paper. My thoughts are like dust on the wind. Every time I try to focus, they scatter, fleeting and swirling so that I can't concentrate. I glance back over my shoulder at Hannah. Surprisingly, she's already writing furiously.

I stare at her for a while, seeing the intense concentration on her face. Finally, I sigh and sit down. I know what I'm about to do would infuriate a few people. They're depending on me. And I've worked hard to come to this spot. But I place pen to paper and begin to write my first line.

Dear Wes, this might not be what you thought . . .

Hannah

I SCRIBBLE ON THE PIECE OF PAPER, BITING ON A STRAND OF MY hair. My hand aches, the barrel of the pen biting into the inside of my finger, but I seem taken over by a demon that's animating my hand.

. . . so when I came to your estate, I thought you were more or less mental. More than mental, I thought you were batshit insane. But over these days, I've learned something during all your madness. So I guess you're not totally crazy, or if you are, you're crazy like a fox.

The simple fact is that I love it here. There is a tranquility, even amongst the chaos of events. I poured myself into each and every one, and yet I found myself also letting go of the anger and angst in between. I found that a man whom I once threw a glass of punch on at my best friend's wedding and thought he was just an arrogant, immature player . . . he's much more than that.

I will walk away from here tomorrow with two wishes in my heart. The first is that I could come back here again some day. This place is magical, and I have never felt happier than I did last night with Tony.

My other wish is that I never, ever see this property again. Because I need to win, my job, and more importantly, Cassie's job, depends on it. But if you declare me the winner, that could break Tony's heart. My winning means that I have to take from him. And that means that no matter what . . . this place would be a place of pain and hurt to me. I don't know how I could come back to that.

Maybe that's the wisdom of all this competition that you've been trying to have us learn. That with every win comes a price, and with every loss a price as well. I don't know. What I do know is that tomorrow, I'm going to cry, regardless of what happens. So I take back what I said above. I would come back here. Maybe there is magic in these islands, or at least magic in this specific place. If there is, then there's hope that the feelings I have for Tony will lead us to happiness and that I can live here for the rest of my life, protecting and caring for this land, for the wonderful people who live here, and loving them as much as they've opened their hearts and loved me.

I'm sure you're interested in what my company would do if we get this contract. I can tell you that my bosses have promised me that they will respect and care for the land as best they can, to do their best to give as much back to the people as they will give to us . . .

I write my heart out. I even tell him that I both like and hate his fucking parrot. When it's all done, I have to use my left hand to unclench my right from the pen, and the moon is high in the sky.

I turn, looking around, and see Tony sitting in the doorway, just looking at me. He has his envelope in his hand, and when he sees that I'm done, he stands up, walking across the room and squatting down. "All done?"

"I think so," I answer, taking the sheets and folding them before sliding them into the envelope. "I'd better be. I'm not sure I can fit another piece of paper in here."

Tony chuckles, watching as I fold over the flap and sign the front with a flourish. "So what do you think?" he asks.

I'm shaking as I look at him, trying to form my answer. I don't know why. I'm sure he said the reasons he deserved the place too. He said so himself. I can't kill myself over it. Finally, I swallow the lump in my throat and answer. "It's all been such a crazy whirlwind. I wish we could both win."

We stand up, handing the envelopes to Wesley, who gives us a small nod, saying nothing as we leave. We walk back down to the beach, where the moon is reflected on the water, and Tony reaches out, taking my hand.

"It's not over yet," he says, brushing my hair off my shoulder, causing sparks to shoot from my skin. "Not the important parts."

We kiss, knowing this is likely going to be our last night in

Hawaii. There's an urgency in each caress, each touch of his hand on my skin. It's an urgency that takes my breath away. His hands find my shirt and peel it up as I do the same to his, tears stinging my eyes as I see the hard, chiseled muscles of his chest and stomach. "Wait . . ."

"What?" I ask him, and Tony picks me up, carrying me down the beach. There's a blanket laid out, probably leftovers from one of the challenges, and he lays me down on it. I smile, unbuttoning my shorts and sliding them down as he strips his shorts off, leaving him standing nude in front of me. I get to my knees, running my hands over his stomach as I kiss his thighs, rubbing my cheek against the velvet hardness of his cock, kissing the tip before he steps back, his eyes full of meaning.

There are no words, at least not those said with our lips as we stretch out on the blanket. Tony kisses me with a tenderness that rips through my soul. Cold and heat run through my body as I feel his hands stroke my ass, running up my back to cup my breasts and massage them even as his eyes burn with loss. I cry out in pleasure as he kisses my nipples, sucking and tugging them the way that he knows I like before kissing up to my neck and lifting my leg. I roll with him, feeling the hardness of his cock press against my pussy.

"Please, Tony," I whisper as I reposition my hips and sink down, Tony's strong hands guiding me as he fills me. "Tony . . ."

His name is the only thing that escapes my lips as I ride him, lifting my hips up and down as I look into his eyes. He reaches up, cupping my breasts as we ride, faster and faster. Unable to take it any more, I lean over, kissing him hotly as he plants his feet and starts thrusting up into me, grabbing my ass and holding me still as I moan into his mouth. My body squeezes him, my nerves on edge as I moan his name one more time. He thrusts hard, his cock slamming deep into me before he comes. I'm pushed over, milking him and holding him tight, clutching at his shoulders as we join fully, pure joy and sadness mixing together in something I've never felt before. All I can focus on is the heat of Tony's cock erupting inside me and the look in his eyes.

Tony holds me, and I don't know what's going to happen. No matter what, once this moon sets and the sun rises, the results are going to come. And one of us is going to be hurt by it. I lose either way.

As I kiss Tony's lips tenderly, getting off him, I'm also scared about what he's become to me. I told Wesley all about it, but I still don't understand it all myself. I know that I've never felt this way about a man before. But . . . he's never told me the way he feels. What if this is just an island fantasy? What if I pour my heart out to him and we make a promise to stay in touch, and daily calls slowly become occasional Facebook messages and status likes before petering out to nothing? I couldn't stand that. It'd kill me.

I reach for my shirt to pull it on, but Tony reaches out. "Please . . . don't go," he says, his voice heavy with emotion. "Spend the night here with me. I need to hold you."

I turn and look into his eyes, nodding. "Then how about a dip in the ocean?"

Tony smiles and takes my hand. "I think a little moonlight skinny dipping sounds great. Thank you for saying yes."

"How could I tell you no?" I ask, my voice cracking slightly as we get up. Walking with him toward the ocean, I'm struggling not to cry, and I'm glad the waves hide my harsh breathing. I don't know what Cassie and Caleb are going to think, finding our beds empty, but right now, I don't care. I need this.

It might be the last night we ever have.

CHAPTER 22

TONY

*H*annah and I walk together out to the waves, holding hands as the waves wash the sweat and stickiness from our bodies. Watching her wade deeper, I feel like I'm watching a myth in reverse, Aphrodite not emerging from the sea but returning to it. But she's taking me with her, and as the warm water laps over my chest and I turn to her, I pull her close. "Hannah, you . . ."

There are no more words as I gather her in my arms, kissing her deeply as the water washes over us. We move together back into the shallows, Hannah tracing her fingers over my face as if she's memorizing me the way a blind person would. I kiss her salty fingertips, brushing her hair out of her eyes as we kiss again, our bodies pressing together and washed by the rolling waves.

I reach down, and she understands, lifting her legs and wrapping them around my waist as I hold her effortlessly in my arms. The water sways our bodies, my legs spread as I hold her. "Hannah," I whisper in her ear as I feel her warmth tingle against my belly. "I don't know what's going to happen, but I want you to know . . . you're the most special woman I've ever met. I knew that the first night I saw you. I was just too much of a fool to say it right. I knew there was a spark between us."

"I—" Hannah says, but I shake my head, running my hand down and slipping a finger over her pussy.

"I don't know if I'll ever have the guts to say this again," I whisper, my cock hardening again as I feel the warm wetness of her entrance. I'm quickly back to full hardness, and I adjust myself, slipping inside her, guided only by the warmth of her body. "You're more important than this contract. You're more important than anything to me."

I thrust my cock deeper into her, taking away Hannah's reply. I don't know if I want the words. I've never trusted them as much as the feeling coursing through my skin and along my nerves as I hold her. The salty water makes her feel almost weightless as I thrust in time with the waves, the backwash pulling her tighter into me as she holds onto my shoulders and back. Our lips barely part, gasps and moans slipping from our mouths as I give her all I can. My fingers dig into her hips as I grip her ass, my cock pumping harder and faster inside her, just on the limits of what the ocean will allow us.

I don't know how long I thrust, my cock aching and throbbing as we move with the ocean, our hips making waves of their own. My breath sears in my chest as Hannah's fingers dig in. She's coming again, and her pussy squeezes my cock so hard that I can barely keep stroking, moving with the pulse of my heart. There's no sound except the crash of the nearby waves and our breaths as I speed up, fighting the ocean now, but I need her. I clutch Hannah to me, her breasts squashed against me as she tries to ride me too, faster and harder. I'm desperate. There's nothing except her right now, and I feel my balls grow tight.

"Hannah!" I cry, my cock bursting deep inside her again. Hannah wails, her fingernails piercing my skin and making the wounds burn as ocean water washes over them, but I don't feel the pain, just the burn in my heart and in my mind as I fill her with my essence.

My knees unhinge, and I start to collapse into the water when suddenly, there's an arm under me, holding me up and helping me toward the shore. I look, and it's Hannah, my angel, a soft smile on her face. We curl up on the blanket, the night air just this side of cool and making it comfortable as I spoon her against me.

"Tomorrow . . . I want you to be happy, no matter what," I say. I don't know what I'm saying, but at the same time, I do. I've waited all this time to hear her say that she needs more than a good vacation fantasy. I've waited for her to say she wants more, that she wants me with all of my imperfections and all of my mistakes.

I've waited, and she hasn't said it. I understand. Neither of us has come out and directly said our feelings, but I hope she understands what I've tried to tell her with my body. She owns my heart, from here on out.

Hannah murmurs something under her breath, but whatever she says is cut off by a large yawn. "Sorry."

"It's okay, babe," I reply, my throat tight. She snuggles against me more, and I wrap my arms around her, snagging our t-shirts to use as a pillow under her head. Within minutes, she's snoring lightly, and I kiss her on the temple. "It's okay, I've got it all . . ."

I can't lie anymore. I don't have it all under control. Watching her snore in the moonlight, the first tears trickle down my cheeks. My heart is breaking in my chest, but everything will be fine if she's the one who wins. I've had the time of my life with her, and I'll never forget this.

CHAPTER 23

HANNAH

*T*he light is still pink in the sky when I make it back to my room. I try to be quiet, but Cassie's already up, sitting on the bed and staring at the doorway. I don't know if she was worried about me or just worried that we may soon be unemployed. Anxiety tightens my throat when I see she's even already packed a lot of things up.

"Everything all right?" Cassie asks, her eyes full of meaning. "I figured you were with Tony but was still a little worried."

Hell no, everything's not all right. "I'm a little down, but I'll be fine," I lie.

She stares at me for a moment and then looks away. "I'm nervous," she finally says. "You know . . . about what the outcome is going to be."

"Don't be," I reassure her. "Everything is going to turn out fine."

Cassie snorts. She knows I'm not a psychic, and I'm just spouting bullshit. "I certainly hope so."

"It will," I repeat, turning away so she doesn't see the tears in my eyes. I want to tell her how I felt this morning, waking up just as the sky started to lighten, being in his arms, enveloped in his warmth. I want to tell her how hard it was to leave his side, knowing it was probably our last time together.

But I don't.

I strip off my dirty clothes and get a quick shower before we get dressed. But there's a pall over our actions. Neither of us wants to be putting on the nicer, professional clothes that feel appropriate for this meeting with Wes. Downstairs at the breakfast table, I avoid eye contact with Tony. He looks handsome as usual, dressed more conservatively in gray slacks and a white dress shirt. No matter what, the next few hours are going to be hard. The tension is so thick you could cut it with a knife, not just between Tony and me but between all of us.

I choke down a grapefruit and wait. Just as someone's watch beeps, the first time I've heard a watch our whole trip here, Wesley comes in with Alani, Mo Mo on his shoulder.

"Good morning," he says, smiling at us. "So I spent the night reading, thinking about what I should do. To say that I was both surprised and touched by what I read is an understatement. After reading what you both had to say, I reflected and meditated. I spoke with Alani about them, and we discussed it for hours more. Hell, I even talked to Mo Mo about this decision."

Mo Mo squawks. "Mo Mo genius!"

He chuckles, while in my gut, I wonder if my entire fate is going to rest on the opinion of a bird that insists on calling me a big booty ho. "Ultimately, I want to do the right thing for Alani and her people. I took into account what was best for them, for the karma of the land, for which of you would do more to ensure that we maintain the spirit of tradition and respect their history while continuing forward on their journey to new sunrises. I wanted to make sure the winner would be the person who will hold this place as dear to their heart as I do. I wanted to make sure they continue in balance with the cycles of Mother Nature."

He pauses, looking at each of us. It's so quiet I can hear a pin drop, and I can see the former industrialist in him. He loves the spectacle of drawing out the moment of the announcement. "I took more than just your performance into account, but I'm sure you already know that. If I were still running a company, I'd offer any of you a job right now. I also looked over your proposals, the files you brought with you that I'm sure you thought I totally ignored. But most of all, I looked at your spirits, your souls, and you've shown me that and more. With all that in mind, I've decided to sell to Hannah and Aurora Holdings."

Cassie throws her fist into the air, and despite my reservation, I get up and hug Wesley before ignoring Tony's offered handshake to hug him tightly. "Thank you so much," I whisper in his ear. "I have a feeling you had a hand in that."

He whispers back. "Congratulations. You deserve it." He has a faint smile on his face as he steps back.

"Tony—"

"Can you tell us what set them apart?" Caleb asks, cutting me off. "You realize they're probably going to tear this place down to put up a fucking resort hotel, right?"

"One of the greatest forces on Earth is water," Wesley says. "Water flows, but at the same time, it can crash. Water and time will even someday reduce these islands to the oceans from which they were born. Change is inevitable, Caleb."

Tony raises his hand. "Caleb, everything's going to be fine."

Caleb turns to Tony. I don't think he really wanted the philosophy speech. "I know that, Tony. I just wanted some answers, especially for Oli. Is that too much to ask?"

Caleb sighs, nodding at us even though he's clearly not in the best of moods "Thank you for your hospitality and this crazy adventure, Wes. Congrats, ladies. You did earn it. I'm man enough to admit that. It just really sucks to be in a tough situation. But it is what it is. I'm going to go get my shit together."

He turns and walks off, Tony staring at him but not following.

"Get your shit together!" Mo Mo screeches.

"I . . ." I begin, but Tony shakes his head.

"I'm sorry about that, you guys. I'll talk to him. He's just a little upset."

"It's okay," Wesley says, smiling. "If you need any help with your bags, we'd be glad to help," he says, nodding at Alani, who hands Tony a package. "Just a book for your flight home and contact information. If you ever need someone to vouch for you . . . just give me a call. Hannah, Cassie, let's discuss business in a half hour or so."

Wesley gives us a nod and a smile before leaving. Tony crosses the room and leans in, giving Cassie a look that she reads perfectly, ditching the room. "I think I'll give Myra the good news, if you don't mind."

Cassie leaves, and Tony clears his throat in the silence. "Can I speak to you for a moment?"

"I'd like that," I reply, while silently hoping he says the words that I've been praying to hear. We go out onto the porch, looking around. The day is searingly beautiful, although on the horizon, I can see rain clouds gathering. I suppose it's appropriate, considering the way I feel. "You know, I'm going to miss this place."

"What do you mean?" Tony asks, leaning on the railing. "You'll be coming back here, I'm sure. Aurora is going to need a top-notch project manager."

I shake my head. "It won't be the same. Things will be different."

Tony reaches over, taking my hand. "Hannah . . . even if the resort thing were true, I want you to forget what Caleb said. I want you to be happy. You fought for this. You earned it and you deserve it. Someone else would've bought this place if it weren't us. Better us, or those we represent, than someone else."

He's saying so many nice things, but each one is like a dagger in my heart. Why won't he say what I want him to say? Why can't he say it first? I come close but back off. The separation is so much, and he's going to have a lot of explaining to do when he gets back home.

I've always been afraid of falling in love. That level of vulnerability seems like a freefall with a mere whispered promise of being caught in the safety of his arms. I've always worried I'd end up hurt, or worse, sacrificing myself to the relationship. Finally, I find a man I think I'm falling in love with, and maybe worth the risk of jumping in, but this feels like the end.

"Hannah, I don't regret saying those nasty things to you that first night we met," Tony says, chuckling. "Because they at least allowed us to get to know each other some. And this time here . . . I wouldn't trade it for the world." He leans in close and pulls me in for a sweet, painful kiss. "I wish you all the best, Hannah Fowler. You're one hell of a woman." He stares at me for a long moment, as if he doesn't want to leave, before letting out a soft sigh. "Give me a call when everything's settled back at work. Let me know how things are going?"

It feels like a brushoff, or at least, a finality, so I nod softly, the pain of my heart cracking and hurting too much to let me speak.

Then slowly, as if committing my face to memory for eternity, Tony turns and goes inside. Moments later, I hear him calling something to the house staff. I don't look up as I hear the doors on Tony's rented car close, the engine fire up, and he drives off. I whip my head up as I hear the tires crunch over a rock, but he's already made the turn, and I can hear him accelerate. I nearly crumble as I round the corner of the house and all I see is the cherry red tail lights. "Tony . . ."

I feel like screaming, like jumping off the porch and chasing after him, but before I can, I hear a quiet voice behind me. "Hey . . . you ready?"

I turn to see Cassie, her face alight with happiness, and I swallow my tears. I still have paperwork to do, stuff to get signed. I feel the happiness too, but it's bitter in my mouth and I swallow reflexively. "Yeah. Let's get those papers signed . . . then . . ."

"Yeah?"

"I just wanna go home."

Fourteen hours.

Now, normally, if I think of doing something for fourteen hours, I'm not this exhausted. I've done fourteen hours at work before, I've done fourteen hours shopping—okay, I was tired then—I even once had an ex who wanted to do a 'sex-a-thon' that lasted almost that long before he tapped out.

In none of them have I been this exhausted. The plane ride was hell, not because of the seats, but just because it felt like every step going through the airport, I had a huge rubber band pulling me back, telling me not to go. I couldn't get much sleep on the plane. Every time I closed my eyes, I saw Tony, and twice, Cassie shook me awake from a nightmare of chasing after Tony and him disappearing into darkness.

Now I walk into my modest apartment, and at the first sniff, I hate it. It's not that it's dirty. I made sure to scrub the place before I left, but looking around the soulless, empty cracker box, I just hate it. It's everything that Wesley's place wasn't. There's white paint on the walls, a tasteful and chic tile floor, steel in the kitchen . . . and I don't even have a plant to water. There's no soul, there's nothing that says *Hannah Fowler lives here*. I don't have any photos on the walls, no mementos, nothing. Except for Mr. Felix's stuff, it's like I'm paying monthly rent on a room at a Ramada.

I sigh again, putting my bag down and wishing for a little bit of beauty. The sunsets were the best, but I can't see a damn thing except the city from my single double-paned, hermetically sealed glass door. I don't even want to open it anyway. It'll let in too much smell of fried hydrocarbons and humanity, when all I really want is rich forest smells, mangoes on a humid breeze, and a kiss of salt in the evening air.

I don't have a home. I have a sleeping box. It's fucking hollow, just like my victory, and now, just like my heart, which has ached constantly since seeing Tony drive away. I look at my bag, I know I should put my stuff away, but fuck it. I have a closet full of things.

My phone rings, and I see that it's Roxy. "Hey, babe, how's it going?" I answer.

"I thought that'd be my line," Roxy says chirpily. "So, how's it going?"

"I'm back," I admit, lying back on my couch. "In the end . . . well, we won. I got the contract."

"Congratulations! Isn't that good news? Why don't you sound happy?"

I feel something unknot in my chest, and in moments, the tears I've been holding back for hours start flowing down my cheeks, and I find myself telling Roxy everything. Every challenge, every tease Tony and I sent back and forth . . . everything. "And now, I've got a feather in my cap that a lot of people would kill for, and I don't care. I love him, Roxy. I love him and he's gone."

"Babe . . ." Roxy says quietly, letting my tears quiet down. "Okay, listen. I know you're wiped by jet lag, but as soon as you can, let's get together and talk about this. I've got a doctor's appointment tomorrow afternoon, but what about tomorrow evening?"

"Maybe Friday would be better, Rox. No offense, but I plan on going to work tomorrow, getting the pat on the back that maybe will make me feel better about this, and then sleep my ass off."

After we finish, I decide I'm too tired to go out and order

some Chinese delivery. When it comes, I'm barely able to get it down. Instead of fresh foods like I've been eating, it's quick and in a box. I get halfway through the sweet and sour pork before giving up and deciding that I need to get ready for tomorrow.

Myra sent me an email. I've got a presentation to the Aurora board, and I need to make sure that's good before I go to bed.

I'm in the middle of my routine when my eyes fall on the picture Tony and me taken at the falls. I set my laptop to cycle through photos as the screensaver. In it, I'm happily in his arms, my smile as bright as the sun. I try, but I can't remember the last time I saw such a lively spark in my eyes. I look genuinely happy in the photo. And so does Tony.

My heart skips a beat as I feel tears prick my eyes. Oh, how I miss him already.

He told me to call him.

I resist the urge to grab my phone and dial his number. He said to call when the contract was settled, but my pain is too fresh. I'll just break down at the sound of his voice.

Sighing, I resume going about getting prepared for tomorrow.

THE NEXT MORNING, I'M STILL FEELING LIKE A SPACE ZOMBIE as jet lag combines with everything else as Cassie pulls around in her little Toyota. "Hey, did you get any sleep at all?"

I shake my head, quickly sucking more homebrew iced

espresso. At least my outfit looks good. I made sure of that. "An hour or two. You?"

Cassie shrugs and puts a hand on my thigh. "I'm so sorry," she says quietly. "I know I gave you some hard times, but you were great over there. I really wish things could have turned out differently for you and Tony."

"It's okay. We got the contract and we both keep our jobs, so something good came out of our trip."

"Yeah, there is that." Cassie pulls away from the curb while I nurse my bottle some more, hoping I don't hit caffeine overload before lunch. I've got some gum in my purse, so hopefully I don't nuke blast anyone with my breath. At the red light, she lets out a big sigh.

"What?"

"I just wish I woulda got to knee Caleb in the balls. At least once, especially after that last little comment of his."

I laugh. "Who knows? You might get your chance someday."

Cassie chuckles. "Come on, we're here."

We pull up to the building and make a stop at our desks on the fifth floor, doing a last-minute breath and mirror check to be ready. I've got on my best pencil skirt, the black one that cuts off right at the knees, and after eating better and exercising on the island, it fits better than ever. I've got my best tight white blouse on, and my hair is swept up just right to balance power with looks.

Cassie stops by my desk, also looking her best, her makeup flawless. "Let's go in here and let the 'suits' know what bad bitches we are."

"Excuse me?" I ask, and I can't help but smile at her enthusiasm. "I'm the bad bitch. Remember, I hit something with my arrows."

"It is not how many arrows you send home. The true bad bitch receives without lifting a finger," Cassie says with a fake Wesley accent. "You're just the wannabe."

I laugh. I can't help it. "Whatever, oh master of the rabbit style."

We take the elevator up to the twenty-third floor, and as we cross the expensive marble floor of the executive reception area, I feel like we've earned the right to walk across such hallowed ground. I know my heels for damn sure appreciate it. "Hey, Ruby," I greet the receptionist, who used to work down on five with us. I hand over the bag of muffins in my hand. "Here, picked these up for you."

"Thanks," she says. "You've got about ten minutes, by the way. Heard you two rocked. Congrats."

We thank Ruby and head in, where Cassie sets up her laptop while I make sure I have all the hard copies ready. Right at ten, Myra comes in, dressed sharp as a tack in her best power suit, the silver piping on the black perfectly matching with her hair, her smile evident as she closes the door behind us. "Have a seat. I'm looking forward to hearing the details."

The meeting seems to take a decade, as before Cassie and I can present, there's seemingly endless board minutiae. Finally, it's our turn, and Cassie and I stand in front of the board. "Ladies and gentlemen of the board, thank you for the chance to deliver the results personally. First, let me say that yes, Aurora Holdings has secured the contract to Wesley Mobber's estate, as you can see from the copies that Miss White is distributing to you all now."

"So, you got Mobber to sign, did you?" asks Lois Zeigler, CEO of Aurora. Just as Myra's been sort of my mentor, Lois was Myra's. "How did you manage that?"

I take a deep breath and smile, while Cassie chuckles. We start our presentation, explaining that upon arriving at the eccentric owner's estate, he was less interested in Aurora's offer and finances and more focused on ensuring that his legacy continued. I described the challenges, showing some of the best photos I took during my stay, highlighting some of the estate's unique features that will benefit Aurora for marketing and development. As we come to a close, I finish up by giving a nod to Cassie. "Cassie was an invaluable asset and more helpful than I could've imagined. I'd like to say that there's no way I could have succeeded without her help."

Cassie's beaming as I wrap it up, but as I look out at everyone, I see stony, unimpressed faces. The comments start almost immediately.

"Games?"

"Mud pit?"

"Hiking?"

Lois clears her throat, giving us a totally nonplussed look. "It sounds more like a spa vacation than any actual work, Miss Fowler and Miss White. But I guess your methods bore results. So congrats, I suppose. Now, moving on . . ."

I exchange disbelieving glances with Cassie. *Did you just hear that?* I want to tell her, and I can see the same reaction on Cassie's face. Didn't they do their homework on Wesley and know it wasn't going to just be a matter of discussing numbers? Did Myra not fill them in at all along the way?

This is most definitely not the response we were expecting.

We were expecting fanfare and to be heroes for scoring an impossible deal, some recognition for working our asses off for this! I didn't even mention Tony and me and how I had to watch the first man I've ever truly loved walk out of my life.

"I can't believe that!" Cassie fumes after we leave. In the elevator back down to five, she explodes. "They didn't care about us. We're nothing to them. I wish I could knee her cunt through her nose."

"Myra didn't even speak up for us," I add, keeping my jaw clenched to prevent me saying more. If I got fired after all of this, I might die.

"Yeah, that was total bullshit too," Cassie says, sighing. "I expected more."

She's telling me. I mean, I didn't expect to be given the keys to the executive washroom, but I did expect at least some sort of recognition. A thank you for your service. Hell, maybe even a promotion. But instead . . . it all just feels empty.

CHAPTER 24

ANTHONY

I let out a sigh, placing my head against the window as the plane begins its descent. Walking away from Hannah and getting into the rental SUV to drive back to Honolulu was the hardest thing I've ever done. I want her to be happy. I hope this brings her the happiness she deserves.

Deep down in my heart, I know I did the right thing. But fuck, I miss her.

Beside me, Caleb is a little quiet. I haven't told him what I'm going through, although I'm sure he can guess. But I don't expect him to understand. I don't think anyone would.

"Yo, dude," Caleb says as we drop through the clouds and I can see the airport. "I'm sorry for acting that way back there, I shouldn't have just ran off. I wish I would've told Wesley that and shook his hand before leaving. I feel bad about that. It was supposed to be business, but it did kind of feel like a vacation, and I had a good time . . . I just couldn't understand. I didn't know why you would give up after all of that."

"I—" I begin to say, but Caleb cuts me off.

"Hang on, let me finish. I think I know how you feel. I could see it in your eyes, and the entire time back, I've been watching you. I know you tilted Wes in her direction."

I stare at him. I figured he knew as much. I just don't know how to respond. I kind of put him through it all and may have cost him a big raise. Oliver surely would've rewarded him, even if he didn't say it. "How?"

Caleb shrugs. "You're in love. You'd do anything for her, and in reality, I can't blame you. I'd probably have done the same thing if I were in your position. I was wrong to react the way I did. I was a poor sport and I wish I could take it back. You may have swayed him in their direction at the very end, but you tried your damndest the rest of the time."

Relief sweeps through me. Caleb's been my friend for over a decade now, and I'm glad to know this isn't going to change anything.

"No hard feelings?" he asks, sticking a hand out to me.

I take it before we smack hands the way we used to, back when we thought Arnold Schwarzenegger movies were the most awesome things ever. "No hard feelings."

Caleb raises an eyebrow. "How do you think Oliver's gonna take it?"

"Dick," I growl. "You just had to remind me about that, huh? No, but seriously, it might be a lost opportunity financially, but Hannah is kind of like extended family. He's not gonna get his panties in a bunch. At least I hope."

He chuckles. "Fuck, I'm gonna miss that place. Wes and his damn speeches. Even the bird."

I laugh. "Well, we'll all miss things." *Hannah most of all*, I think to myself, my heart aching.

Fuck, I hope she calls. But I probably ruined my small chance like I always do. I should have said more before I left.

I'm still haunted by the look that was in Hannah's eyes, like she was trapped. And I'm scared my biggest regret is going to be that I didn't do enough for her.

We land and get our bags. Outside, Oli is waiting for us at the pickup area with a smile on his face.

"Hey, boys, how was your trip?"

Caleb looks at me, uncertain. He's gonna let me take the lead on this. "Awesome," I say with the fakest enthusiasm I can muster, my stomach twisting with dread even after I just told Caleb that Oliver wouldn't completely flip his shit. I haven't answered or responded to Oliver's calls in the past two days. He's probably gotten the point, but I didn't have the guts to tell him over the phone what was going on. I wanted to tell him face to face.

Oliver waves us to put our luggage in the back of his SUV. "Come on, get inside. Y'all must be starving, and it's a long ride back home. We can stop on the way."

We load up, and he takes us away from the airport and we hit up a burger joint. He doesn't say anything about the contract on the way over. I'm sure he knows. It's just a matter of me saying it.

As soon as we're seated, he sits back, looking at the two of us. "Don't be so quiet, you two. Spit it out. Tell me everything."

I relax a little and tell him all about Wes and his parrot, all the funny stuff, all the crazy shit we did over the time we were there. I gave him a complete rundown on all of the challenges, and how Wes seemed to be interested in our character, not necessarily who won. Oli listens, laughing in the right places before sipping his Pepsi and asking, "So, what's the verdict?"

Finally, the question comes. Caleb sputters and gets up to refill his own drink at the dispenser while my mouth goes dry. As he leaves, he gives me a small nod. I understand, he's giving me some privacy. "What's going on?"

Taking a deep breath, I tell him everything, dread growing by the second. But by the time I'm done, I feel like a ton has been lifted off my shoulders. "I'm so sorry, man. I know how much this meant to you."

He sits quietly as Caleb comes back, eyeing me as he sets his soda down. The whole time, Oliver just stares at me. I'm starting to think I might be wrong. I willfully lost. That's a giant 'fuck you' if there was one. He probably thinks I'm a hopeless waste of his time, my carelessness once again costing him.

"What are you going to do now?" he asks quietly, surprising me after the silence. He looks . . . calm.

"I don't know," I say uneasily, not able to read his face and half-expecting him to jump across the table and drag me out the door to curb stomp my ass. "What's the next property you want me to look at?" A part of me feels honor-bound to find the next assignment and deliver for him since I screwed him over. "I promise you, no more conspiring with the competition."

He shakes his head. "No, that's not what I'm talking about. This is more important than that. What about Hannah? You love her, don't you?"

I see the compassion in his eyes. He understands what I'm going through.

"I don't know," I reply. *Of course I know*, I tell myself. I've known it since . . . "What do I do? I mean, we have our own lives. My family is here, and hell, she probably just got a promotion."

"Hmm," Oli says, sipping at his drink before giving me a long, evaluating look. In his look, I see a question I've wanted to ask him for at least a year now, and for some reason, now is the time.

"How'd you know when you loved Mindy?" I ask. "Not when you thought. When you knew."

"That's easy. When you find the one who makes you feel like your heart isn't in your chest anymore but in her hands. When you meet that person who makes you feel like you'd be happy sharing the fifth circle of hell if they were the one with you . . . when you meet her, and you'd be willing to do anything, be saint or sinner or angel in order to make her happy . . . that's when you know."

I can tell he's speaking from experience. It's like he went off a checklist of my feelings for Hannah, and I slow blink a couple of times to ease the burn in my eyes. You just can't cry in front of your best friend and your brother. Totally not cool. "Oli . . . I don't know what she wanted. Neither of us outright said anything. I mean, when it comes to the big four-letter word or if we were going to make an effort to see one another after . . . it was all about our dreams, how we wanted the other person to be happy, how they made us feel good. Maybe we just assumed we couldn't be together."

Oliver's eyes are sad. "Never assume when it comes to love. I know I've asked you to do a lot for the family, but if it meant your being with Hannah, you don't owe me a damn thing. The world's a small place. You can still visit."

His words hit me hard, and I struggle to keep up as Caleb tries to keep the rest of dinner conversation light and as far from the topic of my heartbreak as possible. I hear about how Mindy's pregnancy is progressing, along with Roxy's, although that's sort of hard to hear since I know Roxy's best friends with Hannah. I'm sure the burger is fine, though I barely taste it. It's just mechanical chewing. They could have brought me a block of wet cardboard and I'd have eaten it.

When I get home, I lie in bed, realizing that I fucked up big time. How the fuck did I just leave and not say more? Call me when everything settles down? What a fucking douchebag. I close my eyes, remembering the spark in her eyes. That fiery spirit, her beautiful sense of humor. I've never known anyone like that, nor will I ever find someone like her again.

Reaching over, I grab my phone. Sure, I got the number for a prank, but it's still in my phone, and I type out a message to Hannah. *Hey, I've been really thinking about you. Wondered if you'd like to talk?*

The question is, should I hit *Send*, or do I give her time?

CHAPTER 25

HANNAH

*T*uesday morning, it's back to the fifth floor, and to be honest, I still feel a bit numb and tired. Last night, I couldn't get any sleep, tossing and turning. I was up past two in the morning thinking about him, wanting him. I woke up at six thirty covered in sweat, remembering a fleeting dream about the time we spent together on the beach.

I was barely able to drag myself out of bed to come here. The only trick I used was by spending twenty minutes looking over photos of us together and trying not to cry. Now, I feel like shit, and I can only hope that it's more jet lag than heartbreak.

"Hey, Han," Cassie greets me. Her desk sits across from mine, right next to the small conference area that we use for group work, with Myra's private office down at the end of the room. I look over, and Cassie looks like me, with bags under her eyes and her hair not looking her best. I doubt she's gotten four hours of sleep. I sit down at my desk and open my laptop, typing in the password for my welcome screen.

"Hey."

"How'd you sleep?" Cassie asks, stifling a yawn.

"Not good," I admit. "You?"

Cassie chuckles sarcastically. "As you can tell, I got ten solid hours of pure beauty sleep."

I nod, checking my emails and wondering what I can do to fake my way through being productive for the next eight hours.

"I miss it," Cassie says quietly after a few minutes. She's been typing on her laptop, and I bet she's playing Minecraft or something. Neither of us is in the mood to work.

"I miss it, too," I admit. "Cass—"

Right at that moment, Myra comes out of her office with a stack of files. Dressed sharply as usual, she definitely got all the rest she needs. "Hello, girls. How are my two treasure finders this morning?"

"Hello," we both say in unexcited unison.

"What's wrong?" she asks when she sees our attitudes. "Jet lagged still?"

"Nope," I reply. "But to be honest, I was a little let down when you didn't stick up for us in the meeting. I thought you would've had our backs."

Myra waves off my being so direct. I guess I've earned a small outburst, at least. "I didn't want to take the risk. What you ladies have to learn about the upper board is that they expect results. You're not going to get much praise when you give them. You're just doing your job is how they see it. You girls are heroes in my eyes. And I owe you big time."

Her words are sincere, and Cassie and I exchange glances. I just wish she would've given us a little heads up. "What's that?" I ask, nodding at the folder in her arms. "I hope I'm not being sent somewhere already."

"Nope. This," she says, coming over and setting the folder on my desk, "is what they plan on doing with the property."

I open the folder, my stomach sinking somewhere down to about the second floor as Myra outlines the plan the board has for Wesley's property. Their plans are so misguided and totally against everything that I was first told and what I put in my letter to Wesley. "Myra . . ."

"The latest figures show that Aurora can clear the main compound, reconstruct, and still come in at budget and turn a profit in less than two years," Myra says as my fingers tremble with horror looking at the artist's renditions. The bamboo buildings, the fruit tree groves, everything . . . they're completely sanitizing its personality, turning it into a spa resort just like hundreds of other ones across the world. Nothing special, nothing with tradition and honoring the history of the island.

"Once we clear the locals out, we'll be able to move on with phase two," Myra says, and I look up at Cassie, who looks as horrified as I do. She's talking as if the whole area is in horrible condition and it's not. Everyone knew there was going to be demolition and construction, but this is on another level. There's going to be nothing left, not even the village. It's horrible. They're going to ruin all the best things, bastardizing Wes's legacy.

"Myra, we can't do that!" I cry out when she finishes.

"Why not? Once the contract's signed on both ends and the money's transferred, it's ours to do what we want. Which, by the way, you're both going to be getting a sizable bonus. I can't give you numbers yet, but as soon as everyone signs on the dotted line, I can," Myra replies. "Projections have that it's going to make the company millions a year in profit. So why not follow this plan?"

Oh, my God, what have I done?

"Because it's a beautiful place," Cassie says. "And those fucking profiteering assholes are going to completely destroy it."

Myra is taken aback by the venom in Cassie's voice. "Excuse me?"

"Myra, I know you sent us there to do this job," I say, desperate to keep her rage off Cassie, "but after seeing the beauty there . . ." I can't in good conscience let this go without speaking my mind. I tell her everything about the property, Wesley, even my love for Tony. I pour it all out, the total story, not just the lines I fed the board yesterday.

Myra is white-faced as she listens. "I don't know what to say," she says. "You turned over the letter of intent to the company. They're in final negotiations with Wesley. Once he signs off on the deal, it's over. There's no going back."

"Tell them that this deal can't happen with this plan," I plead with her.

She backs away. "You know I can't do that. Our jobs are at stake."

"Myra, please!" I beg. "They're going to ruin one of the last truly beautiful places on Earth. It's like . . . their plan's like someone replacing the Mona Lisa with some paint by numbers Jesus on velvet!"

"It's done, Hannah, and you're just going to have to accept it!" Myra says with finality. She stomps back to her office and slams the door, silence falling like a curtain between me and Cassie.

"What the hell are we gonna do?" she says after a moment. "We can't let those bastards do this!"

In some karmic way that lets me know the cosmos is jacking with me, at that moment, my computer dings with an email from Wesley Mobber.

Dear Hannah,

How has your return to the mainland been? I hope that the jet lag has worn off. I had a long phone call from the legal department at Aurora Holdings, and while they certainly talked my ear off, it also left questions running around in my head.

You probably wonder what it was that convinced me to choose you. Let me say, it wasn't just your words. I could read between the lines, and I knew that half of what you said about Aurora's plans were corporate bullshit. Oh, you believed it, but it's still corporate bullshit.

You're smart, Hannah, but naïve and maybe not quite as jaded as I am after so many years in the corporate rat race. I thought this would be another lesson worth learning first-hand. Do not be the tool they use to further their cause, know what your purpose is and how to best utilize your own strengths. You are in charge of your destiny.

Beyond your letter and Aurora's proposal, there's something else you need to see, and dare I say, learn from? I think it's more important than anything else that's happened since I first laid eyes on you.

There's an attachment, a PDF file. I open it. It's the letter

Tony wrote Wesley. I see the handwriting, and I read it over twice, letting it soak in.

"Dear Wes, this might not be what you thought, but I don't want to win your competition anymore. When I arrived in Hawaii, I was so different. I was ready to kick ass and take names. Even arriving, my only thoughts were of getting your property, then relaxing with some fine island honey.

Then I met Hannah again. You see, I met her a little over a year ago, at the wedding of a family friend. And oh, man, did I want to lay the pipe on her that night. It was thinking like that, of course, that got a glass of punch thrown on my tux. All of this you know. We've sort of talked about it since my arrival. What you probably saw with your own eyes, though, was that as soon as I saw her again, I wanted her just as much. That first night, after she slipped the Horny Goat Weed into my food, I wanted two things—your property, and to fuck her so hard she never, ever forgot the name of Tony Steele.

Maybe it's your crazy lessons, maybe it's the fact I still want to choke your damn bird, or maybe it's the magic of the land, but somewhere along the way, I realized something. It doesn't matter which company wins, which side wins. As long as this property, the people involved with it like your wife and her family, and all those people in the village who opened their lives up to us at the festival . . . as long as they win, it's all good.

And I realized, as I've thought about it, that this land has to go to someone who needs it. Who will cherish it and protect it and treat it with the honor it deserves. Who will preserve the magic that is here.

That person isn't me. Because as much as I love your property, as much as I love this land and the people I've met, I've come to realize that I love Hannah more. Wesley, if Hannah told me it would make her happy, I'd burn this property to the ground. And you deserve better than that. You deserve better than me.

So I want Hannah to win the contract. She's an amazing woman, beautiful inside and out, someone who will make sure your legacy and the land will be protected with honor. I don't want to be an obstacle to her happiness, and if by stepping back, I can give her her dream, I want to do so."

Tears roll down my face as I read the message again and again, seeing the word that I wanted to hear. *Love.*

"Hannah?" Cassie presses, "What are we going to do?"

I look up, fires hotter than Oahu's volcanos burning in my belly. "We can't let the deal happen."

"You look . . . big," I say, hugging Roxy carefully as Cassie and I come into her penthouse. Cassie's eyes are huge, about ready to pop out of her head as she takes it all in. "Where's Sophie?"

"On a campus visit to Harvard," Roxy says with a smile. "I doubt she's gonna go, but now's the time to explore options. You said it was important."

"Hold on," Cassie says, still looking around. She scrunches up her face, making Roxy look at me with concern.

"Ten seconds," I reply, watching as Cassie squeals softly, hopping up and down before opening her eyes and letting it all out.

"Oh my gawd, I'm such a fan! I love watching you perform, and this is so amazing being in your house!" Cassie blurts out in a single long stream before taking a deep breath. "Okay, fangirl moment over. I barely held it in last time we went shopping together."

Roxy laughs, giving me a look. "I can see why you like her."

We sit down and exchange small talk for a little bit. Roxy shows us some ultrasounds. Her baby is going to be big like the father. Roxy shows me some of the baby clothes that have come in from fans and people at Club Jasmine, and they're adorable. "But . . . tell me what's going on? You said it had something to do with the trip. I mean, I'm not even sure what all went on."

"Oh, it was crazy!" Cassie blurts, grinning. "We met a guy who thinks he's a pirate, there was a tug of war, and obstacle courses . . . oh, and I got to totally be Katniss. I put an arrow in like, a dozen fish—"

"Liar," I say with a snort. "You barely hit the ocean with your arrows half the time!"

"Ooh!" Roxy says, and I can actually see her stomach squirming as the baby moves around. "Oh my, feels like I've got a twerk off going in my belly!"

"Must be a girl then," I tease, but Roxy's eyes darken as she sees me and sees the serious expression on Cassie's face.

"Okay, you two, what's up? I can see something is wrong, and your message more or less said it, too. I see hurt in your eyes, Hannah, and Cassie, you look scared as fuck."

"I think . . . I think I may have made the biggest mistake of my life," I reply, tears stinging at my eyes. "We won the contract, but . . . what Aurora's going to do to the land, to the people . . ."

I can't go on, the pain's too much, and Cassie takes over,

showing Roxy the file folder Myra gave us. Roxy's eyes go wide with the horror as she understands. "Is this not what the plan was from the start?"

I shake my head. I should've known better. "Roxy . . . Tony basically told Wesley to choose to go with me and Aurora. I don't know why, but Wesley showed me the letter Tony wrote. At the end, he said that he'd give up anything to make me happy, and that he thought I'd be the one to make sure something like this didn't happen. But also . . . he said he loves me. I never told him. I never told him how I feel, and now I feel like I'm going to lose the most precious gift I've ever gotten. My heart's a dead lump in my chest and I don't know what to do except fight to protect it all."

"Well, you know me. I spent all that time not chasing my dreams. It took finding Jake to wake me up again, to get me to start doing what I'm meant to do," she says. "So we need to get you back on that track. What do you want most?"

Her question shocks me. It's not what I came here for, but the answer comes to me immediately. "I want Tony by my side."

"See?" Roxy asks with a smirk. "Why work for that coven of soulless vampires? They lied to you, they lied to everyone to get you all to go along with it. I learned that chasing my dream, and singing brought me more happiness than I ever could have imagined. For me, the decision would be simple."

"How can I?" I ask. "My God, I took Tony's dream of helping his family and I almost burned it to the ground. Because of me, he went against his brother. No wonder he left the way he did. He probably dreaded going home to face Oliver."

"You let me worry about that," Roxy says with a smirk. "Remember, Oliver Steele is my brother-in-law now, so

Tony's family too. I'm pretty sure if they don't want me singing about Oliver's little performance at Club Jasmine that time, they'll at least listen."

"Performance?" Cassie, who wasn't there, asks. "What performance?"

"Let's just say Oli looks better in stockings than any heterosexual man has any right to be," Roxy says with a laugh. "But seriously, getting with Jake and following my heart changed my life. I had Mindy, and now you have me."

"Wait . . . what's this about stockings?" Cassie asks. "What type of fun do you people have?"

"Stick around a while, and you'll find out," Roxy says. "Now, I have one question. If you do this, you're out of a job, probably both of you. You understand that, right?"

I look at Cassie, who swallows her fear but gives me a nod of support. It's in my hands now.

"Fuck the job," I growl, looking at Roxy. "Make the call. I'm gonna go get my studmuffin and we're gonna save that property."

CHAPTER 26

"*T*hank you so much, Caleb," Mom says as we finish fixing the water sprinkler. I can't really blame Mom. She didn't know where the pipes for the system ran, but when she decided to put in a tetherball set for her grandchildren and nobody exactly checked, the result was a big mess. So it fell to me and Caleb, sweating our asses off in the sun once again, to replace the four-foot cracked section of PVC pipe.

"Aw, shucks, you're welcome Miz Steele," Caleb drawls, and I swear he's putting just a little extra into his voice. It's almost annoying.

"Did you enjoy your stay?" Mom asks before looking at me and then at Caleb. "You mind telling me what's wrong with my boy here?"

"Nothing that I know of," Caleb says innocently. I gotta give him credit, he isn't ratting me out, respecting that I don't really want to talk about it.

Mom crosses her arms, and I know the look on her face. I want to tell Caleb to watch out, but she's too quick. "Caleb, don't you sass me, young man. You know exactly what's going on, and I'm going to find out one way or another!"

"Ma, I told you a million times nothing is wrong," I say. "Stop embarrassing me." I'm trying to make my voice strong and commanding, but even to my ears, it lacks any conviction. The fact is, I've never been in love before. I've never felt my heart break before, and it fucking hurts.

"Mmmhmm," Mom says. "You know I can smell bullshit from a mile away. But I'm going to go inside. If you boys can finish that up, I'd appreciate it."

Mom goes inside, and I look over at Caleb. "Sorry about that."

"No problem," Caleb says. "You doing okay still?"

I pick up my shovel and plunge it into the wheelbarrow of dirt that we've dug out of the hole. "Hell, no," I admit, carefully dropping it into the ditch we've dug around the new pipe. "With nothing much to do for Oliver right now except scout deals over the Internet a few hours a day, I've had too much time on my hands to think. I keep coming back to the idea of taking a road trip to see Hannah. Calling just won't do."

Caleb digs in too, his shovel scooping up dirt and dropping it down evenly. "You know . . . if you really wanted to, I might be willing to call shotgun."

I stop, leaning on my shovel. "Why?"

Caleb thinks, then goes for another scoop of dirt. "You ever wonder why I flirt with women, Cassie included, but never more than that?"

"The thought has crossed my mind," I admit. "But I never really had an answer on why that was. "Are you not attracted to Cassie? Fuck, are you coming out to me, man? I love ya, but not like that. I'm team pussy forever."

Caleb chuckles but shakes his head. "She's a nice girl, but . . . I've been in love once. This was a few years ago. Her name was Wendy Reinhardt. I'm a little more guarded these days."

"Wendy . . . don't know the name," I admit. "Must have been when I was being a party hog in college."

"About that time, yeah," Caleb admits. "I fell for Wendy pretty hard. I did all sorts of stupid shit to keep her attention, but I got burned. I don't really want to discuss all the details because it fucked me up pretty bad for a while, but just . . . I know what it's like to love and to lose."

"You're not telling me you haven't been with a girl since then, are you?"

Caleb chuckles, shaking his head. "Fuck no. I still talk the talk because I'm a creature of habit, but I'm a little more cautious beyond that. I'm not ready for love again. But you, Tony . . . hell, I lost Wendy because of what she did to me. You've still got a chance with Hannah. I'll tag team drive your ass tonight if you want."

I think about it. I'd love nothing more than to have her in my arms, but if she doesn't want to see me, if I'm going to cause her pain, I don't want to go running to her doorstep. "Listen, man, thanks for having my back, but let me think on it."

"I wouldn't think too long," Caleb says. "I didn't say anything, kept hoping you'd seen it, but maybe you didn't. When we were driving away, I saw Hannah come around the side of the house. She was looking at us . . . she was trying to look for you, Tony. Now, some people say I'm not a smart man, but I know love when I see it."

I reach in my pocket and grab my phone, going to message drafts, finding the text I never sent to Hannah. I can't wait any longer, and I hit *Send*.

"So this property could be the next big deal we need," says Martha, Oliver's property acquisitions manager. She's mainly talking to Oli, because I'm sitting quietly to the side, pretending to look at the big monitor she's rigged up on the wall. I'm sitting quietly to the side, looking at the big monitor that Martha's rigged up on the wall. We're on the second floor of the Flaming Dragon building, above Mindy's Place in the office that is supposedly Oliver's headquarters. Really, it's Martha's office, but it's a good place to talk business. I've been coming in for the past couple of days. I've felt obligated after giving away the Mobber estate to Hannah.

Oliver hasn't said anything, but he understands, knowing that I want to make it up to him and everyone else. I told Caleb the truth. My sleep's been shit. I've been hitting the gym like a madman because I've got a desperate hope that if I tire my body out enough, it'll get pummeled into sleep. So far, all I've done is earn a really sore set of quads. Every time I try to lie down, I'm thinking of Hannah, wondering how she's doing.

I feel like shit.

"Hey, babe?" It's Mindy, sticking her head in the door. "Someone's here to see you, says they need to talk business."

"Show them up," Oliver says. I'm too tired to bother to look. Probably another associate, maybe someone with the deal Martha found.

There's a quiet knock on the door, and it opens. "Hello, I didn't mean to—"

I twirl around at the sound the unmistakable voice, standing up so fast that the table jumps as my aching quads jostle it, spilling Martha's coffee and making her jump back herself. "Hannah! What are you doing here?"

I cross the space to her, stopping up short. "I took a flight here. This is something I had to do face to face. Tony, I got your text message, and I wanted to respond, but . . . listen, I've got three hundred and seventeen dollars in my checking account, a landlord who's gonna be pissed that I don't have my rent, and Cassie's freaking out on me, hoping that I'm not wasting my damn time."

"I'll excuse myself," Martha says, exchanging glances between us, an amused expression on her face. "I think you all have a lot to talk about."

She leaves while Oliver sits back, an interested look on his face as Hannah and I stare at each other, both of us too nervous to reach out and cross that final line separating us. Finally, Hannah clears her throat and looks over at Oliver.

"I'm here about Wesley's land," Hannah says. "What Aurora is planning to do . . . here, it's easier if I just show you. I can't believe that I'm doing this, I'm so gonna get sued, but dammit, it's the right thing to do!"

Hannah reaches into her purse and pulls out the file, showing it to us. I'm horrified. It's the only word I can think of. "A five-floor main building, restaurants, water park . . . what the fuck, they're tearing out the spa to put in—"

"A golf course," Oliver says, shaking his head. "There's going to be literally nothing left."

"Exactly," Hannah says. "And unless we can stop them, after that, their sights are going to be on the village. I can't but help think I bear some responsibility for this. It should've gone to you guys! You'd obviously have to make your money, but at least you guys would have respected the land!"

"We would have." Oli gets up to leave. "Let me start making some calls and see what, if anything, can be done. Legally, my hands are tied, but there might be some options. I might start with calling this Wesley Mobber—"

I cut him off, getting up. "Let me. I have his personal number. It'll be better coming from us. I'll give him a call. The book's back at my place."

Hannah nods. "He's right, it's kind of like Wesley shares a bond with all of us. Besides, I want to say this in front of you first. It's what brought me here."

Oli looks curious as he sinks back into his seat, and I turn to Hannah, curious. "What do you mean?"

She takes a deep breath, and I can see . . . fear? "Oliver, I'm sure your brother told you all about the place and how special it is, I can tell from your reaction. What he didn't tell you is how we fell in love. God, I was so wrong about him."

"Hannah—" I start to tell her that Oliver already knows, but she keeps going, momentum not letting her stop.

"Tony, you're cocky, you're sarcastic, you're a major pain in the ass, and your decision to send me a dick pic, of all things—"

"You bugged me to get Hannah's number so you could send her a pic of your dick?" Oliver growls at me, and I blush.

"It's okay, Oliver. I kinda asked for that," Hannah says, blushing herself. "That's a story for another time. But I was wrong about Tony. He's the kindest man I've ever met. Wesley sent me the final letter he wrote, the final challenge . . . and in it, I read how he sacrificed everything to make me happy. So Oliver, please don't be angry at him. Tony, at the property, I wanted to tell you, but I was too afraid. I thought that there'd be no way I could really feel this way, especially this fast. And just like you did with the property, you saw the truth and did the right thing . . . so I want the world to know that I love you too. You said you'd burn down Wesley's estate to make me happy. Well, how about we work together and save the place where we fell in love?"

"You sure that's what you want?" I ask, my throat tight. Hannah nods, and I get up, going to her and pulling her into my arms, kissing her softly. She wraps her arms around my neck, and I hold her close, tears of happiness trickling down my cheeks as I feel complete again. "Hannah, I swear to God, I'll be the man you deserve."

Oliver looks from Hannah to me and laughs. "Yeah, I guess I looked about that stupid when I walked back into the Bean-gal's Den and went to get Mindy back. Hannah, Tony's told me all about you two. But let me call my lawyers, see what we can do. You two . . . well, go get that phone number because we've got some important business to handle. And guys, don't get too sidetracked," he says with a grin and a raised eyebrow.

WE'RE BACK DOWN IN THE BASEMENT. BECAUSE OF THE TIME difference between here and Hawaii, it's late, but for Wesley Mobber, it's just past lunch. Wesley is sitting in his meditation room, but of course he's going to have good Wi-Fi in that place. it's one of those weird things about him, the balance of ecological with modern high-tech. "It's nice to see you again, Tony. And nice to see Hannah with you."

"It's good to see you too, Wesley," I say, smirking when a familiar squawk sounds and Mo Mo settles on his shoulder. "You too, Mo Mo. I wish I could be saying this is under happier circumstances."

"Wait," Wesley says, smiling that strange little smile of his. "First, before we talk about what you emailed me, there's something I have to ask. Have you two talked?"

"If you mean have we told each other how we feel, yes," Hannah says, reaching over and giving my hand a squeeze. "But Wesley, us being in love isn't the reason we called. It's Aurora and your legacy, your estate."

"You know what a legacy is?" Wesley says, chuckling. "It's what people who don't have anything else to leave behind comfort themselves with saying they have. My legacy, if there is one, is going to be the people I've been able to touch and influence. So tell me, how have I touched you two?"

"You gave us the chance to fall in love," I reply immediately. Behind the computer screen, Oliver raises an eyebrow, but he sits back silently. "You taught me that there are things more important than money, work, and rules. There's people. And the Aurora plan is to eventually take the heritage of Alani's village and destroy it, turn it from something to be treasured into some plastic trinket to be hawked to tourists for ten bucks and a side of fried plantains. I can't just sit by and let that happen."

"They are rat bastards, I agree," Wesley says.

"Rat bastards!" Mo Mo squawks, and Oliver sits up, surprised, and I have to hold back a grin. Welcome to what I had to put up with. It gets better.

"So we have to—" Hannah says, but Wesley grins. "What?"

"You two have taken me to be a man with a lot of money who's more than a little off his rocker, right?" Wesley asks. "Wait, don't answer that." Wesley continues, and I have to laugh. "But I made my money by being the coldest blooded shark in an ocean of sharks. Do you have a copy of the contract?"

"Of course," Hannah says. "Why?"

"Turn to page seven, paragraph 31E," Wesley says. "It's a minor little paragraph, but . . ." As he talks, I can see the shrewd business acumen glinting in his eyes. We might have misjudged him, underestimating him the whole time because he very clearly has a trick up his sleeve.

Hannah's already flipped over her pages, and we read it together. He's right, it is minor, but it's a very clear out, and Wesley can trigger it unilaterally without getting us in trouble.

"Hawaii has some very strong laws on exploitation and land use, and I've added to it here," he explains. "Their plans give me an out. So . . . Oliver, are you there?"

"I'm here," Oliver speaks up, coming around. "It's nice to talk to you face to face again, Mr. Mobber."

"Here's the deal," Wesley says. "I'm willing to sell my property to you, with a few new clauses to the contract."

"What new clauses?" Oliver asks.

"First, I realize that you're not looking to lose money, but the spirit of this land must be preserved. I thought I was careful in narrowing it down to just you or Aurora, but I should've known better. With that in mind, I'm going to require that you have a permanent live-in manager on the estate. They would have to be approved by myself and my wife first."

"I think I can find some people who might be willing to do that," Oliver says, glancing at me. "Although from what I know, they're a pain in the ass at times."

Wesley grins. "Okay. I'll contact Aurora and tell them I am triggering clause 31E. Tomorrow morning, I'll call you. Oh, and one more thing."

"What's that?" I ask.

"You came to me. This time, I'll come to you. Alani would like to see some of the mainland, and I've heard that there's a hell of a coffeehouse in the family, and a hell of a singer. Alani happens to be a fan of *Heartstopper*. Think we can arrange something?"

Oliver laughs. "Wesley, you get here, and we'll make it happen. It's a deal."

When we're done with the call, Hannah hugs me tightly. "Thank you, Studmuffin."

"Studmuffin?" I ask, and Oli grins, getting his laptop and

recognizing his queue to leave. We're alone, and I turn to Hannah. "What is this Studmuffin stuff?"

"That's what I thought of you when I first saw your butt. You were a total studmuffin. I just wanna take a bite of that bubble butt."

I laugh, embarrassed. "Uh, yeah, if you say so."

Hannah laughs, getting up and straddling my legs. "I'm for real. I can teach you how to twerk. I taught Roxy all her best moves. Want me to show you?"

I laugh, putting my hands on her waist before reaching around and running my hands over her ass. "I think I'll pass. I might have something, but not as much as my big booty . . ."

Hannah wags her finger at me to not finish that sentence even as she arches her back to press her ass into my hands more. "Oh, no, buddy, don't you dare say it!"

I laugh. "Sorry, couldn't help myself."

I massage Hannah's ass, and she sighs happily before giggling. "Don't tell anyone I said this, but I sort of miss that damn bird. I'm going to be happy to see her again."

"I knew it," I reply, pulling Hannah into my lap more and drawing her in for a kiss. "But if you really want to show me some dancing, I have a few ideas."

"What?" she asks breathlessly, moaning as I kiss down to the curve of her neck, licking the soft skin, relishing the taste of her.

"Let's see how well you can pole dance . . . on my pole."

"Mmm . . ." Hannah moans, rolling her hips against the hard bulge in my pants. She glances at the door and sees that the lights are off. We're alone. "A little corny, but challenge accepted."

Hannah stands up, reaching for the first button on her blouse and opening it for me. There's no music, but that doesn't make her slow striptease any less erotic as she peels off her blouse and skirt for me, leaving her in just her bra and panties before she reaches for my shirt. "You know, my love . . ." she says before stopping and shivering in pleasure. "My love . . . it feels good to call you that."

"It's even better to hear it," I reply, reaching up to brush her hair out of her face. "I should have told you exactly how I felt back on the island. I was just . . . afraid."

"I was too," Hannah admits, undoing my shirt and leaning in to kiss my chest. She runs her tongue over my nipples, biting lightly and making me moan as her breasts press against the bulge of my cock inside my jeans, their warmth soaking through the denim and making me throb. I run my hands through Hannah's hair, gasping as she kisses back up, looking me in the eyes as she straddles me. "I'm not afraid anymore. I love you, Tony."

Hannah puts her arms around my neck and rolls her hips, riding my cock through her panties and jeans, kissing me deeply as she does. I chuckle. Not this time. Instead, I reach around and pick her up, setting Hannah on the wide wooden topped table that the cafe uses for preparing pizza dough, making her giggle. "Plan on covering me with pepperoni and mozzarella?"

"Don't give me any ideas," I tease back, kissing down her throat as my hands undo her bra. I free her breasts as Hannah runs her fingers over my shoulders and back, gasping when my lips find her right nipple and suck longingly. I devote myself to Hannah's breasts, licking and sucking to the sound of her gasps and light growls of pleasure while I undo my pants, freeing my cock.

"Lie back," I whisper, helping Hannah down before lifting her hips and easing her panties off. I kiss my way down and trace my tongue over her lips. Hannah's hips buck, and I slip my hands under her ass, cupping her cheeks to lift her pussy to my mouth, not letting her get away as I suck and taste her. My tongue slides up and down between her lips before I swirl around her clit, teasing Hannah.

"Tony . . . God, you feel so good," she gasps, and I reward her by letting my tongue flutter over the tip of her clit, tickling lightly. Her breath catches in her throat and choked pleas rip from her lips. "Please . . . please . . . please . . ."

I stroke my tongue over her clit harder, sending her hurtling into the throes of her orgasm. I keep my mouth glued to her, refreshing the exhaustion in my body with every droplet that coats my tongue and dribbles down my throat. When she's done, I stand up, my cock iron hard and pulsing with desire. I lift her knees. The table is at just the right height that I don't have to do anything to line myself up.

Holding onto Hannah's thighs, I push forward slowly, my cock sinking into her in a single long, amazing thrust that leaves both of us staring into the other's eyes. She reaches down and entwines her fingers with mine as I let her knees slide to my elbows, holding her open and vulnerable to me as I fill her all the way up. Her pussy grips me tightly, sending thrills through my cock to bloom in my chest before exploding in my brain, signals that tell me she's the most beautiful woman I've ever known, and that I've finally found my perfect partner.

Slowly, taking our time, I thrust my cock in and out of Hannah, our eyes never wavering with each stroke. My heart beats hard and deep in my chest with every slap of our hips together, and my breath quickens as I pump faster and faster.

Leaning down, I kiss Hannah hungrily, pushing her back further onto the table to climb up, pressing her body into the warm wooden surface and holding her still. Our tongues stroke and twist together, sharing breath and soul as we speed up, my hips driving my cock into her with all the passion and love that I've been holding back ever since I left Hawaii. My fingers tremble as I grab the edge of the table, my cock pumping harder and faster, Hannah wrapping her legs around me and digging her fingernails into my back as her pussy tightens around me, she's so close to coming again. "Tony . . . fuck . . ."

"Now!" I gasp, my balls growing tight and my cock swelling in an instant before I come deep inside her, my heart stopping as I fill her up. Hannah quivers and gasps, crying out my name again and again as she holds me tight. I hold onto her, my heart and soul bared as I stay deep inside her, feeling her pussy milk and squeeze me until not a single drop is left, and I feel myself truly bonded for the first time in my entire life.

As my heartbeat returns to normal, I hold her close, letting my skin just press against hers, the feeling so perfect that I never want to let her go again. "So . . . what about your job? Your apartment?"

Hannah shakes her head, kissing me softly on the lips. "I don't want to go back."

"What do you mean?" I ask, stroking her back and looking in her eyes. "You told me your job was important to you."

"It was, but I found something more important. And I was

thinking . . . if Oliver's going to send you to manage Wesley's estate, you might need a partner."

"Hmm . . ." I tease. "Well, Cassie does know the place pretty well."

Hannah laughs, tugging on my hair. "Don't make me go rough next time. I'll still go Katniss on your ass if I have to."

I laugh, kissing her soft lips. "It'd be a dream come true for us to be back there together."

CHAPTER 27

*T*he clock is just hitting noon as I come into the office the next day after grabbing the first flight home. I was certain I'd have armed security guards waiting for me the moment I walked into Aurora, along with a team of lawyers. Nobody says anything though, but still, I feel certain they'll read all over my face how their plan has backfired.

I was honest with Tony last night. I don't want to come back here. But I need to talk to Myra and give my notice. She's treated me right, and to just bounce in the middle of the night after cutting Aurora's hamstrings isn't right. Still, I'm nervous as I step off the elevator, expecting either icy silence or a hail of gunfire.

As it is, as soon as I step off the elevator to the fifth floor, Cassie takes one look at me and grabs my hands. "What's going on, Hannah? Listen, I know we talked, but . . . it's been a madhouse here this morning. Myra's been upstairs most of the time, and I swear it's like a mausoleum today. Myra came down a few minutes ago, and she looks like she's aged a decade since nine this morning."

"I—" I begin, but before I can fill Cassie in on the details of everything that happened last night, Myra pops her head out her doorway.

"Hannah? You're finally here. I need to see you and Miss White immediately, please."

Cassie's eyes are desperate. She wants details about what happened, but I just shake my head at her as we walk into Myra's office together and sit. Cassie's right, Myra looks for the first time like a woman who's seen her best days behind her. Her face looks slightly lined, and her hair hangs limply. Even her suit looks rumpled. She just looks tired.

"The board received a rather distressing call from Mr. Mobber this morning. He's enacted an obscure clause in the contract that no one realized was there, the legal department included. I'm sure heads are going to roll for that. If I were either of you, I'd avoid the tenth floor unless you want to get blood on your shoes."

"Eww," Cassie murmurs, going a trifle paler. She's looking rather Goth at this point, with her red lipstick and near-ash-white skin.

Myra gives a tired sort of chuckle, nodding. "Yeah. Clause 31E effectively means that he can cancel his intent to sell to Aurora with no penalties other than returning the down payment we already transferred to him."

"That's . . . interesting," I reply as Myra gives me a level look. I can't reveal that I tipped off Wesley. It'd get my ass sued from now until I'm a grandparent, and if it came out that Tony was involved too, Oliver would find himself the most successful coffee shop owner in the welfare office. I have to dance on the edge of a knife right now and pray that Wesley is as much of a shark as he claims to be. "How?"

Myra shakes her head. "Somehow, he seems to have gotten information on our plans for the property. According to Mobber, what Aurora had planned violates local laws on exploitation, and so he triggered the clause unilaterally."

"Can he do that?" Cassie, who wasn't involved last night, asks in shock.

"Of course he can," Myra grumbles. "I just got back from a meeting with the board, and Mr. Thompson, head of legal, was in there. Apparently, he had the nuclear option in his back pocket the entire time and triggered it as soon as he caught wind of what we were going to do. The question the board has right now is how Mobber found out."

"What are they thinking?" I ask, knowing my face might as well be a giant sign that's flashing *GUILTY, GUILTY, GUILTY* over and over.

Myra gives me a look, leaning back in her chair. "There's suspicions flying all around. I'm not going to lie. A couple of those accusations have been leveled at this floor. But Mobber's not saying, and the company had already gotten in contact with quite a few sources in Hawaii, so it could be any number of people. Of course, everyone is denying it. They don't want to have legal on their asses. Do you two know anything?"

I stay silent, Cassie looking at me with her lip trembling. She's been so helpful and loyal to a fault. If she sells me out, she can save herself, maybe even get a promotion out of it. But instead, she says nothing, and I give her a look and a small nod. "I'm sorry, Myra, but I really have no idea."

Myra nods, her face grim. "Well, let's just say that, hypothetically, of course, Wesley got the information from someone at Aurora. The witch hunt is going to get pretty hard and heavy around here, with a lot of eyes on this floor. By the way, corporate's told me that they're going to be going into fire sale mode on the real estate development side."

"Let me guess, they'll call it corporate restructuring?" I ask, and Myra nods. I sigh, knowing what I'm going to say next is going to make this more difficult. "Then I guess I'll get it started early. Myra, I came in today to give you my notice. I'm quitting."

Myra doesn't look surprised and instead leans back. "You know that by doing that, you're going to get a lot of people saying you're the leak. You practically broadcast it to the entire building the other day that you hated the plans."

I nod and take a breath. "Myra, I have learned so much from you, and your mentoring has taught me many things. You taught me how to read people and negotiate, when to show your cards and when to bluff, and most importantly, to trust your gut. But the biggest lesson you taught me, I don't think you've even realized."

"What's that?" Myra asks. Next to me, I can see Cassie watching intently. She's being brave, oh, so brave, that I wish I could hug her right now. But I need to tell Myra this.

"Myra, you showed me, and I bet if you ask Cassie, she'll tell you the same thing—you showed us that sometimes, you just have to do it your way. I don't know, maybe you filtered Sinatra a bit too damn much when you were younger, but you made it by doing what you felt was the right thing. I learned that by watching and learning from you. I'm resigning because it's the right thing to do. This company took my hard work and they perverted it from minute one. Not you, but corporate. They fed me a line of bullshit, played me like a pawn, and then at the end, they didn't even have the presence of mind to say thank you. It's just not the kind of place I want to work."

Myra's eyebrows have risen nearly to her hairline, but she doesn't appear angry, more pleased at my little speech. "Nice speech, Hannah, but your resignation is not accepted."

"What?" I ask, surprised, but Myra's expression gives me pause. "What are you doing?"

"Saving your ass," Myra says with a small smile. "Hannah Fowler, effectively immediately, you are fired. Your position is being eliminated as a budget saving measure for the real estate division of Aurora. Aurora wishes you the best in your future endeavors."

I laugh softly. Myra's covering my ass. If she fires me, she might take some heat, but it'll take heat off me. "You sure about this?"

"I'm sure," Myra says. "And if I may, one last lesson . . . I've always considered myself rather bold, but you have some big clanking brass balls. Use them wisely." Myra laughs and sticks her hand out for a shake. "Best wishes, Miss Fowler. I'll give you a glowing recommendation anytime you need one."

With a clap, she turns to Cassie. "Alright Miss White, now with our office being shorthanded—"

"I'm leaving too," Cassie says, her mouth set in that same line of determination I've gotten used to seeing. This is the same Cassie who fought like a mongoose on speed during the tug of war. "I can't stick around—"

"Yes, you can," I say, reaching over and taking Cassie's hand.

"Cass, I've got something else lined up." I'm sure Myra knows it, looking over at her. "But you? You need this. Stick around a little while, help Myra get the fire sale going, get the ball rolling. Cash your paychecks and make connections. Protect yourself."

"Listen to Hannah," Myra says quietly. "Stick around, and I'll make sure you're taken care of. Besides, I was going to say, you just got a promotion to my primary assistant. Real estate's going to work as a two-woman shop until we get either absorbed or closed down. Give me three to six months, and I'll make sure there's a good severance check in it for you. Just make sure you're prepared for what's next."

Cassie looks determined, and I give her hands another squeeze, leaning in to whisper to her. "Say yes. I just had an idea, and we'll talk about it in my office. Let me go clean out my things."

"Fine, fine . . . pair of crazy ass bitches around here," Cassie mutters. "Okay, but that means I'm done cleaning out the coffee pot around here."

I give Cassie a quick hug and collect a few things from my desk before waiting. Cassie comes out a few minutes later, looking afraid but still brave, willing to do what needs to be done. "So, you're packed?"

"Yeah," I reply, patting the small box of stuff. I never kept a lot of personal things in the office, and my office laptop, I just made sure was scrubbed of any personal files. "Listen, when things are done here with Aurora, give me a call. I suspect that with what's happening, I'm going to be meeting some new people. Between your charm and a sparking recommendation from Myra and me, I'm sure we can find something you'd be perfect for."

Cassie laughs and comes over, giving me another quick hug. "Well, if that's the case, maybe I can cash a few checks. Don't become a stranger, okay?"

"Stranger? I'm planning on taking you out to dinner tonight!" I tease. "Us fired people, we've got all the money we need. I'm getting some pizzas and then you're helping me pack up my stuff!"

"Moving too, huh?" Cassie asks, and I nod. "I can guess where. Probably won't need that heavy leather jacket where you're going."

"Not in the long term," I agree. "In the short term, who knows? I'm just going by my gut and faith. Give me a call when you get off work, and we'll make some plans."

I head back to my apartment, not as bothered by its emptiness this time because I'm just here to gather up my bare necessities. I'll have movers pack and ship the bulk of my things and donate the rest because my new life awaits in Hawaii.

CHAPTER 28

ANTHONY

"This place had better have some good rum and whiskey, otherwise I don't think I'll be able to handle all this riff raff!"

I grin as I look over at Ivy Jo Price, who's scowling in her seat as the hum of the plane engine drones in the background. Armed with her cane and wide brim hat, she looks like she's ready to do battle.

"What riff raff, Grandma?" Mindy asks, who's sitting beside her and cooing softly to her daughter to keep her quiet. "You're surrounded by your grandchildren and great-grand babies. Isn't that wonderful?"

Ivy Jo stares at her granddaughter as if she's gone nuts. "I am, but then I keep having to listen to Mary Jo go on about that damn dog! I told her she couldn't bring the thing and she's not letting me forget it! Like it's my fault that dog wasn't allowed as a carry-on!" She shakes her head mournfully. "So disrespectful. Why, when I was younger . . ."

Caleb, who's been getting his ear talked off between Mom

and Ivy Jo, gives me a look of suffering. Okay, so it was a little unfair, but that was the way first-class was laid out, three and two. And he seems to put up with the eccentricities of older women like Ivy Jo better than the rest of us. "Tony?"

"Hey, it could be worse," I reply, pointing behind me, where Roxy and Cassie have been going since takeoff. Thankfully for Jake, he was willing to sit between two baby carriers, so Justin, my new little nephew, and Mindy's newborn baby girl, Rachel, had plenty of care and Jake could get some sleep.

"Hey, Studmuffin, you hush before you're in my next song!" Roxy teases, reaching around and ruffling my hair. "Gotcha!"

"You're a mother now. You'd think you'd grow up some!" I protest, trying not to laugh. Now that I've got Roxy not only as a sort of sister-in-law but also as my girlfriend's bestie, I've gotten to know her a lot better, and she's been a real trip. I can see why she and Hannah get along so well.

We land and get our rental vehicles, leaving Honolulu behind to head directly to Wesley's property. There'll be time for touristy stuff later.

When we arrive, there's stunned silence as everyone takes in the beauty. They've all seen photos—Hannah's gigabytes of memories have helped—but there's nothing like the real thing. Wesley's waiting as we pull up, Mo Mo on his shoulder. "Pleasant greetings, travelers and friends! Welcome to what's soon not going to be my home!"

I laugh, getting out to shake his hand, only slightly surprised when he gives me a huge embrace before hugging Hannah as well. He goes around shaking hands with everyone else until he reaches Mindy and Roxy's grandmother. "What in the Lord's name is that on your head? Looks like you took my kitchen mop and decided to use it as a hat!"

Wesley chuckles. "Well, Alani has been asking me to get it shaved off, so I guess that makes it unanimous. Would you like to have one of the locks, like they do when they cut a retiring sumo champion's hair?"

Ivy Jo makes a face and then looks at me. "Tony, if you let your hair grow into a rat's nest like that, I'ma take a butane torch to your head!"

"Rat nest!" Mo Mo echoes. "Don't need no water, let the motherfucker burn!"

"I like this bird," Roxy says, chuckling. "Good taste in music."

"Shake your rump!" Mo Mo says, starting a little boogie on Wesley's shoulder, and we all laugh. I let Wesley take the lead, transferring us to quad runners for the post-natal women and Ivy Jo as he shows off his property. Everyone's enchanted, and more than once, Oliver gives me a look that says he's counting his lucky stars.

"And right up that trail is where the hiking challenge took place," Wesley says. "I was planning on taking you all up there for sunset. The view is fantastic."

"Just a moment," I interrupt. "You know, I wanted to grab a midday photo from up there. Hannah, if you don't mind?"

"Sure," Hannah says, not seeing as I give Wesley a wink.

Hannah gets off her quad runner, letting Gavin take over while Cassie takes mine. It gives them time to go around the long way and still get there ahead of us. I take Hannah's hand, and we start up the trail, relishing the clean, wonderful air. "I'm glad for the quiet."

Hannah laughs. "You know, I can't believe how everything

worked out. I'm going to be dead broke for a while longer still, but that's okay. In the end, the right thing happened."

"What about Cassie and Myra?" I ask, and Hannah smiles.

"Cassie says that for a little while, at least, she's gonna help out Roxy and Jake until she figures things out. Apparently, they need a fill-in bartender over at Club Jasmine, and she's still got her server's license from back in college," Hannah says. "She'll be fine. She says she's happier this way. Myra's moving on too, striking out on her own. I don't know what all she's got planned, but knowing her, she'll come out just fine."

We reach the top and head over to the blue rose bush. I wrap my arms around Hannah, kissing her neck. She moans lightly, humming with happiness. "You know, I'm all sweaty. That walk wasn't any easier this time around."

I chuckle, wrapping my arms around her tighter and licking the salty tang off her skin. "I happen to know a nice little pool and cave where we can go cool off."

"Mmmm . . . I was thinking the same thing," Hannah says, taking my hand and placing it on her left breast. "I was thinking some other things, too."

"Like what?"

"Like the bathroom in the airplane was too damn small to do what I wanted," Hannah says, tilting her head and giving me a warm kiss. "Come on."

We walk hand in hand to the pool, where the birds are quiet but the water's crystal clear. "This place is gonna be special to us," I say as we draw closer. "Hey, what's that?"

"What's what?"

"That," I say, pointing. "Something in the shallows behind you."

Hannah turns, seeing the glinting light. "I'm not sure . . ."

Hannah kneels and reaches into the water, and I try to hold onto my serious expression, waiting for her reaction.

"It's a ring . . . and it looks like it's got one hell of a diamond in it," she says. "I wonder who it belongs to?"

"Let me see," I say. She hands me the ring, and I grin, getting down on a knee. "It's yours, if you'll have me. Hannah Fowler . . . will you marry me?"

Hannah's shocked, barely breathing as she looks at the ring, and a quiet voice comes from nowhere. "I would accept. According to some of the villagers, you're already married."

Hannah looks over, a startled gasp coming from her as Alani leads everyone to the other side of the pool. "What?"

"That place we went to the night of the festival," I tell her, grinning. "According to Alani, it's an old native temple. Basically, by doing what we did, we told the gods that we were one. So . . . how about making it legal in the eyes of modern law too?"

She's shocked, and tears trickle from her eyes. "Oh, my God, yes. But . . . when? We're going to be so busy with—"

"And I'm booked to sing at your wedding tomorrow," Roxy says. "Sorta my comeback performance. I haven't sung a wedding in . . . well, ever. Hope I don't screw it up."

Hannah blinks, then looks at me, grinning. "You mean the tickets, flying everyone out . . . you knew this all along!"

I don't have an answer. I just grin. It's a surprise to Cassie, though, who laughs. "How did you know she would say yes?"

"Because she knows I'd do anything in the world for her. Because she's the light in my heart, the breath in my lungs, the blood in my beating heart," I reply, standing up and taking Hannah's hands. "Because I love her more than life itself, and the only thing that would make me happier is when we have children together."

Hannah knits her brows, scowling. "Oh, so you want me barefoot and pregnant, do you?"

"Barefoot is how a lot of the locals go around," I point out, and Hannah lets go of her mock anger, laughing.

"I wouldn't have it any other way."

We kiss, to the wild applause of everyone, until Grandma Ivy Jo comments how her old bones are ready for a trip to the spa that she heard about. "And I heard something about cabana boys? Is that true, Caleb?"

Caleb groans, looking at Cassie. "I'm so gonna toss you in the ocean before we leave."

"Hey guys, think we can meet you back at the house in about an hour?" I ask. "We've got a few things to talk about."

They leave, and I look at Hannah, who's grinning. "Well?"

"Well, what?" she asks before pushing me in the pool. "Race you to the cave! Whoever gets there first is in charge!"

Hannah scampers over the rocks, laughing as I'm forced to swim. Even with her speed advantage, Hannah has to pick her path carefully, and I plunge through the water with abandon, loving the feeling of the competitiveness we had together before. I gave her the obstacle course. I sure as hell am not making that a habit. I pull hard through the water, feeling the waterfall pound onto my back as I emerge . . . and find Hannah just sitting down on the blanket.

"Guess who gets to be in charge?" she teases me, leaning back and letting her body stretch out in the dim magical lights from the crystals.

I open my mouth to protest but realize I don't have to anymore. I move across the pool and hoist myself out, grinning. "You're lucky I don't have a water balloon handy."

"Lie down on the blanket," Hannah says, "and get those shorts off. Now . . . where did I put that butt plug Cassie gave me?"

I laugh lightly, pushing my shorts down and lying back. As Hannah takes off her bra, straddling my head and lowering her pussy toward my eager lips, I feel a surge through my body that has my cock standing at full attention. "Now, if you're good . . ."

I don't need any more encouragement, and I reach up, tracing Hannah's lips with my tongue before sliding it deep inside her, tasting her and making her gasp. I feel her wrap her hand around my cock and pump lightly, moaning as I suck and tease her, dragging my tongue deep inside her before sucking on her clit. Hannah grinds her pussy over my mouth, stroking my cock and moaning. I can't see anything except the glistening pink of her pussy, and I don't care. I devote everything I have to her as I let her control everything.

With a gasp, Hannah pulls away just as I thought she was about to come. "Wait," she says, her voice shaking as she repositions.

She straddles my hips while facing away from me, reaching down and lining my cock up with her pussy. She sinks down, my cock enveloped in the tight, clingy warmth of her body. Her ass is right in front of me, and I reach down, massaging it as she starts riding me, moaning happily. "You know just how to please me."

Watching Hannah's ass as she rides me is mesmerizing, each flex of her hips in perfect timing of my cock sliding in and out of her tight pussy. My cock throbs as she rolls her hips, gasping when I smack her right butt cheek lightly. "And I know this feels good," I add.

She looks back, a gleam in her eyes and a smirk on her lips as she clenches her pussy around my cock. I start thrusting up to meet her, and Hannah groans, throwing her head back and I grab a fistful of her hair.

We fall into a perfect joining, my cock thrusting up to meet her exactly, both of us adding to the speed and electricity crackling through the air. Keeping one hand tangled in her hair, I use the other to squeeze and spank her ass as we go harder and faster, the glimmering lights from the crystals making everything look surreal and sensual.

"Fuck…oh Tony, give it to me," Hannah begs, and I thrust up, our hips smacking together so hard they echo in the cave, and I feel my balls grow tighter, my cock swelling. We're close, so close, and I thrust as deep as I can, Hannah groaning as I bottom out inside her. I can feel her pussy tighten before she cries out, and I unleash myself, coming deep inside Hannah as she milks me, her body quivering as we come together, riding it until our bodies collapse.

"We're going to have to come up here often," Hannah says when she can speak again. "This place is magical."

I shake my head, sitting up and gathering her in my arms. "Magic is what we make together. This place, this land . . . it's important, but nothing will ever replace the magic that I have with you."

Hannah turns and kisses me tenderly, and I hold her tight. She's right, this land is special, but what I have right here, the love in my arms . . . that's the true magic.

EPILOGUE

HANNAH

*M*orning dawns and I stare out at the ocean, the sand pristine and glimmering in the brightening light. There's a soft wind coming off the water, and as I look out, tears come to my eyes.

"Hey, what's wrong?" Roxy asks, rubbing my shoulders. "This is your wedding day."

I smile, looking at her. She's gorgeous, her island wrap picked out by Alani so that all of my 'maids of honor' look like they coordinate. My wrap is all white, of course, and I wipe away the tear. "I'm just so happy, you goof. Back when you and Jake got married, I remember thinking to myself that if I ever got married, I'd want a ceremony as beautiful as yours. Well . . ."

"I'd say yours beats the shit outta mine," Roxy says with a quiet laugh. "Although I'll still claim the reception. I didn't have a foul-mouthed parrot at mine. Hmmm, on second thought... would that be a point in your favor or mine?"

I look up at the altar, where Wesley's waiting. He's going to be the minister. Apparently, he is ordained some way or the other. Caleb and Tony are up there too, Tony looking so handsome in his full tuxedo except for the flip-flops, while Caleb decided to go a little more casual, rocking some Bermuda shorts under his tux jacket. Alani is the musician, and Mo Mo, of course, sits on Wesley's shoulder.

"I wouldn't have it any other way," I promise Roxy. "And I promise not to throw a glass of punch on Tony today."

Alani starts up the music, playing *Can't Help Falling in Love* on a ukulele, of all things, and Roxy and I go up the 'aisle' in the sand. Everyone's here—Brianna and Gavin with their kids, Jake with Roxy's baby, Mindy and Oliver with their kids . . . even Myra showed up this morning. She took her golden parachute when Aurora's property division closed down, and while she's not ready to retire, she's going to be okay.

I reach the altar, taking Tony's hands as Wesley looks over us both, smiling that sort of wide, slightly vapid smile that tells me I'm glad I'm used to him by now. "Fellow carbon-based inhabitants of the Earth, I welcome you all here today to see the spiritual and physical bonding of Tony and Hannah into a fellowship that transcends the limits of our limited perception."

"Did someone test him for drugs before this?" Ivy Jo asks, and I can't help but chuckle. Wesley doesn't mind, and for the next five minutes, he rambles on with a speech that's part Captain Kirk, part Captain Jack Sparrow, part The Dude, and truly heartfelt. Finally, Alani clears her throat and Wesley stops short.

"Okay, okay . . . so, Tony, do you take Hannah to be your old lady, to hold her hair out of the toilet when she's got morning sickness, to rub her feet when she's got blisters, and to smile and put up with it when menopause turns her into a total bitch?"

Tony blinks. I'm shocked too, but he immediately nods. "I do."

Wesley turns to me. "And Hannah, do you take Tony to be an annoying pain in the ass who needs a man cave, will probably play video games at the worst times, develop an innocent crush on some pop princess, and will eventually get a pot gut and morning breath and bellybutton lint?"

"I do," I say, thinking I may have gotten the better of the vows. I mean, I could hang out in a man cave. And my best friend is a pop princess. Hell, I could develop a crush on her.

"Good. Now, the rings . . . the rings . . . uh . . ." Wesley says, patting his pockets. "Hold on just a moment."

Grandma Ivy Jo speaks up again. "Now, I've known a few people who were a little off their rocker in my life, but this man takes the cake. He makes me look as normal as blueberry pie."

"Yeah, well," Wesley grumbles before searching every single pocket of his cargo pants. Of course, they're in the last one. "Oh, there they are!"

He pulls out a plastic baggie with the rings inside. Tony and I exchange rings, and a single kiss later, I'm now Hannah Steele. We all go to the main house and change clothes for the reception, which is in the same village square where the festival took place. I change from my white wrap into something much more native inspired, a hula skirt and tank top that, while nowhere near as revealing as what I wore for the competition, is still wavy and sexy, just like I want it to be.

"You look smokin'," Cassie says, grinning as she comes out of the room she's sharing with Sophie Stone, who is taking a few days off school for a free trip to Hawaii. Cassie's got on a bikini top and a wrap skirt, looking as beautiful as ever and just at home. "You know you got him now. You don't need to dress up."

"I've got something special planned," I tell her. "I sorta jammed it with Alani last night. She stayed up until nearly midnight with me, working all the moves."

"You do know the only move you need is to drop it low, bring it up slow?" Cassie asks, and I laugh, shaking my head.

"Not for this. This is a special dance, just for Tony. Come on, I made him promise to get changed and head over there with the guys, so it's just us girls for a few minutes on the way over."

Our SUV is filled with ladies, and I find myself slightly squished next to Brianna Adams. She and I haven't talked much, but she seems nice. "So, what do you think of the property? I mean, you do practically own a timeshare here now."

Brianna laughs lightly. "I think we'll enjoy coming out here. Although that Wesley . . . he's a character."

I groan. "What did he do?"

"Oh, last night as we headed out for a walk, he asked Gavin if his sperm count was, how did he put it? Oh yeah, 'as impressive as the equipment delivering it'. Just when Gavin thought he'd lived down that video . . ."

I laugh. It's Wesley. "Don't worry, I think he'll end up asking every man in the family about his sperm count at some point. Wesley's very big on virility. I'm kinda curious what he'll do if someone says they're suffering a little bit in that department."

"Probably something herbal and illegal," Mindy jokes from shotgun, resting her stomach. "Phew, I think I'm taking a baby making break for a little bit. Three might be enough for me. I'd at least like to let the stretch marks fade a little before adding new ones."

"Still looking hot to me, sis," Roxy says as she drives. "And you don't need to wear a crop top on stage."

We get to the reception, where Tony looks handsome as hell in a Hawaiian shirt, Bermuda shorts, and a white silk scarf around his shoulders. I hug him close, kissing his lips and feeling the ripped body that's going to give me decades of love. "Mmmm, you look good, Mr. Steele."

"And you're the most beautiful woman on the island, Mrs. Steele," Tony replies, kissing me again. "Alani said you had something planned?"

I chuckle, nodding. "A first dance. Go sit down with the guys. You and I will have our couples' dance next."

The music starts, and I'm glad for Alani's help as she plays lead ukulele again. I'm so nervous. Still, the moment I take my first step, I just look at Tony and dance for him, an ancient wedding hula that Alani taught me. Every sway of my hips, every motion of my hands is done with as much love and grace as I can do, and when it's over, Tony comes over, pulling me in for another kiss as the crowd explodes in applause.

The reception is a lot more normal after that, with a Hawaiian luau spread, plenty of drinks for everyone, and the village square becoming a large street dance. Alani and

Wesley put on a hell of a show themselves, dancing, of all things, a classical flamenco in the dirt square before Wesley literally tosses his wife into the air and catches her to the wild applause of everyone.

"A final show before I start the next stage," Wesley says with a smile.

"What is that, if you don't mind us asking?" Tony says, offering Wesley and Alani drinks. "I mean, Alani's already said she wants to help out with the transition."

"You're taking over our village's sacred grounds, so of course I do," Alani says. "I may have forgotten to mention . . . I'm sort of the traditional village chieftain."

"Oh, now she tells us!" Caleb laughs. "I'm so lucky I didn't get fed to the sharks."

"I'm honored, then," I tell Alani. "I look forward to learning as much as I can from you. But where will you go?"

"We'll build a small house for ourselves in the village, but I want to spend the next decade or so traveling the world," Alani says. "I've never seen snow, and I figure a decade will give you two time to have some children and get them to just the right age that they'll be able to learn from mine about what could be expected of them."

"You mean you're pregnant?" Tony asks, and Wesley grins, kissing his wife on the cheek. "Congratulations, both of you."

Even with all the good feelings, there's still plenty of drama, even if some of it's silly. About two hours into the party, a now familiar yell cuts through the air. "Someone get me a damn BB gun!"

I look, and Roxy's trying to calm down Ivy Jo. "Come on, Grandma, you've had enough to drink."

"Oh, hell no, I'm gonna shoot that damn bird!" Ivy Jo protests. "I was just trying to get my groove on with some nice boy when it started making fun of me! It called me a big booty ho!"

I try not to laugh, heading over. "Ivy Jo, Mo Mo makes fun of everyone she likes."

"Yeah, well, she keeps on fucking with me, I might have to take my cane upside her head! I might be old and crusty, but it doesn't mean I can't throw down!"

"Old and crusty!" Mo Mo squawks, and I wonder if the bird is suicidal. I peel Ivy Jo away as Roxy takes over, grabbing a microphone and doing a short three-set of songs, starting with *Drunk in Love* before *Heartstopper*, and finishing with her new ballad that she's going to release soon, *Forever is Our Love*.

Tony and I dance, and as Roxy's voice powers her way through the bridge, he leans in. "I'm ready to go to our special place."

"You mean . . .?" I ask, and Tony nods. The circle, the ancient temple. I'm sure he's cleared it with Wesley or Alani . . . it's ours. I nod, smiling. "Give me a minute to say goodnight to everyone."

The song ends, and I give Roxy a hug, telling her about what I'm planning on doing. It's no big deal, the party's going to go all night, I suspect, and Roxy gives me a smirk and a pinch on the cheek. "Good. I want to be back here within a year to meet your new babies."

"We'll see," I say with a chuckle. Just then, Cassie runs up, looking desperate. "Whoa, whoa, what's going on?"

"I just saw you . . . and I wanted to tell you that I didn't do it!" she says, looking over as I see Caleb looking around furiously.

"Didn't do what? Seriously, you two still at it?"

"He's fun," Cassie says. "Listen, I overheard you saying you're leaving. I just wanted to tell you that I'm going to follow Wesley's advice. I don't want to end up like those bitches in the boardroom, and with Aurora shutting down, I took my severance package. I'm going to think a little. Jake says I can stretch it some by helping out at Club Jasmine a little. After that, I'm going to strike out on my own."

"What are you gonna do?" I ask, and Cassie grins.

"I don't really know yet. I like the real estate game, but I want to make sure I'm ready. Tony said something about coming to work for Oliver, but I'm gonna let that percolate a little before I jump in. You go do your wedding thing, and I'll tell you what I can as soon as I know. And Hannah?"

"Yeah?"

Cassie gives me a quick hug. "I love you, babe." She lets go, tossing a quick look over her shoulder. "Gotta go!"

She takes off running, Caleb following her, and I just shake my head, seeing Tony and taking his hand. We walk through the night, not saying much as we make our way toward the old temple circle. Parting the trees, I can see the remnants of the old foundation. It was built of stone, I bet, and I turn to Tony, putting my arms around his neck. "Shall we honor Alani's ancient gods again, husband?"

Tony's hands encircle my waist, his right hand cupping my ass as he kisses my neck. "You don't have to ask me twice," he murmurs into my neck, his cock pressing against my thigh. "You will always be my heart and soul, mine to love forever."

"And you'll always be my heart and soul," I reply before giggling as Tony's fingers find a ticklish spot on my hip. "And one more thing."

"What?"

"You'll always be my studmuffin."

Want the FREE Extended Epilogue? Sign up to my mailing list to receive it. If you're already on my list, you'll get this automatically!

Irresistible Bachelor **Series (Interconnecting standalones):**
Anaconda || Mr. Fiance || Heartstopper
Stud Muffin || Mr. Fixit || Matchmaker
Motorhead || Baby Daddy

PREVIEW: MR. FIXIT

BY LAUREN LANDISH

Cassie

*T*he blistering heat envelops me as I step outside with a glass of cold water in my hand. Immediately, the humidity makes my thin cotton tank top cling to my body even before I'm halfway down the steps.

"I get it, I get it," I mutter to myself, glancing up to the heavens. "I've been such a bad girl that I have to spend the summer living next door to the gates of hell. Doesn't mean you have to throw in the mugginess too."

At least the weather's good for one thing, I think as I feel a droplet of sweat trickle down the back of my thigh. I can barely stand to wear anything at all, so I've spent most of the past few days in nothing but crop tops and Daisy Dukes. Sure, I might be looking just a tad bit skanky, but I think I can pull it off. And it's done wonders for my tan.

I hear the buzzing of the small gasoline motor, and I come

around the corner of the house, knowing what I'll find. After a delay in getting some of the materials that we need, Caleb and I decided to tackle something else. A friend of his was willing to let us borrow his big riding lawnmower, so we're tackling the one-acre space behind the house, taking it from a jungle to a half-tamed space. We'll worry about making it a lawn later, but today's all about at least getting it so that I'm not worried about snakes or other creepy crawlies if I want to take a walk back here.

Caleb and I have been working together all morning to try and get the lawn done, alternating between driving the mower and using the other tools. We've been through six gallons of gas in the big mower, but the ten huge bags of cut grass stand as a monument to the amount of work we've accomplished. But now, he insists on running the weed whacker, saying my bare legs are in danger. The way he keeps looking at my legs and ass, I'd say he's the one in danger . . . and that's just the way I like it.

"Do you need some wa—" I yell, but the words freeze in my throat at the sight in front of me. Caleb's peeled off his shirt while I've been inside, leaving him in just a pair of jeans that hugs his lean hips like a glove, and I get a full view of the long muscles of his back and the swell of his arms and shoulders as he shuts off the motor. Just looking at the sweat glistening on his tanned skin makes my internal temperature ratchet up a few more degrees, and I'm tempted to drink half the glass of water myself. I'm burning up inside.

"Hey," he says, turning all the way toward me and shrugging off the gas trimmer. Watching his chest and arms flex with easy strength and the bead of sweat that trickles down his pecs before coursing its way over the deep ridges of his abs has me gasping for air.

I've always known that Caleb was a fine, sexy specimen of manhood. But the recent change in our relationship has me looking at him differently. I'm shocked at how turned on he makes me. These past few days, I've noticed him not as an opponent, not as a playmate, but as a man. And no matter how much I want to deny it, I want him with every fiber of my being.

Why couldn't I see this before? It makes sense. From the moment I saw him, I wanted to beat him, to show him that I was worthy of his notice. Every mean trick I played on him, every time I've tried to show him up since we've started working together, it's always been to get his attention. Sometimes, I've been subtle, like with a slight joke or making sure I wore my thinnest bra today underneath my thinnest tank top. Other times, it's been as in your face as a bucket of water poured over his head. Yeah, I did that too.

And now, I can't deny it. I can't get enough of him.

The corner of Caleb's lips curl up into a cocky grin as he watches me, and I realize I'm staring at him, the glass of ice water frozen in my hand. "You okay?"

I tear my eyes away from his sweaty abs. "Yeah, a bead of sweat just fell in my eye." I lie my ass off, trying to maintain at least a little bit of control of myself. I'm not quite that desperate that I want to fall on my back in the freshly mown grass and spread my legs, begging him to plow me. At least, not yet. I wipe at my eyes with the back of my hand, holding out the glass of cold water. "Here. You look like you need it."

Caleb reaches out and takes the glass from my hand, my eyes fixed on his Adam's apple as he downs half the glass, his throat making me even more breathless before he stops and gives me a curious look. "You sure about that?"

He steps closer, and he's so close I can feel the heat emanating from him, heat that has nothing to do with the blistering sun. I swear my internal thermometer is rising through the roof. Standing next to him, the only image I have in my head is of my entire head exploding like a cartoon thermometer, but I can't tear my eyes away from him.

"I'm sure," I finally reply, my voice husky. "How much more do you have to do?"

"Not much," Caleb admits, not looking anywhere but at me. "There's a few bushes that need trimmed, but that won't take long at all."

If you want to see a nicely trimmed bush, I've got one for you, I think, but instead, I nod. "Okay."

The sounds of the summer fade away as I watch him finish off his drink, a trickle of water running from the side of his mouth and down to his chest, making me want to lick the clear droplet off his skin. He licks his lips, and all I can imagine is feeling his hands, his lips, his tongue licking me that way, and I moan lightly, my thighs trembling with desire.

Caleb finishes the last bit from the glass before crunching one of the ice cubes that I'd put inside, smiling. "Delicious. Just what I needed."

Please, please, PLEASE run that ice cube over my nipples, I want to beg him, my heart pounding in my chest like a sexual drum. "Yeah. I was just going back inside. I was going to get that list of stuff for the bathr—"

Trying to keep my eyes in a safe place, I fail utterly. Every glance at Caleb makes me want him more, and I stammer, unable to find a single square inch of his body that doesn't leave my heart fluttering, my stomach twisting, and my pussy aching. Finally, in a desperate bid for keeping control, I turn to leave, but I freeze when I feel a powerful hand grab my wrist.

"What are you doing?" I gasp as Caleb pulls me back around, my body pressing against his. I can feel his heart pounding against my chest, and between his legs is a throbbing, thick heat that leaves my knees weak.

Caleb grins at me, his eyes twinkling in a way that I've never seen before. "You didn't call me names like you normally do."

"Oh," I whimper weakly. "I just forgot. This heat has me burning up."

Caleb lowers his lips until I can feel his breath on my ear, and I whimper again, my nipples hardening inside my top. "I think you're burning up all right. And I know just what to do about it."

"Oh, is that so?" I ask as my hands clutch at the full, hard muscles on his chest.

"It is," he purrs, pressing himself into me. I can feel the rapidly hardening growth of his cock, and my legs seem to spread on their own to let him have access to me. I want him so damn badly I can taste him already.

He pulls me tighter, and I moan, unable to form words. He's got me right where he wants me. Caleb whispers in my ear, "You have a problem, and I have the tool for the job."

He grabs another one of the ice cubes from his glass, gently dropping the glass to the grass. I bite my lip as he brings the ice cube to my jawline, tracing the line and then letting the drops run down my neck. He dips his head down to lick at the river of drops from the quickly melting ice, humming in satisfaction.

"Mmm, even more refreshing than I thought. Are you cooled off now?"

Knowing it'll drive him crazy, I smirk and shake my head. "Not even close. In fact, I might be even hotter now."

"We can't have that, now can we?" he says as he trails the little bit of remaining ice down toward my cleavage. I press my tits together, creating a little crevice for the water to puddle, and Caleb's eyes focus there. Moving his hands over mine, he cups my breasts together even higher, lowering his head to dip his tongue into the pool, lapping the water up and running his tongue along the upper crest of my breasts. My head falls back as I groan. The water gone now, he moves to slip the neckline of my tank down, giving him more access. Kissing down, he slurps my nipple into his mouth, swirling his tongue over the peaked tip. He's driving me crazy, and I know my panties are already soaked.

I'm this close to letting him take me right here in the back-yard, whoever can see be damned, when I hear my phone blare out. *"Work hard, play hard."*

"Shit," I gasp, pushing away from Caleb and going over to his truck to grab my bag off the tailgate. My phone's still singing its digital ass off, and I know from the ringtone that it's work. I pull it out and see that it's Martha. "Fuck!"

"Well, that was sort of what I had in mind," Caleb teases, grabbing my hips from behind and pulling me closer, but I pull away before I can be swept away in the sexual passion coursing through me.

I hold up a finger to signal for him to hold on a second, answering the call. "Hey, Martha, what's up?"

Caleb realizes it's work and is professional enough to not do anything too naughty. Good boy. "Hey, Cass," Martha says. "I hope you're not waiting on me."

Oh, shit, I forgot . . . Martha is supposed to come to the house today. It's a good damn thing she didn't pull up just now or she would've gotten a bit more show than she'd planned on. "Oh, um, no, Martha, not at all," I quickly reply while trying not to facepalm myself. I've done that before, and it's not a good thing to do while you have your smartphone to your face. "Actually, we're just finishing up the yardwork. Why?"

"Well, I guess we're both lucky then," Martha says with a relieved sigh. "I was getting my hair done, and you know how the salon can get on the weekends. Is there any way you could meet me at the office in an hour instead of my driving out there?"

"Yeah, no problem," I say, relieved. "I'll see you there."

We hang up, and I turn to Caleb, who looks disappointed. "Sorry."

"Work?" he asks, and I'm counting the minutes in my head even as I look down. An hour. That means we have about ten minutes to . . .

No, stop it, dammit, I tell myself.

"Yeah, work. I promised Martha I'd go over some documents with her. She's gotta send them off Monday morning or else."

Caleb sighs but nods. "I understand. Well, at least I know I can make you lose all track of time."

I laugh, shaking my head. "Probably because you're so boring you put me to sleep."

"Is that what you call it when you scream my name and pass out? Boring. I'll remember that."

Want to read more of Caleb & Cassie's explosive antics? Get it HERE or visit my website at www.laurenlandish.com

ABOUT THE AUTHOR

Irresistible Bachelor Series (Interconnecting standalones):
Anaconda || Mr. Fiance || Heartstopper
Stud Muffin || Mr. Fixit || Matchmaker
Motorhead || Baby Daddy

Connect with Lauren Landish!
www.laurenlandish.com
admin@laurenlandish.com

Made in the USA
Monee, IL
15 November 2020